BUSISEKILE KHUMALO

His Baby Maker

First edition

ISBN: 978-1-997459-67-5

This book was professionally typeset on Reedsy.
Find out more at reedsy.com

Why does it feel right every time I let you in?
Why does it feel like I can tell you anything?
All the secrets that keep me in chains and
All the damage that might make me dangerous
You got a dark side, guess you're not the only one
What if we both tried fighting what we're running from?
We can't fix it if we never face it
What if we find a way to escape it?
We could be free

"Free." K Pop Demon Hunters

Contents

Foreword

Some stories bulldoze their way into publication, and this is one of them. I love a despicable villain; cue Scar from The Lion King, Maleficent, Ursula from the Little Mermaid and Hades from Hercules. I often root for the villain to find happiness, because I believe that everyone is a villain in someone else's story and all the villains needed was a little love, a little understanding and a whole load of healing. I love when a villain redeems themselves and this is Daniel and Candice's redemption arc.

That being said, I want you to know that you cannot fix someone who does not want to be fixed, no matter how hard you try. At times the best way you can help them is by walking away before they break you further. Trauma bonds are intricate, dangerous and I tried to handle this one with the grace and understanding that I often lack.

His Baby Maker covers many layered themes of sexual trauma, childhood traumas, and if this is too much for you, please proceed with caution. If you have been here since The Harvard wife, look how far we've come my darling!

As always, if you have anything to get off your chest regarding this book or any of my work, I'm only one DM/Email/Tag away. I appreciate your feedback.

Love and Light.

Busisekile Khumalo

Preface

Candice

6 December, 1995

Every time I visited my mother, I always imagined myself as Sarafina. The movie had found a soft spot in my angry heart, and I often posed the question: 'What would Sarafina do?' whenever my mother was yelling at me or beating the crap out of me for something I hadn't done. At times, it felt like the biggest crime I had committed against my mother was just being alive.

Unlike Sarafina, I didn't have a hoard of siblings to fuss over, my grandmother was dead and my uncles and aunts couldn't care less whether my mother and I were alive or dead. It was just my hateful mother and I. But, just like Sarafina, my father wasn't in the picture; I didn't even know if he was alive or dead. The mere mention of my father often left my backside smarting with welts and yet stubbornly, I kept asking after him, his family—just anything to get me away from the bitter, guaranteed eruption of my mother's wrath.

The only time I got to breathe and be free was when Gladys—she didn't allow me to call her 'Ma'—was at work. I was no social butterfly either, because my pale skin made the other kids wary. My mother often looked for reasons to whoop me with her belt , so I didn't roam the streets of KwaThema as my age-mates did; I stayed home and I studied. My grades were high; at times, I took First Place but even that didn't please my mother.

The only time I ventured out of our tiny box red brick house in Mohlala Street, Phomolo Section, was whenever I went to collect money from Gladys after she'd received her fortnightly wages. On the last day of school of my Standard 9 year, Gladys had instructed me to come see her. As I sat on the bus, leaving behind the sectional houses that all blurred into dots of red bricks, I wondered how many buses Sarafina had to take to get to the posh side of the city where her mother worked. I took three buses, and when I got there, I wasn't stupid enough to mess with a house that Gladys cleaned or brave enough to talk to her the way Sarafina spoke to her mother. Though, I wish I were.

Gladys was curt and not outwardly hostile whenever she was around her employers and their children; ironically, they loved my mother. It was always, 'Oh, what a ray of sunshine Gladys is!' and how well she took of and loved those ugly, entitled brats of theirs.Visiting her at work, even if for two measly hours, often left me raw and exposed. It wasn't that Gladys didn't have the capacity to love, she just didn't love me. And it stung!

After seeing Gladys tenderly nursing her employers' oldest daughter, who was almost the same age as me, I left with her wages carefully tucked in my bralette and a lump lodged firmly in my throat. The bus was full, as always, and I gave up my seat to a pregnant lady two stops from where I'd gotten on.

The bus lurched unexpectedly, and I teetered dangerously before falling on the lap of a man sitting by the aisle. Mortified, I made to stand, but he gently pushed me down.

'I don't mind carrying you,' his voice rumbled at my back with a richness to it that did weird things to my stomach.

At first, I was perched on the edge of his long legs, and I tried to steal glances at him from the corner of my eye but I couldn't. The bus's sharp turns and lurches brought me lower, until my back was plastered against his chest, my body feeling his heat seep into me. He smelt nice and clean, masculine, with a scent that had the hint of money. He smelt like the crisp notes that Gladys had handed to me. When the bus stopped to drop us off in town, he let me down his lap almost reluctantly.

I turned to thank him, only to stop short and gape at him. He was the most handsome and polished black man that I had ever seen, his clothes weren't expensive but they were crisply ironed. It was in the commanding way he carried himself, as if he was someone important, even though he was more on the lanky side without much muscle definition. I finally collected myself enough to stutter an apology and make a hasty retreat but he easily caught up with me.

'Wait, at least walk me to my work. You owe me that much, I have cramps in my legs,' he said, then grinned cheekily down at me and I was a goner, my heart lurching just like the bus did when it caused our worlds to collide.

He looked to be around nineteen to twenty years old; which I later found out that he was actually twenty-two about to turn twenty-three. I lied and said I was eighteen years old, copying the age of the only girl in the neighbourhood who bothered to talk to me, Mapura. I was yet to turn fifteen. Due to the unrest leading up to independence, it wasn't unusual for one to be that old and still be in Standard 9.

'I'm Daniel,' he said, his smile reminding me of Nelson Mandela. Or, maybe it was because of his haircut, with the side-parting.

As we walked, I almost bumped into someone and Daniel tugged me by my hand until I was plastered against him. He was an apprentice at Luthuli House and he was telling me how he was going to be in parliament one day. His voice was animated with conviction. Even though I didn't understand a thing that he said, I hung on to every word. He was charming, too, holding my hand and shielding me from the throes of pedestrians rushing about. For a moment I forgot all about my mother and how it hurt to watch her loving other people's children.

With Daniel, I didn't have to try and speak boldly like Sarafina, because he found my shyness endearing; and besides, I couldn't think while his thumb was stroking the pad of my palm. I remember laughing a lot, too, but I'm not sure if it was because he was funny or I was smitten. He had a dry sense of humour. By the time I left him at Luthuli House, just standing outside the sidewalk and watching me walk away, my heart was gone. Daniel had charmed the pants off of me.

Prologue

Daniel

6 December, 1987

My sister Phindiwe ran our household like a drill sergeant, and I was her shiny brass boot that she had to keep polished and shiny. I accepted my fate at the first school award ceremony I ever attended. After sweeping up as many of the awards as there were in the rundown hall where our school held its 'award ceremonies'. It was pathetic, really; the teachers tried, and the community chipped in with their meagre funds but it was a shit-show. The partially-burnt hall was cramped, mostly with mothers. The fathers were either those on the run from the government, immersed in politics, toiled to the bone and too tired to care, or there were those who were like my father, who were so deep in the clutches of alcohol to care. The awards were printed on paper that looked like it was ready to disintegrate, but Sis' Phindi held them as if they were gold. After the ceremony, Sis' Phindi held my chin firmly in her hands and the words she spoke that day became etched in the fabric of my soul as soon as she uttered them.

'You... You are our ticket out of here. You focus on keeping your grades up, and leave the rest to me.'

I nodded solemnly, even though I was sceptical, because there really was no way out of the poverty we were born into. One thing I knew was if Phindiwe got her mind fixed on something, she would move mountains to get it. On the days when my mother was too drunk in love over the pathetic man she chose, to the point of neglecting us, Phindiwe stole, lied, and tricked people to get us fed. My mother worked four to five jobs concurrently, and yet, she easily handed over most of her wages to her husband. Sis' Phindi often stole money from our mother's purse for our upkeep, before it all made its way into my father's grubby hands.

After my first award ceremony, my sister took a sudden interest in Bantu education, even though she had dropped out in Form 1 when there became too many mouths that she had to feed—our older sister, Nothando, the first-born, had succumbed to malnutrition, leaving Sis' Phindi in charge. A point she was bitter about, and made sure to remind us of as much and as often as she could.

When the unrest in schools escalated, my sister called for and arranged meetings after meetings with the parents, the liberation fighters, students, teachers, or so she told me but the only room I saw her coming out of was Bra Scorpio's—who was known as the top dog in our little shanty settlement. Sis' Phindiwe even hustled the Sowetan from people; how she did that, was a miracle, because we were the shanty's laughing stock—something to do with our surname and our father's inadequacies.

I remember one of the cut-outs that Sis' Phindi placed on the large piece of broken mirror that rested against the rickety wardrobe in the centre of our shack. It said: "Bantu Education cannot be improved. It has to be eliminated, and buried with its origination. Liberation with education certainly bodes far better for all of us in this country. Let us go for it."

'Daniel, take this, scrub yourself thoroughly. If you don't, I will! Quickly!' Sis' Phindi barked at me one December afternoon.

Schools were closed, and while I could hear the noise of other kids playing just outside our shack, I was burning inside the tin that we called home as I pored over a book that Sis' Phindi had brought home after one of her outings with Bra Scorpio.

I took the soap and loafer that she handed me curiously. I was in the thick of the awkward part of adolescence: All gangly legs, my voice had deepened but it still squeaked whenever I was afraid or agitated. I made sure to scrub myself twice over, just to be sure; I didn't want Sis' Phindi washing me and I knew she would make good on her threat. I knew better than to ask when she handed me clothes that were a size bigger and instructed me to wear them. The way she primped and plucked off any hair that was out of place, you would have sworn she was taking me to see the president.

I got into Bra Scorpio's Cressida for the first time ever. I perched in the middle, where I had to watch as he groped between my sister's legs with one hand while he drove with another and told me all the inflated stories of his importance in the 'struggle'.

It felt like forever before we pulled up in front of what, in my young and impoverished mind, looked like a monster mansion—huge and scary. We left Bra Scorpio lounging in his Cressida as Sis' Phindi frog-marched me up the long winding driveway and knocked boldly on the door.

'You are a man now, you have to do what you can for the family,' Sis' Phindi told me and before I could ask what she meant, the door was swung open.

I remember the disdain of the butler who opened the door, his long hook nose scrunched as if we smelt like his leathery pale skin. If anything, I fought to keep from pinching my nose to evade his smell. He led us to the living room, and that was the first time I met her. Her skin was already hanging off her neck, reminding me of the wild turkeys that sometimes found their way to the fringes of our shantytown. She had the same beady eyes too, even though hers had a coating which gave one the image of creamy mucus balls. She sat on a leather armchair as if it were her throne and we were commoners bringing homage to her, just like in the book I was reading, only, instead of there being a scroll next to her, there was a glass of whiskey that she kept twirling her long, bony finger on the rim of the glass.

'Come here, boy.' I didn't want to go, so I looked at Sis' Phindi for direction and she nodded before pushing me towards the tough birdie woman.

I looked at Sis' Phindi as the woman made me splay my legs and then turned me around, and she felt me up before nodding. I looked at her when the woman with her long fingernails prodded and pinched me until I let out a high-pitched yelp, Sis' Phindi nodded. I looked at her when the scarecrow announced shrilly, 'He'll do!' Sis' Phindi didn't nod that time, she turned around and left, closing the door firmly and leaving me to face my fate alone.

I made sure to wipe my tears before I got out of that monstrous house. I got into Bra Scorpio's Cressida and found him necking my sister heavily; he didn't stop on my account, so I sat there staunchly, trying to get rid of the smell of whiskey and musty sweat that seemed stuck in my nose. I was a man, I didn't say a word the whole drive back to the little section of land which was allocated to us. Sis' Phindi wouldn't meet my eyes, and yet, I didn't blame her.

When everyone was asleep, I carefully snuck out of the shack from my position near the door. I went to the tree that was close to the tavern, it was also in front of where everyone dumped their garbage. I didn't mind the acrid stench because it overpowered the smell of whiskey. I waited and just like I knew he would, my father came stumbling—swaying and swearing. He kicked and tried to claw at my hands, just as I had just a few hours before, it was satisfying hearing his pleas and cries mirroring mine. He was still bigger than me, so, even drunk, he managed to break free, and his eyes widened when they met mine in the darkness. He swore at me and turned to look for something to hit me with. I didn't give him the chance to accomplish that mission, I shoved him hard and he fell and hit his head on the large rock I had been sitting on while I waited for him. I felt nothing. At fourteen, I was a man. And, we didn't need him burdening us anymore.

I

Part One

Dancing with Ghosts

Chapter 1

Candice

"Today's guest has been topping the headlines this week ever since she came out with her debut book, 'His Baby Maker', and that is not because of her book, which, from the cover alone, is promising all kind of scandal—"

Appreciative whistles and clapping fill the studio from the live audience, and I try my best to keep the wide smile pasted on my face and relax my hands on the arm of the plush leather couch that I am sitting on the edge of. Scandal is exactly what I am here to circumvent but maybe coming here was a bad idea... The over-light is so bright, I feel like a deer caught in headlights.

I told Sibo, my publicist, that holding an interview was a bad idea; especially with Fifi, known for her scandal-breaking show 'Mamgobhozi Live'. It not only has a wide viewership but this show is right smack in the middle of prime TV!

"Any publicity is good publicity. Just drive them towards the book, be vague enough to forestall any lawsuits, and you should be home free. What do you have to lose?"

My first daughter.

Sibo doesn't know this, none of my publishing team know this, but this interview can make or break the relationship that I have been painstakingly building with my daughter. Sweat breaks out on my back at the thought of losing her, again. I barely survived handing her over when she was three days old, I won't survive losing her again because it's no longer just me in the firing line.

Denise adores her sister and I have come to rely on her a lot, too. I wouldn't have done this interview if she hadn't told me she was fine with it. But I know the unspoken rule: Should this interview do anything to hurt or implicate her mother, then our relationship is as good as buried.

Feeling my heart constrict at the mere thought and my air circulation becoming restricted, I try to let go of the web of familial ties that hang delicately on balance and focus on the web of lies that I spun together for this interview.

"...please put your hands together for Candice! Welcome, Darling. Let's not beat around the bush now, is this book about one of our most prominent members of parliament? And, are you the mother of his first daughter and heiress?" I smile back at her beaming face, her fangs ready to sink into my throat and suck the scandal that would bring a nation to its knees.

If I could afford the luxury of truth, my response would be 'Yes', but even as I laugh a little and flash her my most dazzling smile, I can feel the acrid bitterness of lies rising up my mouth.

"Wouldn't that be some story?" My voice is measured and a bit playful but my insides are quaking in trepidation, because I know that if Fifi catches even a whiff of the real story, then I'm a goner.

"I wish I could say I have lived such a high-end life, filled with glitter and power, but I'm just a simple girl from Ekurhuleni with a penchant for fiction. I live in a small apartment in Turffontein, with my beautiful babies." I turn to the screen when the picture of Denise, her brother, and I in the dingy apartment that I found after I finally swallowed the bitter truth, that I was never anything more to the love of my life than just his baby-maker.

"You make beautiful babies, Darling, but then, how do you explain your uncanny resemblance to the heiress in question?"

Oyama's picture takes up the screen and it feels like looking at me in college; only, I didn't do something as prestigious as Medicine. The only time I wore scrubs was when I worked on a holiday boat and they were nowhere near the green ones that Oyama has on in this picture.

As if I willed it, a picture of me in white and navy blue scrubs comes up and it looks like one person in two different quality pictures. I have to push past the lump in my throat and the deep yearning to announce to the world that I made that stunning and exceptional young lady.

But you didn't make her, you only gave birth to her, the sneer in my mind is enough to make my voice come out.

"I don't. I can not explain how we look so alike. I've always heard that we all have our doppelgangers somewhere in the world but I was so shocked when I first met my publicist and she called out the resemblance. It was so uncanny, as you said, and we reached out to Oyama and she was a sport enough to agree to meet up with me and we immediately clicked. Her mother was also gracious enough to meet me. I understand where Oyama gets her intelligence and the ability to live by her own rules, she gets it from her mother, Nompumelelo Ndinisa-Levine, not from me; I am just a stranger who happens to look like her."

Even though the words cut me up inside and leave me bleeding, it feels like a huge burden has been lifted from my shoulders. I don't mind loving my daughter in the shadows, I've been doing that her whole life but at least now, I can meet up with her and actually go out to grab some ice cream.

"Tell me about Daniel. I mean, Dakalo in the book. What, or who, inspired that character?" Fifi is not willing to give up her pound of flesh just like that, the mention of his name wasn't a slip up on her part and I won't lie about the buzzing hearing his name caused to my stupid heart. I smile and lie some more; I already denied my daughter, denying her father who strung me along since I was fifteen should be a breeze.

* * *

The headache that was threatening to consume me when Fifi wouldn't let up during the interview has reached its pinnacle by the time I drag myself up the stairs to my apartment. The elevator is so old and rickety, I'd rather go up several flights of stairs on these heels that are pinching my toes than be caught dead in it.

The shrill cry of my phone makes me jump. I have been nervous ever since I left the studio; it's felt like someone has been watching and following me, but maybe it's just my paranoia. I swallow my nerves when I see that it is only Sibo.

"That was a fantastic interview! I already have channel 403 on the line, they want to interview you!" Her excitement goes over my head and I no longer have it in me to pretend to be excited, but somehow, she takes my silence for shock.

"I know you didn't expect this, but this is huge! Sales have gone up on Amazon... we have so many clicks on your website. You did good, Kid. Now, get some rest because we are meeting up tomorrow to go over a few things."

By the time she hangs up, I am already unlocking my door, grateful that Oyama took her siblings for the weekend. The lights are off and I almost jump out of my skin when a familiar voice calls out my name. He turns on the study lamp next to the armchair that he is sitting on. No, I can't call it sitting, he is lording over my armchair, turning it into his throne.

Something about the way his legs are splayed sends shivers of déjà vu tingling down my spine. The sire of my children is also my prosecutor and adjudicator. Like a cat of wild, he eyes me as if I am his prey and I have to force a nervous laugh out of my dry lips. It comes off too high, shrill, and off-key.

"You scared me there. Why are you sitting in the darkness?"

I don't dare ask the other questions which are at the forefront of my mind; like, how did he get the keys to my apartment? I paid for this apartment with my own money after I gave up the cosy duplex he had set up for me and his children. The most burning question is, why is there a gun beside the untouched glass of whiskey, just within his reach? My heart is thudding way too loudly in my ears, and I fear that he can hear it just as clearly.

"You hesitated." I don't ask him for clarification because I know the precise moment he is referring to.

Fifi had stopped hedging and straight out asked me if I knew Daniel Sisulu. Images of how I know him in the Biblical sense, how he doesn't drink alcohol but likes to pour a glass of the most expensive whiskey and set it beside him, images of him beaming as he held our son for the first time after cutting his cord. All those tiny images, even of the day I first met him, flooded my mind and it couldn't have been for more than 30 seconds but it's all it took to rouse Daniel's ire.

"I gave you everything, Candice, everything I am, Baby. You know and had me, not the minister, not the honourable man I have to be, and I thought it was enough. That I was enough for you. So, why do I have to learn about a book that you've written from a colleague? Why are my children living in this dump, when the property worth millions that I bought for them, for you, is empty?"

I hate how scared I am right now, but I can count on my hand the number of times he has been this unhinged before. I take a deep, fortifying breath as I consider my response.

"You know why. It wasn't enough for us anymore, it wasn't enough for me. My children deserve more than to be your dirty secret. I deserve more than to be your baby-maker in secret, popping your children while other women get the privilege of being your wives to the world!" My voice is shaking, but so is my whole body even before he switches off the safety on the gun and cocks it while pointing it at my head.

"Give me one good reason why I shouldn't blow your brains off right now."

Anger lends me the bravery to walk up to him until the cold barrel is kissing my upper stomach.

"You couldn't go through with it with Mpumi, you came to me." Nompumelelo Ndinisa-Levine is Daniel's ex-wife, the one the world knows and still links to his name even almost a decade later.

What the world doesn't know is that Mpumi had an affair with the white man that she gave her virginity to while she was practically engaged to

Daniel. They don't know that when Daniel found out, he held her at gunpoint pretty much the same way he's currently holding me at gunpoint. What the world and even Mpumi don't know is Daniel was so cut up over the whole thing. He was a crying mess, snort and all; he even vomited from what he had done, and I took care of him.

"You are not Nompumelelo, you will never be her." The quiet certainty in his voice cuts deeper than if he was shouting at me. Just like he meant it to. Daniel is like a vicious puppeteer, he knows which string to pull and dig into when he needs to rip a person apart.

"I have the real manuscript; with names, not the fiction I was talking about today, anything happens to me and my source will make sure it gets published. Oyama has the other copy."

I am the mother of your children, should have been enough, but it has never been enough—not with him and not for me. I see the hurt behind his eyes and I steel myself against it as he wavers a bit. He instructs me to get the manuscript I am speaking of. He thinks I'm bluffing. My hands aren't shaking as I open the locked compartment of the TV stand and I take out a printed manuscript.

He gestures with his gun for me to bring it to him and I do, woodenly. He browses through it, showing no reaction besides tightening his fist over his gun. His gun shepherds me to sit on the couch next to him and he tosses me the manuscript that never made it to print.

"Read."

Chapter 2

Daniel

"Running on the dry, red soil of Maebani, shrieking and bare-chested, with a stolen mango dripping down my ashy face and already-sticky hands used to be my ultimate haven, until it wasn't. And, being with Daniel Sisulu used to be my haven... until it wasn't."

Candice's voice wobbles over the words, shaken and sounding foreign to me. I know she's conscious of the gun still trained at her and my dark gaze boring into her. If I were a better man, I'd put the gun away and reassure the mother of my children that I just want to understand. I'm not a good man on a good day, I'm a selfish prick and it's magnified right now by the anger that I'm trying to get a handle on. I've been seeing red ever since I heard her name falling from the lips of another man.

'Candice,' that punk, Joshua, a new contact I just made in Australia, had said, and even though his face didn't shift, I could hear the mockery loud and clear from his voice because he had found the one person that can bring my world to its knees.

That meeting with Joshua and my Zimbabwean contact promises to elevate my career beyond my wildest dreams, but all I could think about was Candice and the book that Joshua mentioned. The moment the meeting ended, I called Candice, and I was bloody pissed when I discovered that she blocked my number and she wouldn't pick up private calls. I had to pull some strings, accumulating owed favours in the process, and I was in the air in a private jet an hour later. That's how I missed the notification that Candice was going to do that dreadful interview with that gossip-monger. By the time my team managed to get ahold of me, it was too late to pull the plug on the whole thing.

The first thing I did when I landed was to drive to the gated complex where I thought I'd find Candice and persuade her to stop this madness. I got there three hours before the interview was supposed to start and I almost had a full-blown panic attack when I couldn't find a trace of Candice nor my children in the house. Security said they hadn't been seen in two weeks. Weeks! My anger intensified as I watched her interview alone in the house that I bought for her and my children, waiting to get a lead as to where she moved to. My information guy didn't have to dig deep to find this dump. When I got here, my anger reached apoplectic heights and it hasn't even been improved by seeing her flawless skin, or by inhaling the heady scent of her shampoo.

"I didn't know you came from Limpopo," I ask in a voice that bellies all my frustration and anger, just how my great-uncle taught me. May his soul rot in hell.

"You never asked."

I catch on to the bitter undertone in her voice and it grates on my ears. I look at her, trying to find my sweet Candice underneath all the stoic bitterness, but her face gives nothing away. For the first time in a long time, I feel a wide chasm between the mother of my children and I. The feeling scares me.

"I didn't know you write," I scramble for something to say that will mend the rift between us but from the narrowing of her eyes, I know I said the wrong thing.

"Yeah, well, besides my vagina, you didn't care to know much about me."

Images of Candice's slippery wet vagina, gripping my cock, squeezing me in its moist heat with each thrust I make, pop up unbidden in my mind and I'm instantly hard. Over two decades later, and just thinking of her vagina still gives me a painful erection, so yes, I do care about it, a lot. But that's not all I care about when it comes to Candice.

I care about her softness, the way she mothers, and I tell her things I'd never tell anyone else, I care about her happiness, hence I bought the dream house that she wanted and watched, content, as she turned it into a home. I care about her sharp intelligence hidden beneath her insecurities; Oyama definitely took her smarts from her mother. I almost burnt this city down when I couldn't find her at home. I would skin alive anyone who hurts even a single hair on her head; pity I can't flay myself for hurting her—though not from lack of trying.

Tat' Xhamela, my mentor, told me that Candice was a loose end that could unravel my whole career and that I needed to terminate our relationship, permanently. In the Sisulu language, that meant sending a hitman after her. It was the first time I openly defied Tat' Xhamela after he begrudgingly took me under his wing. I didn't care then if Candice ended my career, and I still don't care now, I can never let her go.

I watch her as she straightens her shoulders and goes back to reading.

"Masase, wee! Inwi Masase!" Makhulu, my grandmother's chanting chasing me and my tinkling laughter echoing her is one of the happiest sounds of my life; topped only by the shrill cry of my baby girl, my first-born, as I held—"

"Masase. Is that your name? Jesus, Candice, what do I know about you?" I can't disguise the hurt and bewilderment in my voice. I thought I knew her, the same way she knows almost everything about me. I thought wrong.

Candice lets out an impatient breath of air at being disturbed, again, and she gives me a pointed look, fully intending to continue reading. She must see the tortured look on my face because she sighs, relenting as she always does when it comes to me. Maybe I haven't fully lost her.

"It was never on my birth certificate, only my grandmother called me by that name."

"What does it mean?" I need to know.

A pang hits me because even with a gun between us, this is the most intimate conversation we've had in a relationship that spans over two decades and three children.

"You would know if you just let me read without interrupting. At least let me finish this chapter without saying anything. Can you do that?" she throws the challenge at me, and I shrug before leaning back into the armchair and putting the gun on the armrest. It doesn't escape her notice that I didn't latch on the safety.

She takes a deep breath and starts from the beginning—becoming lost in the words and I am lost in her voice, lost in her story, lost in her.

Chapter 3

6 December 1996

Running on the dry, red soil of Maebani, shrieking and bare-chested, with a stolen mango dripping down my ashy face and already-sticky hands used to be my ultimate haven, until it wasn't. And, being with Daniel Sisulu used to be my haven... until it wasn't. It sounds so simple but most parts are hazy, lost in a sea of what could have been, should have been, and regrets. Still, I hold on to the memories of happiness, of when both were still my haven.

"Masase, wee! Inwi Masase!" Makhulu, my grandmother's chanting chasing me and my tinkling laughter echoing her is one of the happiest sounds of my life; topped only by the shrill cry of my baby girl, my first-born, as I held her in my arms for the first time.

Exhausted, in pain, and overwhelmed by harrowing labour at the tender age of almost-sixteen, it all faded as I looked into her wrinkled face with its splotches of amniotic fluid before she was whisked away to be cleaned. When they brought her back, wrapped in that soft baby material cocoon, I couldn't stop marvelling at how tiny she was. She had skin so pale, it was almost translucent; I was even afraid to touch her, in case it broke and blood seeped out.

I could imagine Makhulu exclaiming as she held her, "Lukanda lutete lu no nga naledzi ya mutsho."

I know for a fact that's what she would have said and I swear, at that moment, I heard her voice whisper it, even though it was only me and my baby in that private room.

"Skin so fair that it looks like the morning star."

That's what she always lovingly said as she braided my hair and my skin turned red around the edges or when she was scolding me for playing in the scorching Maebani sun without a hat.

"Naledzi ya Masase."

She only called me that when she was very happy, when she had gotten more money from the market for her plants than she had hoped for or when I did something that pleased her, like the time I came first in my class. She put me on her back and carried me the whole afternoon. I was in Grade Five. She was convinced I would be a doctor.

With the bitter-sweetness of retrospect, I realise that she spoke that blessing onto my little girl. The great-granddaughter that she never got to see, hold, and kiss loudly on both cheeks. The great-granddaughter that would have disappointed her because she saw so much more for her Masase--her little star.

I always think about Makhulu a lot when it comes to the big moments in my life. Makhulu in her no-nonsense manner of fisting her hands on her waist handles, bangles dangling on the loose skin on her wrists as she shouted at me out of bed every morning. Makhulu who would turn my backside blue-black with lashes from a peaches stick whenever I was late coming home from Luvhivhi Primary School.

There was nothing extraordinary about Makhulu; except maybe for her strength, which younger me mistook for invincibility. She was as tough as nails and maybe that's why her death blindsided me. It came so suddenly and gave me my first heartbreak.

My grandmother embodied unconditional love. I was her Naledzi ya Masase--the one star that comes from the east in the morning, signalling dawn. I think she and God have a good laugh over that choice of name when they look down at my life... a series of darkness with only glimpses of dawn that are quickly snatched from my bleeding fingers.

I thought of Makhulu in that hospital bed and I wished she was there to hold my hand, and I wondered what name would she have given her. My mother came in shortly after, heaving from the walk

from the taxi rank to the hospital.
"Why would he book for you a hospital in Park Lane? What is wrong with Bara? I gave birth to you there, and you were fine."
No greeting or asking how labour was, if I had any stitches, (I had several)--just straight to complaining. I could have given birth at Bara and she still would have had something to say. My relationship with my mother had always been... difficult. Only because 'harrowing' sounds too cruel a word to use to describe it. I resented her for the longest time for just upping and leaving me behind with Makhulu when I was four, with a promise to come back for me. She never did. She only came back when Makhulu died. They had their own hard relationship, that's why Makhulu stubbornly refused to call me 'Candice', the name my mother gave me, and why my mother never spoke in tshiVenda, her mother tongue.
When the nurse placed my daughter in my mother's hands, a swift transformation happened right before my eyes. The usual tight and pinched look around my mother's eyes and mouth stretched into a beam and for the first time in a long time, I saw the gap between her teeth clearly as she cooed and aah-ed.
"Nzukulu kaGladys nzena... Look how gorgeous she is, look at those tiny puckered lips." Her voice was thick with emotion and a fleeting sheen covered her eyes. "She looks just like you when you were born."
It was like all the months of being told I am a failure had slipped away, the years of quiet resentment ebbed away in that instance. We were united in our love for the little person among us. Naively, I thought that it was the dawn of a harmonious family.
"Kungentando, that's her name. God willed her into our lives." I bit back my need to give her a Venda name in honour of Makhulu. The moment was perfect and I didn't want to ruin it. I figured I would just slip Naledzi into her birth certificate; besides, Daniel would likely approve of 'Kungentando'.
"I know I have been hard on you, Candice. I hope you know it's not because I hate you, you had so much potential and I wanted to see you do and become better than me." She wasn't looking at me as she said the words that made my heart constrict, she was looking at Kungentando and smiling serenely.
Click!
I didn't get a chance to respond because Daniel came in then with

his camera, a glorious bouquet in hand, and my heart fluttered. That moment in that hospital room, after he kissed my forehead and thanked me for our daughter, when he and Gladys became engrossed over my baby and I felt my grandmother's spirit hovering over us as well... That moment is etched in my soul, tucked away in my infrequent bubbles of happiness. My life was perfect in that moment, and I stupidly thought the stars were finally aligning.

Then my mother said she was going to buy some clothes for the baby, Daniel gave her money to buy more and she hugged me, kissed me on both cheeks loudly, just like Makhulu used to do, and she left. That was the last time I saw her--no goodbyes, nothing. Her death hit me just as hard as Makhulu's, I was desolate, even more so when Daniel dropped the bomb that he was married and he... no, they--he and his sister--thought it best that my child be raised by his wife.

All the blinkers left my eyes and the dawn I had glimpsed turned into murky waters. I wasn't getting the chance to make my mother proud of me. I was never going to be the doctor that Makhulu wanted me to be. I wasn't the love of Daniel's life as he was mine. No, I was nothing more than his baby-maker.

Chapter 4

Candice

Silence hangs thick between us, punctuated by my heavy breathing as I try to contain my emotions. My mother's death is a huge trigger for me. I wish I had appreciated her more; I wish I hadn't disappointed her so much, I wish— The shrill cry of my ringtone breaks into my thoughts, breaking the silence.

"Don't answer that," he commands sharply.

Any other day I would listen, but my emotions are currently all over the place and my nerves are taut, so I snap at him just as sharply, "I am a mother and something might be wrong with the kids." Idiot! I add silently. Even in my highly-strung state, I know that I can only push him so far. He grunts and commands me to put it on loudspeaker. The controlling ass!

"Candice—"

"Mummy!"

Denise pushes to speak at the same time as her sister and they both dissolve into fits of giggles, and that makes some of the tension gripping my heart loosen.

"How are you girls doing?" My voice is rough with emotion and I try to clear my throat.

"We are doing great. We just finished watching The Princess and the Frog, again." The soft exasperation in Oyama's voice makes my lips twitch.

Denise is obsessed with that movie and Amandla is obsessed with Moana. The last time they had a sleepover at my place before we moved to this dump, I was just as exasperated. I half-listen to their happy chatter while trying to get my emotions under control. I can hear Oyinqaba's excited chatter as well; my little boy is so grown and he can speak a mile a minute, even though most of his words aren't clear. His speaking development has been slow but we are getting there.

"Candice, are you okay?" Oyama's question makes Daniel raise his eyebrows at me.

"Just a sore throat and a headache, I think I might be coming down with a cold." The headache part is true. Oyama tuts kindly and tells me what remedies I should take.

"I saw your interview." She's lowered her voice, even though the children have long lost interest in our conversation and I can hear them badgering her husband in the background. "I want you to know how proud I am of you. I finished reading the other manuscript, your life story, and I—"

"We can meet for lunch sometime and discuss it without the kids' prying ears," I quickly talk over her, not wanting Daniel to hear this. It's personal, just as I originally wrote my life story just for Oyama, not for him.

"You're right, I just... I want you to know that I love you, Candice. I know our beginning wasn't great but I want us to break the cycle and have a full mother-daughter relationship. If you'll have me."

I forget about Daniel and his gun, about everything, and I hold on to the words that I have been longing for... for so long.

"I would love that very much." I can't help the tears even if I tried.

"You're crying, aren't you? You should have been Lola's mother, not mine," she teases, and I can't help the bark of laughter that escapes.

"These are happy tears." Well, mostly.

When the call ends, I have a smile on my face and I feel lighter than I did before answering it. Light enough to ignore Daniel's snarl.

"You gave my daughter this?" He points derisively at the printed pages. He thought I was bluffing and now he's like a bear with a sore tooth. I smile deviously at him and flip to the next page. I start reading the next chapter while he fumes.

Chapter 5

7 December 1996

I was young and couldn't make sense of my grandmother's death. One minute she had been chasing me for taking some of the mangoes that she wanted to go and sell at the market, the next, she went to sleep early because of a headache and she never woke up. I was still young and couldn't understand how my mother left with a promise to get baby clothes and the next, I got a call to come and identify her body. I was in pain, the stitches throbbed every time I moved and my heart felt like a truck had rammed into it, just like the truck that rammed into the taxi that my mother was in.

Daniel found me struggling to get off the bed, the moment I got down despite his misgivings, a dizzy spell engulfed me, the floor spinning, until darkness pulled me under. When I came to, his face was looming over me, creased with worry.

"You had me scared, the doctors say you are anaemic. Why didn't you tell me that you collapsed after giving birth?"

The whole birthing process had been a blur of pain for me and I was put on bed rest for that day, even after I had tried telling them that I had to go and identify my mother's body.

"Let me carry this burden for you, Baby." And carry it, he did. From identifying my mother's body to arranging the funeral... making sure her death certificate was secure. I don't know how he

did it all but it gave me time to heal and cry.
I was let go on the second day; they wanted me to stay longer but Daniel got me discharged. He hired a cab for me so that I wouldn't have to take the many taxis to KwaThema. His sister was there with me, holding Kungentando. I was drowning in my own bewilderment and sorrow, I couldn't cope, so much so that when she started crying, I cried too. My nipples hurt, and every time Sis' Phindi told me a remedy or how to hold my daughter, I just thought it should have been my mother or grandmother teaching me all this and they were gone.
Grief is a funny thing. My mother's death awoke all the grief I felt when my grandmother died and it felt like I was being swallowed whole by the sheer magnitude of my grief. It got worse when I got home and I found my aunts and uncles had taken over our tiny resettlement home.
It reminded me too much of my grandmother's funeral. They had come then and instead of allowing me to grieve the love of my life, I was sent to and fro from dawn until dusk and as soon as the burial was over, they couldn't wait to get rid of me. I found my clothes packed when we got back from burying Makhulu.
Seeing them again in my mother's house, acting like they owned the place, broke me further. Kungentando cried that night. She cried until she was blue in the face and I was there, crying with her. She needed her mother and I needed mine. I tried breastfeeding her but she latched on too tight and when I yelped in pain, she cried with renewed vigour. I felt like ending it all that night, taking my life and hers seemed like the way to go but I was just in too much pain. We were woken up by my aunt, the headmistress of Luvhivhi Primary School, just an hour after we had finally collapsed into sleep, exhausted by our tears.
"I knew you wouldn't amount to anything, just like your mother. Get up! You are only good for opening your legs. Your peers are going to college, starting businesses, and you are struggling to feed a newborn baby. At least my mother is resting, this child would have been her burden as well. Do you even know the father, you yellow thing?"
I had thought I was numb but her words pierced my grief and all I could do was cry silently and try to hush my angry baby. We had slept on the floor, they took my mother's bed. My body ached and my stitches felt like they were about to burst. When Sis' Phindi

came, she was appalled that none of my aunts had helped me sit on salt or massaged my back with a hot towel.

I hadn't bathed because none of my aunts or cousins would hold my baby. I tried wiping Kungentando but she was so tiny and I was afraid that I would hurt her tummy where the umbilical cord still sat as a pegged stump. Her aunt wiped her and applied spirit around the stump and then attended to me.

When Daniel came, he found my aunts and uncles having a shouting match over who should take the responsibility of burying my mother. I was sitting quietly in the corner, crying, while Sis' Phindi attended to Kungentando.

"Elders, I have taken care of the funeral arrangements," he assured them and my uncle, he was still a soldier then before he rose quickly in ranks, shot him an accusing look.

"Who are you?"

"I am the father of Candice's baby."

There were grumbles among them, then they wanted to know when he was coming to pay damages and the bride price. I wished the ground would open up and swallow me. All they wanted was money, yet they weren't even willing to give their sister a dignified send-off. I was relieved when Daniel asked me to take a walk with him. I was feeling suffocated and all I wanted was the burial to be over so that they would leave.

He took me to Zibas Garden Square and he looked nervous, nothing like the self-assured young man that I had fallen head-over-heels in love with. I put it down to him experiencing my family for the first time and their demands. He asked me how I was feeling and I told him everything but he was still fidgety. I was starting to worry and trying to figure out what could be the matter. I was never prepared for what he blurted out next.

"I had a fiancée when we met but she was studying in America. She came back two months ago and we got married last weekend."

I felt the world spinning out of control again and darkness mercifully claimed me.

* * *

When I came to, it felt like someone had sucker-punched me right in the gut, knocking all the air out of my lungs. I was floored and I couldn't breathe. It felt like my heart was fighting to break out of my chest.

"We need to get your iron levels up." The care in his voice which I cherished before had turned into mockery and I shrugged his hand away.

He was crowding me. I wished I had woken up without the memory of what he'd said but the words still threatened to crush me. I looked at him, Daniel, hoping that he would laugh and say it was a joke. If anything, he looked guilty as hell.

"But there was no sign of her in your apartment," I managed to wheeze, after what felt like an eternity of me gaping at him and him evading my eyes.

"She hadn't been to the apartment. When she left, we had just graduated from university and I had just started working."

There wasn't much to say after that. He wasn't pulling my leg; he was married, had gotten married right under my nose. I tried to think of a weekend when he hadn't been available. He was always there, like clockwork, every day--with my cravings, with a massage at hand, and he took me for my daily walks. Had he been distant? I wrecked my head, trying to think of any indication, any sign that he had been living two lives and that he was anything but the older boyfriend who was loving and attentive almost to a fault. I couldn't find any.

"Nowa yo vhonalaho a i lumi." Makhulu used to say. A visible snake doesn't bite; it's the one that you don't see coming that strikes. At that moment, those words made the most sense to me. That was my first inkling of the way Daniel Sisulu could embody and play a role. It should have warned me about the depth of his psychosis back then but I was an emotionally overwhelmed, desolate teenager who felt like the world she had painstakingly built up in her mind had unexpectedly come tumbling down like a house of cards.

"We just had a baby." I remember the anguish in my whisper vividly. My voice was choked with so much emotion but my eyes remained dry. Maybe I had spent all my tears or I was just too stunned to cry.

"I know, and our baby is the reason why I needed us to talk.

Look, Candy, you snuck up on me and got under my skin. I love you so much but it has always been Mpumi--she was always going to be my wife, the mother of my children. What we had was supposed to be fun, a girl that I met on the bus but it grew into more. We have a baby together and now, we have to think about that baby."

I often sit and think back to this conversation. I can see myself--my body ravaged by giving birth, my eyes red-rimmed from crying for my mother and lack of sleep. I was in one of my mother's chunky jerseys because my breasts were too full of milk and they kept leaking. I was a mess, figuratively and literally, while he was his usual suede, sophisticated self with his Mandela cut, shiny brown shoes and cardigan thrust carefully on his shoulders over his Polo shirt. He looked like he was going to one of his golf games where he slithered his way into parliament.

He wouldn't meet my eyes, that was the only indication of any discomfort he might have had or maybe he just hadn't perfected the art of manipulation yet. He didn't have to be perfect at it to get to me, though, he had me at 'I love you so much'.

My therapist and I have spent years unpacking our conversation on that park bench, years trying to unravel where my need to be loved comes from. Is it from the space left by a father I don't even know? There were whispers about who my father is or was but my mother clammed up whenever I brought up the issue of my paternity, until she died. Or, is it to fill the void left by Makhulu? No one can ever fill that void; that much, I have learnt over the years. Or, is to fill the gap left by the dysfunctional relationship that I had with my mother? So many possibilities but one thing I know for certain was that at that moment, everything else was a blur--except that he loved me so much.

Not enough to break off his engagement or annul his marriage but he--the put-together lawyer and Mandela-in-the-making--loved me, the girl who didn't even have a high school diploma at the time.

"I know this must all be a shock to you, and I wanted to talk about this with your mother, but unfortunately, she's not here anymore. I know how overwhelming everything is to you right now, so we thought... Sis' Phindi and I thought that it would be best for everyone if I could take the baby and raise her," He was silent for a moment, as if unsure of his next words, "with Mpumi."

I remember how deranged my laugh was, it felt like the wheels were coming off in my mind and I was going crazy. I laughed until tears seeped from my eyes and he was just staring at me the way one stares at a bomb that's about to go off. Petrified. The laugh bubbled from deep inside my stomach, I felt like I was going to be sick. When I finished laughing, I felt depleted of all emotion, hollow.

"You took everything away from me--my virginity, my future--and now, you want to take the only person I have left in this world? I haven't even buried my mother yet." My voice was robotic and grew into a soft plea at the last sentence.

"That's what I mean. This will give you a chance to go back to school, finish your Matric, and make something of your life while I look after the baby."

I looked at him blankly and didn't say a thing. I might have been thinking about ways to kill him and bury him with my mother. No one would be the wiser.

"So, when I get my life together, will I be able to get my child back?" He wouldn't meet my eyes and he kept shifting the cardigan on his shoulders.

"I already took her birth record and wrote down Mpumi as her mother."

Whatever little sanity I had left snapped. I got up from the park bench in a huff and I all but flew down the street to my house with Daniel hot on my heels. He had planned it all down to the dot, the bastard!

I felt used and cornered, I needed to get to my baby. He kept telling me that it's for the best, I was in no state to look after a child. I kept going, fuelled by the fear that I might find that my child had disappeared. No one would have fought for me, that baby was all I had.

Sometimes I wonder at the convenience of my mother's death. She would have been the only stumbling block between Daniel getting what he wanted, the perfect little family to spearhead him into parliament. With her gone, I didn't stand a chance in hell against him, I didn't fit in the image he was building for himself and he wasn't afraid to squash me to get his way. I see it all now that I never stood a chance against him not without my mother, but back then, I was fired up. He would get Kungentando over my dead body.

Chapter 6

Daniel

"Candice how could you accuse me of killing your mother? How could you even put such thoughts down? You made my daughter read this filth!" She is too engrossed in reading her words to realise that I'm now standing right in front of her.

Anger is seeping out of every pore of my skin. I was the one running around trying to make sure I gave her mother a dignified funeral. I had nothing much then but I had to ask a favour from the woman who molested me since i was fourteen, I dubbed her 'the scarecrow', and I paid the price, even though I hated every second of it. I did what I could because I couldn't stand to see the broken, empty look in Candice's face. I took care of her as best as I could and now she has the guts look at me calmly, while accusing me of such cruelty without flinching.

Candice pushes past me and picks up the glass of whiskey before downing it in one go before I can stop her. The smell crowds me and it feels like I'm suffocating.

"You don't have a conscience, Daniel, not since you killed your own father. Anything that stands in your way, you remove; just like you removed Mpumi's unborn baby. You killed an innocent soul because it stood between you and your perfect family. How would you explain away a white man's child? You wouldn't have been able to just add your name to its birth certificate and claim it as yours..." She's all up in my face with her whiskey breath and something in me breaks.

I'm fourteen again, my eyes are leaking, and I'm trying to think of all the ways I'm going to strangle the scarecrow for what she's done to me. I fantasise about putting my hand around her turkey neck and squeezing until her face is a violent shade of red.

'You took everything from me! You worthless piece of shit! I am ridding the world of filth.'

She would try clawing at my hands, because with each sentence, I would tighten my hold and shake her neck to emphasise each point. I want to smell her fear over the stench of whiskey that clings to her like a second skin. I want to watch as her air circulation is being cut off permanently, until she doesn't have the strength to claw at me anymore.

"Da...Da...niel..." The sound of Candice's scratchy voice drags me back to the present where I'm squeezing the life out of the love of my life.

I quickly let go of her neck, as if my hands are being electrocuted by her skin. I watch in horror as she slumps back onto the couch and gulping down as much air as she can to fill her most likely burning lungs. Each feeble cough is like a stab to my heart, my hand hovers above her and she recoils away from me.

I leave Candice crying silently and I move to the tiny bathroom to look for ointment. When I don't find it, I check on her nightstand. The walls in this tiny shithole are closing in on me. I find myself on the floor of Candice's bedroom and violent shudders have rendered me immobile. I almost killed her. I almost killed the one person who, despite all my shortcomings, continues to look at me with stars in her eyes.

Oyama and Denise's faces pop up in my mind and make the shuddering even worse, it feels like I cannot breathe.

* * *

When she flinches, in fear and pain as I hold her neck to the light, pain and shame cuts me deeply. We've done this dance many times, Candice is the only woman I feel safe enough to do choke-play with whenever I have steam to blow off but this is only the second time we are doing this because I snapped and became violent. I want to tell her about the scarecrow and the real reason behind all the other women, but shame always stops me. Dammit! I almost killed Candice.

The topical arnica ointment should feel cool against the burning of her skin. It will reduce the swelling but she'll still have to wear a scarf or polo neck for a week or two this time around because I went too far. I know this because at times, the scarecrow would whip me, and she's the one who introduced me to the ointment.

"Wami…" My voice is hesitant as I call her by my favourite endearment, 'Mine'. Candice looks at me blankly, waiting for me to continue.

"How did we get here?"

Candice sits up, clearly having not expected those words and the thickness of tears roughening my voice. I have done a lot of shitty things in my life that I do not regret, but seeing the imprint of my hands against her pale, slender neck makes me sick to my stomach. For the first time in my life, I regret coming after Candice, maybe I should just let her go. And yet, the thought makes my stomach twist painfully.

Chapter 7

Candice

"I thought you were happy, that I was giving you and the children everything. I've been trying with Denise... Oyinqaba only sleeps after having spoken to me. I asked for a little more time. The people I have discovered now can set us up for life, then I won't have to worry about politics and public image. We can be a family. Then you just had to go and complicate it."

I slump back onto the couch, exhausted because I had hoped that he genuinely wanted to know what went wrong between us, what got us here. I hoped for too much, too soon, and right on cue, he came right back.

Thank God the bite of winter still lingers, even though we are in the middle of August. The daring part of me dares me to not hide my bruises and let the world see the kind of monster that Daniel is. That would only hurt my babies the most, just as exposing him would, so I let the thought go as soon as it enters my mind.

Liar, you don't want to hurt him.

My subconscious is on a bitchy roll today and I'm too exhausted to even think about my need to keep Daniel safe, his image intact after all that he has done to me. The silence stretches as he tends to my neck, and my mind wanders. At times, I think I provoke him to get a glimpse of this tender side of him when I am not pregnant. I think at this point, even my therapist is exasperated by me.

I feel his thumb wipe away the stray tear from my cheek, a slight mildew smell lingers on his hands from the ointment. I resist the urge to lean into his gentle touch because then I would have folded. I meet his beseeching eyes and I keep my stare icy.

He never says 'Sorry'; well, not out loud but he usually follows me around like a wet dog until the bruises disappear. After giving me the most intense orgasm numbing sex, of course. He doesn't lavish me with gifts but gives me something that I crave even more: his loving and attentive side.

I watch as he goes to the kitchen. His presence somehow makes the apartment seem smaller, shabbier. He is in there for a while, I'm even dozing off by the time his steps startle me. He comes back with a huge mug and I can smell the spicy scent of cinnamon.

Oh, he made a honey chamomile latte, my favourite reducing-swelling-from-throat beverage. I take the mug wordlessly and I take gentle sips of the scalding coffee. I even entertain the thought of pouring it at his face, for him to feel a fraction of the pain that I'm in.

I clear my throat, and just that tiny action hurts, then point at the manuscript where it lies forgotten on the couch. He picks it up and when he makes to give it to me, I point at my throat. My voice is gone. He sighs dejectedly then sprawls back on the couch and flips through the pages until he gets to where we were before he strangled me.

It's weird hearing my words coming from his mouth. His voice starts clipped but cultured and I take the time to look at his face, the light cuts off rough planes on his face and highlight the grey streaks in his neatly-cut hair.

I notice the haggard lines around his eyes and mouth and I realise that his Armani suit pants are wrinkled, a far cry from the put-together man that I am used to. I stop ogling him and start listening to him read.

Chapter 8

9 December 1996

In the end, I didn't try to fight giving up my child. When we got home, I found Phindi pacing with my baby, who was burning up, while the rest of my family moved around my mother's house as if they couldn't hear my child's insistent cries.

I tried taking the baby and shushing her but she only cried louder as if, like me, she didn't want to be anywhere near that house. I held her tight, slowly reaching the hard realisation that I didn't have anything or anyone to give to the precious soul in my arms.

How was I going to bathe her? What was I going to feed her? Without a high school diploma, finding a job would be hard. My tears trickled, joining hers, and I handed her back to Phindi, I gave her little forehead one last lingering kiss, then went into my mother's room and locked myself in there; The decision I had taken already haunting me.

Was this how my mother felt when she left me with Makhulu? At least she had had four years with me but I only got three days--a measly, miserable three days--and I already felt like I couldn't cope.

I was shivering and I tried wrapping my arms around me but that didn't erase the gaping, cold prism lodged firmly in my heart. It was the best decision, I tried to convince myself, but I knew in my heart that I should have fought, at least, or tried something, anything, instead of just handing the baby over.

I didn't open the door when my aunts kept knocking. I didn't open when nightfall fell and they wanted to sleep. I couldn't open, even if I tried, not when I felt like I was a zombie, every part of my body didn't feel like it belonged to me anymore. I don't remember sleeping that night but I do remember the insistent wails of an infant tormenting me, my breasts throbbing with punished milk, and twisting around Mama's bed with my fists firmly covering my ears.

My mother's funeral passed in a blur. I don't remember how I got out of the bedroom. I do remember Sis' Phindi bathing me like a baby, though. I wanted to ask where she left Kungentando, wanted so badly to demand that they take me to my daughter, but it felt like my mouth was sewn shut; all emotions and words locked securely away.

I remember stumbling as I went to throw some soil into the grave, and Daniel's strong hands hoisting me up when my legs finally failed me and I slumped on the dusty red soil when everyone else had left.

'Leave me alone.' Those were the first words I uttered and reluctantly, he left me next to her freshly-covered grave.

I didn't say anything as I sat there, just brushed the soft soil and sat there for hours, until Mapura came to get me. Mapura was an older friend that I hung out with. We were in the same class but she was older than me by three years. My mother hated her because she was brazen but on that day, I was grateful that I defied my mother.

'Kuzodlula, Ntwana.'

It will pass, were all the comforting words she gave me, then she passed me a bottle of Savanna Dry. Distell had just recently launched it in May of that year, and I hadn't had a chance to taste it yet because I was pregnant then.

I took my first gulp and the alcohol exploded in my mouth in a foreign taste and I almost spit it out but Mapura told me that it would numb the pain, so I kept on drinking. After the first bottle, I felt light-headed; I hadn't eaten anything in two days. It was a nice and mellow feeling, and I agreed when she suggested that we go to a party that she had been invited to. Anything was better than going back to my mother's house and listening to them

passing my care-giving to each other.
Three bottles was all it took to get me bawling my eyes out for my Makhulu and Mama. Mapura and her friends were sympathetic and they let me cry it out while giving me more bottles of Savanna.
I didn't return home until two days later, and I was relieved to find everyone gone. There was an angry letter from my aunt, that I only read a paragraph of before tearing into tiny pieces and throwing in the bin. I had been summoned to my uncle's house in Limpopo, but there was no way in hell I was going there.
Being home proved to be a double-edged sword, as it reminded me of my mother and Kungentando's cries. I flipped my mother's bed and I found, tucked away, some of the money that she always kept for rainy days and I went to buy two bottles of Savanna, which had become my new drug, and it knocked me out. Mercifully, in my knocked-out state, I didn't have to face Makhulu's disappointment, my mother's wide smile as she held Kungentando, and my daughter's angry little red face as she wailed.

Chapter 9

31 December 1996

The loud knock felt like it was inside my head. I stretched and tried to hold my head as the room swam around me. This was the part of alcohol that I didn't like much. The insistent knocking again had me crawling out of bed and I almost fell flat on my face.
I had to wait for the room to stop spinning before I cautiously ventured outside of the room that I was in. After what felt like ages later and walking through an active minefield, the knocking hadn't abated; if anything, it had grown even more persistent.
I flung the door as hard as I could and winced when I came into contact with the bright beams of the sun and Daniel's glowering face. I moved back to get away from the sunlight and he let himself in and closed the door with a loud bang, causing me to whimper as I held my throbbing head.
'I've been looking for you for three weeks now!' It sounded like he was screaming from inside my head.
'Not so loud, please,' I protested, as I closed my eyes and put my head on the kitchen table to cool it; it felt like it was about to combust.
'Don't tell me to keep it down. Look at you! You smell like a distillery! When was the last time you showered or ate anything? When was the last time you cleaned? Look at this place, it's a

mess!'
With each line, I firmly placed a fist over each ear. It did nothing to help with my splitting headache. Daniel let out a long-suffering sigh before frog-matching me to the bathroom, thrusting a toothbrush and toothpaste at me, then instructing me to bathe and look presentable.
I took my time in the cold shower, until my skin was faintly pink and wrinkled. I felt better and braced myself as I got into the bedroom. My mother's presence still lingered and I could only bear it when I was drunk.
After shrugging into the closest thing that I could lay my hands on, I hightailed to the kitchen, only to stop short when I found Daniel with my mother's apron on and the sleeves of his shirt rolled up his arms as he cooked on my mother's old Moffat stove. The kitchen was now sparkling clean and so was the sitting room. Come to think of it, the bed had also been made. I perched gingerly on the kitchen chair, the headache back with a vengeance. No word was spoken as he cooked and afterwards, he dished up for me and handed me some Asprin and a glass of orange juice. I ate as if my life depended on it, took the Asprin, and waited for the lecture. It didn't take long in coming.
'Drowning your sorrows in alcohol won't make them go away but only add to your troubles.' Stern lines etched on his face, reinforcing his reprimand.
'What do you care?' I mumbled, breaking eye contact.
'You are the mother of my child--'
I didn't let him finish, 'No, I'm not. You made sure to erase me from your child's life, so don't come here and pretend like you care because you don't.'
He sighed and looked at me, he looked nervous.
'Mpumi would like to meet you.' It felt like he had sucker-punched me in the lungs, stealing my ability to breathe. When I didn't answer, he went outside and came back with a plump woman; her ebony skin was glowing, while mine was pasty from too much alcohol, dehydration, and not-enough sleep. I understood immediately what she had that I didn't.
She was classy, even in her discomfort, what with the briefcase she held with both hands in front of her blue collared dress, with a tiny red belt that cinched her waist perfectly, matching the red bow in her afro as well as her shoes. I didn't even want

to think about what I looked like next to her in one of my mother's old t-shirts.

'Hello.' Her greeting was pleasant enough, but I just stared at her blankly, intimidated and bitter that she got to live my dream life while I spiralled.

'I promise I will love and take care of her as if she were my own,' she blurted out, and I watched as Daniel stood behind her, brushing her shoulders in comfort. They made a striking couple and I could see that with her, he had an image that he would never have with me. For one, I wasn't as articulate or sure of myself as she was. She gave off 'high society wife' even back then. When I looked into her eyes, though, their sadness mirrored mine. I wanted to ask what she had to be sad about, but my tongue was stuck to the roof of my mouth.

Daniel sighed before taking out the briefcase that she had slid under the table. I watched him snap it open then turning it to me.

'It's not much, but we thought it should be able to send you back to school and be enough to live on until you get to college.' It didn't escape me that he'd said 'we'... They had sat down together and discussed poor orphan, fatherless Candice who had been their incubator, and decided to pay me off.

When I just looked at the money without moving or blinking, Daniel sighed again and tried again.

'Look, I know that you are angry, hurting, and scared but this will work out for the best. You are young, Candice, and you have the rest of your life to find yourself, make more babies if you want them. But, go back to school first.'

I listened but didn't make any move to acknowledge his words, and when he tried to hold my face, I shrugged his hand away. Mpumi got up abruptly and left. Dejected, Daniel stood up to follow his wife, probably to assure her that I meant nothing, and I only spoke when he was at the door.

'How is she?'

He stopped with his hand on the doorknob and turned to look at me, I tried hard not to cry again because I knew that if I started, I wouldn't stop.

'Her fever has gone down. It was colic but she's fine now.'

I nodded past the lump in my throat and closed my eyes until I heard the faint click of the door. When I opened my eyes, I was alone with a pile of money. I looked at it, not seeing the

neatly-stacked notes, only Makhulu's disappointed face--the way she would suck her teeth and turn the sides of her mouth down.
'Ni a shonisa, Masase inwi.' Her face might have faded from my memory but her voice always remained the same in my mind.
She would be right to say that I was an embarrassment because I had amounted to nothing, I couldn't write my exams because I fell pregnant and I didn't even have the baby to show for it, just a pile of money.

***

The leopards on top of the notes were all staring at me blankly but I could feel their condescending censure. I had just snapped shut the briefcase when there was a swift knock and the door was flung wide open. It could only be Mapura. She eyed the briefcase with curiosity, it was made of worn-out leather that looked like it was about to give in at any moment.
'My mother's,' I lied, hoping that would assuage her curiosity and it worked, then she quickly moved on to why she had come.
There was another party. This one was a festival held by Studio Mix at Lotlamoreng Dam in Mafikeng.
'How the hell are we getting to Mafikeng?'
She brushed off my question with a simple answer but wouldn't meet my eyes, 'My uncle and one of his friends is coming to fetch us. Between you and me, I think his friend has taken a liking to you because he asked me to bring specifically you with.'
I would learn later that Mapura's uncle was actually her sugar daddy and she had recruited me. But on that day, the festival was just what I needed to alleviate the pain that throbbed in every part of my body. I agreed to go and she excitedly went to her place while I dragged the briefcase and hid it at the back of the wardrobe.
'We need to do your hair!' Mapura shouted as she came in with the clothes that she insisted I should wear.
I plainly refused to wear the bralette that she insisted we both

wear because my breasts were not only bigger than hers but also still full of milk and prone to occasionally leaking. A baggy shirt over a very short, flared skirt and thick-soled boots that were tied up at the front was what I eventually agreed to.

'You are lighter than me, you should do the blond,' she insisted, and even though I didn't care much for the colour, I went along with it.

I had nothing to lose. I had no one to tell me what I could or couldn't do. No one cared and neither did I. That's a dangerous mental space to be in at the age of sixteen. My place was our dressing place because Mapura's mother wouldn't be there to tell us off, my neighbours kept a wide berth away from me and those who did try to meddle, I cut off very quickly.

Bhut' Mandla--he insisted on the 'bhuti' when I mistakenly called him 'Malume'--arrived in a cloud of fumes from his Dolphin without his friend, whom he promised we would meet up with in Mafikeng. I sat at the back while Mapura sat in front; I pretended that I couldn't see how his hand was riding up her plaid skirt and I drank my Savanna, which had quickly become my sanctuary.

When we arrived at Lotlamoreng Dam, it was already teeming with people. We set up our cooler box some distance away from the dome and just where we could see the sun's sinking rays lazily stoke the dam's surface.

I was relieved that Bhut' Mandla's friend didn't have the same stubborn pouch that Bhut' Mandla had. His hair was greying on his temple but that was the only indication if his age. He had a fit body, muscular than Daniel, he was shorter and stockier and it didn't hurt that he drove a Mercedes SL 500.

After my third Savanna, I was bouncing up and down his lap as Boom Shaka performed Thobela. So started my life of debauchery on the eve of 1 January 1997. It was a slippery slope from there, that parts of still remain elusive in my mind, flirting in recesses of my memory.

I remember kissing Bhut' Mandla's friend, his clammy mouth suctioning my lips until they felt like they would bleed as, around us, others drunkenly groped and the rest screamed, welcoming in the new year.

Chapter 10

Daniel

I stop reading when she falls asleep, I can imagine where the story is going and my vision is already darkening around the edges at the thought of that disgusting old man with his hands all over my Candy. My hands itch to tell my investigators to find him, but with nothing to go by except 'Bhut' Mandla's friend', there isn't much I can do besides kill him a million times in my mind for daring to paw over what is mine.

When she's asleep, Candice is an endearing mix of Oyama and Denise. I lightly brush my thumb against her pouty rosebud lips, loving their full and lush softness. Her breaths are even, until she encounters something in her dreams that has her long, doll-like eyelashes quivering. I ease the frown-lines from her forehead, not wanting her to worry even in sleep.

Candice is the most beautiful woman in the world. I'm not thinking this in a subjective or besotted way. It's fact. Her features are porcelain, she looks breakable, like that precious china set that is kept locked away in MaNtuli's lounge display unit. MaNtuli, who is my ex-wife Nompumelelo's mother, would kill anyone who goes anywhere near what she calls her room divider, and I will kill each and every person who has gone anywhere near my Candice. I just need to note down their names and have them hunted down. The thought gives me some pleasure, until I see the angry red marks around her neck, then the self-loathing settles around me like a worn and familiar mantle.

It takes a while to fade and when it does, I place a lingering kiss on her high forehead and I brush off the stray tear that splashes on her cheek. I pick her up from the sofa, and I realise that she's gained some weight. She snuggles up to me, placing her hand on my heart as she always does and I lean over and catch a whiff of her smell as I always do. Her bed covers most of the tiny bedroom and I'm relieved that she bought the same bed as the one she left behind, at least they sleep in relative comfort. When I put her in bed, she clings onto me, and I let her while I stroke her curly hair.

Long after Candice's limbs have loosened and she's blowing small bubbles through her mouth, I can't get myself to stop stroking her hair and staring at her. My phone's flashing notifications, making me reluctantly let her go. I pull down the notification bar and see that there's a bunch of notifications.

Mandisa: I told you to put your bitch on a leash. Look now she's live on TV, making a spectacle out of me.

Mandisa: Where are you????

Mandisa: Since you can't deal with that whore, I'll ask Daddy to deal with her.

Fuck! I clear the notifications when I see a bunch from her father, Sis' Phindi, and my team. I can already feel the darkness moving in. I'm about to place a call, when an incoming call starts flashing across my screen—an unknown number. I curse silently and move out of the bedroom, making sure to softly close the door behind me. I accept the call, but the caller doesn't say anything.

"Mkhulu was too lenient with you. He felt guilty about his nephew and he tried to turn Shanty Town trash into something fit for parliament, and this is how you shit on his grave," my cousin's nasally voice grits against my ears. I clench and unclench my teeth before I respond.

"What do you want, Mbuso?"

"I want to take out the trash, but since you are tucked away in your fortress, I'll settle for doing what Mkhulu should have done in the first place: Get rid of your sperm dish. Now that she's gotten out from under your thumb, it will be so easy to crush her. But I'll toy with her first, maybe sample those creamy thighs that have you losing your mind..." I cannot control the explosive anger that grips me as I listen to him speak about Wami like that. Candice is my kryptonite and I hate that so many people are now aware of that fact.

"Listen here, you piece of entitled shit—!" Mbuso cuts off my menacing threat with a taunting laugh and he hangs up just before I hear glass shatter.

On high alert, I rush back into the bedroom and I'm greeted by the whole window blown and scattered across the floor and bed. By some miracle, Candice is still peacefully sleeping, without any cuts. I shelve the burning anger as I carefully take her from the bed and put her on the sofa, she mumbles something in Venda that I don't quite understand, reminding me of how much I never knew about her. I also shelve the sting of pain that that reminder brings, and I activate my proactive mode.

My top priority is keeping Candice safe while I get rid of all the threats against her. After the interview she did, that number probably tripled. She didn't fool anyone important with her denial, I doubt if she even managed to fool the masses. While I strategise, I move the table and couches, the rug is fluffy and deep enough to sleep on. I go back into the bedroom and find something to cover her with. In the built-in cabinets, I find the kids' comforters and some blankets. Once Candice is carefully tucked in, I make a call. The number rings twice before a bored voice rumbles over the line.

"Speak." I've noticed that my new colleague is a man of few words, he always gets straight to the point. I find it refreshing after spending more than half my life around people who enjoy hearing the sound of their own voices.

"I need a favour," I state, and the brute chuckles as if he finds me cute.

"Mr Candice. I'm impressed that you managed to get my number. For every favour, you'll owe me two," Joshua informs me in the same bored tone.

I ignore how much I like being called 'Mr Candice' and ask for cleaners, I need them to install shatter-proof windows and reinforce the security in this shithole as much as they can, while I figure out my next move. I also request the blueprint of the building's floor plan to figure out an exit that won't draw anyone's attention. I could use my team, but I have a niggling suspicion that someone in my team is either working for Mbuso and the Sisulus or Mandisa and her father. Both options mean that if I use my team, I would be putting Wami in danger.

"Done. The cleaners should be there in ten minutes. I'll also have the jet on standby should you need a quick escape."

The line goes dead before I can thank him or ask any more questions. There's a brief knock on the door nine minutes later. While I make sure Candice is comfortable on the fluffy rug, the cleaners work discreetly. For once, I'm grateful that Candice is a deep sleeper. By the time I let out the cleaners and lock the door, the first rays of the sun are peeking through the clouds as I inspect the windows in the bedroom.

Everything looks exactly how it was before Mbuso's attack, they even remade the bed. I shelve the thoughts of dismembering Mbuso as I reach out to my contact eSwatini; we'll need to disappear for a while, to give me time to regroup and put some plans in motion. I wasn't sure about getting into bed with Joshua and my Zimbabwean contact, but Wami has taken that decision out of my hands. I would lay down with the devil if it means keeping her and my kids safe. I know the kids are safe with Oyama, I just have to focus on their mother. I find it easier to strategise with one hand gently massaging Candice's curls while the other flies over the screen of my phone, placing all my chess pieces in position.

Chapter 11

Candice

I wake up feeling warm all over and the weight of a familiar body against me. I snuggle closer before I open one eye and peek at our surroundings. The coffee table has been moved across the lounge and so have the couches—weirdly, pushed against the door…and we are sleeping on the fluffy rug. One of the kids comforters was put down and my blankets are covering us.

I must have fallen asleep after he read the third chapter. I try to move but he murmurs something and clings even tighter around me as if, even in sleep, he still holds me hostage. The lines brought about by age have slipped away in his sleep and he reminds me of the young man I met on the bus.

"Why are you smiling with that dreamy look on your face?"

His rough morning voice brings me back to the present. Still hung up over my reminiscing, I let my hand trail his morning stub. He watches me, eyes slightly widening as if he wants to be sure if it's really me. Satisfied that I mean no harm, he leans into my touch and revels in the way I keep stroking his beard. We don't say anything, we just stay in this position as the minutes trickle past.

Our bubble is burst by a loud knock on the door. Daniel looks at me with narrowed eyes and I shrug my shoulders, I have no idea who it could be or what time it is. He presses his finger to his lips and I roll my eyes before pointing at my throat, I can't scream for help even if I want to. Whoever is by the door is persistent.

"Candice, open up, Kid. It's me." Oh, shit! It's Sibo, my publicist. We were supposed to meet for a breakfast meeting and discuss the interview I had and the ones she has lined up.

Knowing Sibo, she won't give up. And, right on cue, the banging starts again. She knocks for another minute before she gives up. Relief washes over me as the clicking of her heels fades as she walks away.

"Get up, we have to leave."

I shoot an angry look at Daniel. He's crazy, I'm not going anywhere. He is the one who has to leave and I will call Sibo and claim a severe cold; my hoarse, almost-gone voice will collaborate my story. He tries hoisting me up but I shrug off his hands.

"No." Even saying that one syllable leaves a trail of fire in my throat.

"You either go to the bathroom and freshen up before we leave or be difficult, and we leave without you brushing your teeth."

The horror of walking around with unbrushed teeth has me springing up and I'm halfway through my shower when there is knocking again. I close the tap and listen. The knocking is persistent but there are voices as well. I step out of the shower and with a towel wrapped around me, I go to investigate barefoot.

"… Ma'am, we can't open the door without the owner's permission or a police warrant. She's probably somewhere else and she forgot that you arranged to meet." The caretaker's gravelly voice carries undertones of irritation that are mirrored by the scowl in Daniel's face.

"It's not like her to just switch off her phone and the security guard said he didn't see her leave. I need to check if indeed she's not laying in a pool of her own blood in there."

"Ma'am, we don't make the laws. Go and open a case with the police and only then will we be able to assist you. Our guards change shifts, what if she left last night or before this guard's shift started? I have work to do, if you'll excuse me."

At which point, Sibo loses it. Her angry voice trails the caretaker as she gives him the stats of women dying while people wait for the police and people in authority to act. Daniel's shoulders are rigid while my eyes are moist; Sibo cares, and it's a foreign feeling.

Once their footfalls have silenced, Daniel takes out one of those old phones that have gone out of circulation and he calls someone as he paces.

"I'm beginning to think you have no friends, Mr Candice," the gruff voice cackles over the phone, and I see Daniel pinch the bridge of his nose.

"I wouldn't call if it wasn't an emergency. I need your help. Again." He is trying to rein in his irritation and I wonder who is on the other end of the line. If it was someone on his payroll, Daniel would have snapped at him by now.

"I am not your errands boy." Whoever it is isn't super chatty, at all.

"Please, Joshua, I need all traces of me erased from the CCTV footage, and a way to get out of here now without being detected," he rounds off by making the request, and the person on the phone didn't interject or make any sound throughout.

"Give me fifteen minutes." The line goes dead, then Daniel is dialling another number.

"Hlongwane speaking. Hello?" This one sounds short of breath.

"It's me. Change of plans. I need to leave right now." Whoever is on the other end of the line curses before promising to call back in ten minutes.

I have so many questions but Daniel is on Minister mode now and I know better than to ask or challenge him anyhow when he is.

"Go and get dressed. We are leaving in twenty minutes."

As I get dressed, I wonder where my phone is. I just know that Daniel took it because I never switch my phone off. I'm about to put my scarf on when he comes in and takes a small suitcase and starts throwing in some of my clothes. He's freshened up but still in yesterday's clothes.

"Wh... Why do... you have... to leave with me?" It takes a lot of effort to say the words and he barely looks at me before moving on to pick some of my shoes.

"We still have a book to read, remember?" I huff at his condescending tone.

I had to go and fall for the world's worst prick and have his babies. He tosses me a wide-brimmed hat and my largest sunglasses and orders me to wear them, just as his burner phone goes off. My life should be a movie.

Chapter 12

Candice

My mother must have dropped me a lot when I was a baby. That is the only logical reason as to why I am dressed up as one of Ocean's Eight cast and being snuck out of my flat in a back exit that I did not even know existed until now. Keeping my head down, Daniel's hand on my back is the only thing guiding me. There is a grey Sedan parked a block away from my flat and when we get to it, a driver opens the back door and I am let in by Daniel before he follows me in.

There is terse silence in the car as it weaves through the traffic of taxis headed to town. I can see the downside turn of Daniel's lips, as if he's never been in a taxi going into town at one point in his life. He wants nothing that reminds him of his poverty, and 'poverty' is the one word to describe his upbringing. He never talks of it but his sister, Phindi, told me everything when we were still on good terms. My upbringing was a bed of roses compared to theirs.

I never once stayed in a shack and I didn't have to go around doing people's gardens and working in the shebeen where my father was a regular.

When she told me all of it, it made me understand his obsession with anything that showcased his wealth, and why he never touches alcohol—because to him, it's synonymous with a downward spiral to poverty. I understand why being in my flat made him so cagey—because he has never wanted his children to have anything less than the best that money can buy. If only he knew that what they need can't be bought with money. They need their father's presence, his unconditional love.

Denise ran to me the other day in our old flat waving the universal house remote and turned on the TV in Oyinqaba's nursery. I was distracted, trying to get Oyinqaba to take a bath is hard. He wiggles around and you have to concentrate, otherwise he can fall or drench everything around him in water.

"Mummy! Mummy, look! There is Daddy on the TV!" I don't remember what half-hearted response I gave her as I scooped her brother out of the water but I remember the angry scream she let out.

That got my attention because not only did it spook the baby, but also, one thing about my middle child is that she is the sweetest of all my children and she is not prone to tantrums or meltdowns.

"Denise! What is the matter with you?"

Oyinqaba was now screaming, and I was trying to calm both of them down and get to the bottom of what had upset her.

In a tremulous voice, she pointed out that her father was with Monwabisi on the TV, and asked why he never went with her to the TV, then maybe the girls in school wouldn't say she makes up tales when she tells them that Daddy is her father. My heart sank that day and it made me realise that the words that Oyama said, though hurtful, were true.

I will never forget the shock turned into disgust on her face when she discovered that I was pregnant with Oyinqaba.

'Please don't tell me you allowed him to knock you up again. What are you, his baby-maker?' The words stung so much, I lashed out but Oyama held my hand in a vice-like grip and gave me a piece of her mind.

'You don't get to hit me for calling you out on your bullshit, Candice, have a little self-respect. That narcissistic man will never make an honest woman out of you. You'll always be his dirty little secret. If you can't think for yourself, at least consider Denise and now the little poor soul in your belly. They have to grow up as secrets, unfortunately for them, his new wife won't take them in and mother

them like I was mothered. Grow up, Candice.'

Seeing Denise crying over seeing her father on TV with his public son made me want to grow up and finally protect my kids. My exit strategy was set in motion that day.

Yeah, you are doing a great job standing your ground and growing up, Candice. Kuddos on your exit plan, my subconscious sneers and I want to shrink into the seat. I have no excuse for not putting up more of a fight and being here right now. No excuse.

Fuck!

Oyama might be looking for me. I clutch at Daniel's arm, drawing his attention to me.

"Need to text Oyama."

The alarm on his face gives away to a gentle expression, the softest I have seen on him since last night.

"I texted her and said you had to go away for a while and clear your head. That you went on a writing retreat."

I slump back into my seat, not surprised that he thought to cover every angle. Sibo alone can't kick up enough fuss about my disappearance but Oyama, with the backing of the Levines, could raise hell—even for him. I think, after Mpumi and Phindi, Oyama is the only female that Daniel Sisulu is intimidated by.

"Are you going to kill me?" My question makes him whip his face around to gape at me incredulously.

"*What*? Why would I kill you?" he asks, as if he didn't almost strangle me to death last night. And, as if he suddenly remembers too, his face becomes shrouded with shame.

"Look, I know I haven't always treated you right but I would never kill you, Wami. I thought going away would make us reconnect and maybe reading what you wrote would make me understand because just last week, we were fine, Baby. I told you that I had to go to Australia, and I had to cut my trip short because you left and you didn't even tell me. You took my… our children to that dump, and I'm just trying to understand why."

"You could have just asked me, instead of kidnapping me." Pouting like

Denise when she's sulking probably isn't helping my case.

He scrubs his face and expels a frustrated breath, before taking my hands in his. I keep my eyes on our entwined hands, refusing to meet his.

"Nowami." A shiver goes down my spine at the gruffness of his voice as he calls me by the name that he gave me.

"When it comes to you, I'm often rash in my words and my actions. When I cut my trip short in Australia, I had a plan, until I got to our flat and I found all the furniture there just sitting alone and no sign of you and the kids. I felt like I was losing my mind. I thought you had taken the kids and skipped the country. This fear crept over me and I haven't eaten or slept since; until last night, when I was in your arms. I'm a mess and I'm sorry—for laying my hands on you, for putting you through all that pain when you were just a kid. If you don't want to go, I can ask the driver to turn around and go drop you off."

The sagging in his shoulders and the way his hands are shaking slightly as he clasps mine give me a hint of the turmoil that he's trying hard to contain. Daniel hates showing any emotion, hates not being in control but he's also a world-class manipulator. I'm torn.

"Would you let me go back?" I look into his eyes and he holds my questioning gaze steadily, his beseeching.

"I wouldn't want to, but yeah, I shouldn't treat you like you are some common slut. You are the mother of my children, you are mine, Nowami, but please don't punish my children for my sins. That flat and area are unsafe. At least go back to our flat. Or, I can buy you the house you've been asking for. Anything, just don't take them back there. I won't be able to live with myself knowing that my family is staying in that dump."

I'm telling you, my mother dropped me one too many times when I was a baby, because that is the only reason why I am freeing my hand so that I can wipe the stray tear that has snuck to his cheek.

"Will you let me go? Let me and the children start over in another country?" His nose widens and he bristles at the question.

"No. Not without me."

It was a test and he passed it, or at least he was honest with that. As the car draws to a stop and I realise that we are now at the airport entrance, I try to wet my dry throat.

"Where are we going?" His shoulders sag in relief this time and his hands stop shaking.

"Eswatini."

I know that is all I'm getting, so I don't bother probing; instead, I ask for my phone back. I want to call the girls. He hesitates and I look at him with a raised eyebrow. He sighs when he sees that I'm not budging and he digs for it in his pocket before he hands it to me. I call Oyama and she sounds relieved, stating that my text sounded weird; I assure her that I was drunk on meds because of the cold that is messing with my voice. Hearing my kids voices gives me a sense of peace.

I even call Sibo and apologise; it's not right to have her worry while I act the fool. She's disappointed but understands that I'm overwhelmed by everything, I'm not her first author client. She gives me a week, saying that she will hold off the interviews until then.

Mistake or not, I'm walking into this with my eyes wide open, just as I allowed Daniel back into my life a year after my mother's burial. A year after he took my child and gave it to his wife to mother. A year into my slippery slope of alcohol, drugs, and sex.

Chapter 13

The Black Hole

The year 1997 saw the Constitution of South Africa come into play: Winnie Mandela was re-elected as the President of the ANC Women's league, Douw Steyn bought a luxurious home for Mandela and Grace Machel after his divorce from Winnie Mandela--and I remember none of it. At times, I think that year is a big gaping black hole because I'm so ashamed of the things I did, my therapist says it's my brain's way of protecting me from the trauma. My experiences were so traumatic, my brain refuses to remember them. I was caked out of my mind half the time.

After Bhut' Mandla's friend, there was a string of other men--some old and some young, some rich and some thugs. One thing I am grateful for is that losing Kungentando made me not want children, ever. So I was always armed with condoms to protect myself from pregnancy but it ultimately protected me from AIDS. Mapura wasn't that lucky, I heard that she died in the early 2000s from AIDS. There was still a whole lot of stigma back then and not a whole lot of medical intervention.

Some men became violent when I insisted on condoms; this one, in particular, I remember well because he beat me to nearly an inch of my life.

By December 1997, I was a regular in Hillbrow, Razzmatazz, Club Gemini, and in downtown Jozi, Lee Club, and Crystal Palace--all the bodyguards at the door knew my name, Candy or the nicknames they dubbed me, which I don't remember but I do remember that I was famous.

The day I nearly lost my life was, ironically, the anniversary of my mother's death, and Kungentando's birthday had been the previous day. I woke up feeling like something was gnawing at my heart on Kungentando's birthday, I curled myself in a ball and refused to leave my bed. The whole day was spent with curtains drawn and the door locked. Mapura knocked until she gave up and eventually went away.

Because I didn't drink on that day, the pain was acute and I felt like it was drowning me. I wondered how she was like. Could she talk yet or walk? What were toddlers like at that age? Did they throw her a birthday? What cake did they make for her? What did they call her? Did she look like me at all? The questions plagued me until I felt like I was going crazy.

That night, my grandmother visited me in my dreams. She hadn't ever since my downward spiral, or maybe I was too drunk to remember any dreams. But I remember that one.

Makhulu towered over me in a threatening posture, her tshotshwane bangles dangling on her wiry arms and hanging over the fists bunching her nwenda around her waist. Even though she was bent over slightly from the weight of the pfunelo neckpiece, her presence was scary. My grandmother rarely wore her full traditional attire but when she did, it was daunting--to say the least.

In my dream, she stood in all her domineering glory, her mouth downturned and her voice, when she spoke, cracked like lightning in an angry storm.

'Ndila ine na vha khayo i do ni isa lufuni, Masase. Humelani hayani!'

I tried to tell her that I had no home, that I stopped having a home when she passed on, but my lips were sealed shut and my heart heavy with her warning,

'The road you are on will lead you to death, Masase. Go back home!'

The warning was clear but I didn't hear it. I was angry. She left me! Makhulu left me with her daughter, who also left me when I needed her the most. I had no one. No home to speak of, just a house that my mother left and every time I slept there, I felt suffocated. Kungentando's cries seemed to bound off the walls, taunting me.

So, I did what I had now perfected in order to stop feeling. I woke up early, bathed, and went to call Mapura over and we bought some Savanna bottles and meat on our way back. I still had over three quarters of the money that Daniel had left me, because most of the alcohol I drank was sponsored by men who wanted sex in return.

Later on that day, we got ready to go out. Makhulu's voice still echoed in my mind in warning but I shoved it into the box in the furthest corner in my mind, then closed it shut.

'Candy!' the security in his blue uniform that was almost similar to the SAPS uniform greeted me with enthusiasm and I greeted him back with the same enthusiasm.

We got in to Mdu's 'Tsiki Tsiki Yo!'. By then, my dance moves preceded me and I was asked on the stage. I left Mapura screaming my name in the crowd, and that was the last I saw of her. Sweaty and feeling flushed after gyrating and getting down on stage, I went out to get some fresh air.

'Those were quite some moves back there.' I looked up to see a guy who looked like he fought for a living--he had the body of a fighter and the scars to back up my conclusion.

'I try,' I responded, then went back to fanning myself.

'Wanna take a hit?' He proffered his expertly-rolled blunt, and I hesitated a bit before taking a deep drag. I remember coughing a lot, it was stronger than the cannabis that I was used to. I would later learn that it was laced with crack cocaine.

I spent the rest of the night with him dancing and going outside to smoke. His Zulu sounded a bit off but I didn't care, I had nothing to lose. I tried looking for Mapura but she wasn't there; it wasn't unusual for her to leave with a man, and I always found my way home.

I was high and drunk, everything made me giggle. I remember stumbling with the guy to a flat not too far from Razzmatazz. It was a dingy flat, and no one took notice of us as we groped each other on the narrow rusted staircase.

By the time we got into his flat, we were panting and his vest had come off to reveal even more scars and the tattoo of a skull covered the better part of the left side of his chest. He was squeezing my breasts too roughly but I didn't feel anything under the intoxication. Everything, I took--besides raw sex and anal sex.

'Wait! Condoms.' My voice came out sounding disembodied but I asked for condoms.

'Don't worry, I'm clean,' he said, before biting my nipple sharply and guiding his huge penis towards my vagina.

'No. It's not just that, I don't want to fall pregnant. No glove, no love.' I hiccuped on the last part and he looked at me with this sudden anger, making his face look scarier than it already was.

'Are you accusing me of something, you little ?whore'

He didn't even wait for me to answer before he let out a slap that had my nose bleeding. I was slow to react, since I was blind drunk and as high as a kite. Before I could touch my nose to clean the blood, he had picked me up by the scruff in my neck and tossed me onto the floor. My body connected with the floor in a loud thump and as I tried to crawl up, he kicked me like he was kicking a stray dog and I yelped in pain. He was just getting warmed up.

I remember laying there in foetal position, trying to cover my face as the blows and kicks kept on coming. All because I refused to have sex with a stranger I had just met that very night without a condom.

I lay there whimpering and wishing that he would just finish me off--maybe the home that Makhulu was talking about in the dream was heaven, with her. I couldn't feel the extent of his battery, but he must have done a great job because I slipped into unconsciousness and only woke up a week later, in Johannesburg General Hospital, my whole body bandaged and pipes stuck in my body.

I tried turning my face but the move made me dizzy and violently sick, and I vomited blood all over the floor. The nurse who was attending to me was kind and sympathetic.

'You were found naked and beaten within an inch of your life in Joubert Park by one of the ladies who clean there. Do you remember how you got there?'

Shaking my head was the hardest thing in the world. I remembered who attacked me but what would it help except bring me more shame? Even death had rejected me, was I not worthy of anything? My heart constricted when she asked me if I had any family that I

would like them to call on my behalf.
The police had been notified that I was awake. Daniel's number was the only number I knew off the top of my head but I wasn't sure if he would come. He had gotten what he wanted from me and I hadn't seen or spoken to him in a year. I still gave her his number, though, and I then looked to the other side and allowed the tears of despair to fall.

***

He came. Daniel came looking like he was being chased by wild hounds and only stopped short when the nurses pointed me out. He hesitated when he was at the foot of my bed and then called out my name. When I tried to gaggle my response, for the first time ever, I saw him cry. He let his tears fall as he looked at me all banged up, and when he tried to touch me and I flinched, I saw his mouth press into a thin line.
'Who did this?'
Telling what happened to me not only embarrassed me but it was impossible with my voice almost gone; even breathing was labour on its own. He trailed his hand on my bandage and it shook with emotion.
He looked up, blinking his tears away, and I saw him shudder and blink rapidly before he could look at me. His eyes were bloodshot, and glistened with tears. It made me feel like I was less alone, like he understood and felt some of my pain.
'I shouldn't have left you alone.' His whisper sounded tormented and I tried to smile and reassure him that I was fine, alive, and still there. Barely hanging on by a thread, yet still alive.
He mopped his face with his hands, something that, as I came to learn over the years, is what he does when agitated. There wasn't much reassurance that I could give him because I was in pain.
'I need to get you to a better hospital. Are they even attending to you here?' he muttered, but mostly to himself, so I let him be.
He paced while murmuring, then he would stop, look at me and

curse under his breath. Unlike the private room where I gave birth, this ward had about twelve other patients in it but they were all critically ill and had throngs of family around them while I had only Daniel. He wasn't comfortable being around so many people, even though none of them knew who he was and were too focused on their ailing loved ones.

After some minutes of pacing, he left my bedside to look for the doctor assigned to me.

He was gone for a while, I was even dozing off when he came back--this time, propelled by anger; I could see it from the fire in his eyes and the scowl on his face.

'Crack cocaine, Candice!' When a few heads turned his way, he regretted his outburst and leant over to hiss close to my face.

'I gave you a chance to go back to school, that's why I'm raising our child. I didn't free your time up so that you could do drugs, alcohol, and have sex! The doctors found copious amounts of alcohol in your system, they are even amazed that your liver isn't fried yet. But crack cocaine, Candice? They found semen, too. Who were you sleeping with? Is it your boyfriend? Did he do this to you?'

I couldn't see his face clearly past the moisture in my eyes, but I could hear the scorn in his voice, the disdain. I couldn't think past the fact that that guy beat me to a pulp and proceeded to penetrate me raw while I lay unconscious, bleeding to death. I felt like the walls were closing in on me. I wouldn't be able to survive another pregnancy or any diseases, I couldn't.

Daniel cursed me out some more but I wasn't listening, I couldn't get over the part that there were drugs in my system and I was not only beaten up but also taken advantage of by a stranger.

When he didn't get any response past my tears, Daniel clicked his tongue and left me drowning in my misery. I didn't think he would ever come back again after what he found out; I clearly disgusted him.

I was surprised when he came back during the evening visiting hours. He wasn't boiling angry anymore and he brought a leather-bound photo album which was to become my lifeline. He still wasn't happy with me but he was now cold instead of spitting, raving mad--which was worse. He then, as stiffly as he possibly could, asked about my health, but I still couldn't respond, and my eyes were swollen from all the crying that I did,

so he carried the conversation.
'Look, Candice, you could have died, and it made me so mad that you are throwing your life away. One day, Oyama is going to grow up and start asking questions, do you want her to know that her birth mother is a crack whore?'
For a moment, I stared at him blankly, wondering who Oyama was and then it clicked. They had named Kungentando 'Oyama'. My heart got heavy at the reminder that she wasn't mine anymore; she didn't even go by the name that my mother gave her.
Daniel helped me up and I had to grind my teeth as the pain in my back escalated sharply, but all thoughts of pain disappeared when he put the leather-bound photo album in my hands. 'Oyama Kungentando Sisulu' was inscribed on the front cover and I felt this weird feeling settle all over my chest.
When I tried to fumble open the album with my bandaged hands, Daniel opened it for me and the first picture almost made my heart stop. There was my mother holding on to Kunge... Oyama, and she was beaming down at her, the gap between her teeth that she'd inherited from Makhulu showing. I had to blink back my tears to look through the photos.
She looked like a tiny version of me. She was a bubbly baby, a happy baby, judging from all the toothless grins captured in the pictures. It was all there: Her first steps, her in a bath, her birthday party where she was in her little princess dress for her birthday. She was so beautiful, it made my heart heavy and light at the same time. Heavy, because I would never get to hold her or kiss her. Light, because she was happy and healthy; something I doubt she would have been with me. I was a mess.
'One day, when she learns that you are her mother, what do you want her to know about you? That you are late because of a fast lifestyle or that you went back to school and made a name for yourself? Do you want her to resent you or be proud of you?'
I knew he was telling the truth, he was also giving me something to live for. I had to be the kind of woman that my daughter would be proud of one day, so I didn't protest when, after three weeks in the hospital, Daniel had me committed to a rehabilitation programme. I finally had something to lose.

Chapter 14

Daniel

"Please fasten your seatbelts, we are about to descend," the air hostess says, smiling sweetly at us before she turns back towards the cabin. Only then do I put down the manuscript.

As soon as we ascended into the air, I started reading. The crew was told not to come in, unless to make important announcements; they didn't come in and I read, only stopping to sip on some water. Now I'm staring at the manuscript as if it's a live snake that is about to gobble me up. I look over at Candice, the tip of her nose is red and her eyes are glassy, she looks emotionally wrung out, like she's been in a box with all her past demons and they knocked her out. Reading this also woke up some of my own demons, but I focus on her, the mother of my children, the wife of my heart. It doesn't matter who the world knows as my wife, Candice has always been the one I've selfishly held onto.

"Ma kaOyama." She looks up into my eyes and I know the anguish in her eyes is reflected in mine because she quickly looks down, hiding her raw vulnerability from me. I fight against the urge to demand that she look at me, that she allows me to share her demons. Everything about Candice is mine and I'm greedy for it all—her smiles, her soft laughs, her sadness, her tears; mine.

"I didn't know, I thought..." The excuse sounds lame and Candice cuts me off vehemently.

"You didn't want to know, you did what you do best... You left a bag of money and thought it would make the problem go away. That's what you are doing with my children." Her voice is a little more audible but it is shaky and hoarse as hell.

I've done unspeakable things to make sure her life was easier than mine. The bag of money that she carelessly speaks of? I got it from a night of being whipped and chained for the pleasure of vapidly old white women with leathery skin, their claws pawing every inch of my body. Every time I think about the little blue pills that they kept feeding me so that my penis was so engorged that it hurt, I throw up a little in my mouth. They had butt plugs in my arse and I had to crawl to them like some animal; at some point, they had me caged like an animal. I did all that because I thought it would give Candice a chance to go to school and make something of herself. Thirty thousand rands, that was how much I got paid for being a sex toy for the scarecrow and her depraved friends. I gave it all to Candice.

I don't regret it, and I would never burden her with those details, but hearing how she still suffered after all my efforts is driving my demons to the surface. I mop my face with my hands and rub my eyes almost manically, bristling with the need to lay my hands on the man who hurt her. When I find him—and I will—I'll flay the skin off him until he almost dies from the pain, then I'll bring him back to life long enough to watch me cut off his manhood.

I take a deep breath, counting backwards and pushing the demons back to the recesses of my mind where they always freely torment me. I cannot afford to snap like I did yesterday and hurt her again.

Think happy thoughts. Think happy thoughts.

Seeing Candice beam as she held each of our kids for the first time—Oyama, Denise, and Oyinqaba. Killing my father. Taking all the scarecrow's money and watching her realise that it was me who took all her family's money. The heart attack came too swiftly but the gods loved me enough not to allow it to kill her. She also suffered a stroke and as the executor of her husband's estate, I took pleasure in tormenting her until her last breath.

Feeling calmer, I turn to Candice and I find her looking at me, conflict shining behind her eyes. Her natural instinct is always to comfort me and she's fighting it. The thought that she will always have this wall up against me makes my voice shake with emotion as I speak.

"I... I was angry when the doctors told me that you could have died, that it was a miracle that you survived... I... Tell me how to fix this, how do I go back in time and fix this?"

There is no way to fix anything now, we both made our choices back then. There is terse silence as we descend and I know her stomach turns as it always does during this part of flights. I hold her hand and by some luck, she lets me. Touching Candice always makes me feel warm, and I need all the warmth I can get right now.

Mercifully, the runway isn't too long and is made of grass. When we get off the private jet, we find Ntsikelelo Hlongwane waiting for us. Hlongwane is a tall man, a shade lighter than me, with cold granite eyes, a fascinating shade of grey that I've seen sparkle with the same unhinged madness that I constantly have to lock down. If there's anyone who can find the people who hurt my Candice, it is Hlongwane. We met when his arms cargo was intercepted at the Durban harbour and he needed someone to pull some strings. We quickly hit it off, his savagery calling to mine.

He was eager to get out from under his father's thumb and his brother's shadow. He was the second person I ever told that I killed my father. He didn't look at me with the sad, heartbroken eyes tainted with sympathy that my ex-wife Nompumelelo had looked at me with. In Ntsikelelo's eyes, I was a hero, a god among mortals. While Nompumelelo's look had made my heart burn with unwanted emotion and bile, Ntsikelelo gave me the courage to admit to myself how proud I felt at the moment I heard that my sperm donor was dead.

He had failed in his role as protector and I had to become man of the house, just as Phindiwe had ascended to the matriarch position over our mother. Our mother was also a lovesick weakling, she didn't last a year after her precious husband died; the doctors said it was pneumonia, but

Phindiwe and I knew that she died from a broken heart.

Ntsikelelo barely acknowledges Candice, keeping his eyes trained on me. I feel my shoulders relaxing, one of the reasons I kept Candice out of people's sight once I had her back in my life, is because I always have the unhinged desire to gorge out the eyes of anyone who looks at her sideways. Hlongwane's face softens in welcome as we step in front of him.

"S'khulu, welcome to Piggs Peak," the arms dealer says with much more warmth than his face portrays as he half-embraces me but he winces when I clasp him.

"Hlongwane, what mess have you gotten yourself into?" My tone softens as if I'm talking to one of my nephews, and Hlongwane just grimaces.

"It's a long story. Come, let's go. My brother and our wife have borrowed you their house in Maphalaleni." Our bags are already being put inside the boot of the huge SUV that he came in.

I haven't seen this bastard in a minute and our conversation is animated. Candice zones out once we start talking politics and weapons, staring at the looming mountains as we speed down the winding road. I keep my eye on her, worried about the blank look in her eyes.

The house we drive up to, perched on top of the mountain, is nothing short of breath-taking. We arrive at dusk, when the house is draped in the husky hues of sunset, making it look rustic and picturesque. Candice's breath catches in her throat when she looks up at it as we drive up the winding driveway. I make a mental note to ask Hlongwane's brother to draw up a design for the next house I'll gift her once I've killed everyone who hurt her or wants to hurt her now to get to me.

Chapter 15

Candice

The greenery surrounding the house looks even more gorgeous in the morning light. I am restless, probably because I slept early last night so just before dawn breaks, I decide to discard sleep totally and take in the view.

The mountain behind and the hills around us are bathed in mist, with the lazy rays of the rising sun dancing gloriously on some parts, weaving a pattern that is both enchanting to look at and calming. The other homesteads appear like dots from up here, assuring you that you are not alone but far enough from everyone to make you feel like you are lording over them. I can imagine living up here and getting to see this view every day.

I take it in until the sun begins to warm up the trees and the chirping of the birds becomes louder.

My grumbling stomach reminds me that I cried off supper last night and opted for bed instead. The room I chose is draped in pretty pastel colours, giving it a little British vibe but the vibrant art of the Swati culture, young girls dancing, a boy herding cattle and an old lady smoking on a pipe, give the room an ethnic vibrancy, as does the leopard skin rug next to the huge Queen-sized bed.

I make the bed before going into the bathroom and washing my face. The minty taste of toothpaste takes away some of the dry bitterness of hunger from my mouth. I hesitate when my hand reaches the doorknob.

I didn't get to tour the house when I cried off supper; I just asked to be brought to my room and left Daniel with his friend to their own devices. He didn't kick up a fuss because they were too caught up in their conversation. I square my shoulders and venture out, I just need to find the staircase and go downstairs.

While the outside is rustic and screams 'money!', the inside of this house is intimate and screams 'family!' from the blown up pictures donning the walls. Most pictures are of the lady of the house—alone, at their Reed dance, and with little twin boys with the same grey eyes as the demigod but theirs are darkened by laughter and seem like charcoal.

I linger in front of one particular photo of a tall, distinguished man with greying hair holding a much younger version of the lady of this mansion in the crook of his arm. She was chubbier, with youthful bashfulness and had on a princess gown but it's the man next to her in the Swati cloth and full regalia that has captured my interest. He looks so familiar but I can't place his distinguished features.

I give up and keep going, there is another full-blown picture taken at the beach of her in a flowing ivory gown that clung to her chest, she was barefoot and looking up adoringly at the Hlongwane guy. They were probably renewing their vows.

The pictures all tell a story of how close-knit their family is. There is one I assume was taken at a maternity shoot, she has such glowing deep-chocolate skin without a drop of cellulite or stretch marks but she was heavily pregnant and from the next picture, I deduce that she'd already had the twins.

The pictures guide me to the staircase and keep me company until I reach the last step. The camera loves the matriarch of this family and most of the pictures seem intimate, like they were taken by someone who knows every little detail about her.

The kitchen isn't hard to locate in all its modern glory; it looks lived in, with an apron draped on the cookbooks stacked neatly on the granite counter. There are only pictures of the children in here—the twin boys as toddlers, then the twin boys with a girl, the twins, girl, and another baby boy. All these kids are under the age of six. I'm not the only busy one in the baby-making industry.

The thought makes me smile as I check the huge fridge and my smile widens when I see that the fridge is fully-stocked. I take out the ingredients for a full greasy breakfast. I'm starving. The aroma of the beef bangers and bacon sizzling in the pan draw Daniel from wherever he spent the night and the hairs on my neck tingle in awareness before I can even hear his graceful footfalls.

"Something smells nice…" I'm about to turn and tell him that breakfast is almost ready when he sneaks his arms around me and nuzzles my neck.

The immediate heat that that action brings between my legs, that throbbing of longing, is the reason why I chose to sleep in my own room—locked and bolted. He steps away after a husky morning greeting and I glance at him, my breath hitching when I see him.

Oh, boy! He looks almost boyish in his shorts, a V-neck tee, and leather sandals. Laid-back Daniel is a whole meal because not a lot of people get to see him like this. He has that boyish and devilish grin on his face when he catches me checking him out. I'm in trouble.

"Breakfast will be ready soon." I hate how breathless my voice sounds right now, but at least I can talk now.

We eat in companionable silence and Daniel raises an eyebrow when I add a second serving on my plate and pour more tea for myself.

"What? I didn't eat last night," I snap, and he chuckles before popping some cherry tomato into his mouth.

"How do you know Hlongwane?" I ask as he clears the table. I'm too full to even move, and he offered to do the dishes.

"He's an arms dealer. Took over from his father, the Beast, who has connections in the ANC and almost every other leading political party in Africa. When Hlongwane took over, he reached out to me when some of his shipment was intercepted at the Durban Port. I bailed him out, he got to supply his customers, and the rest is history."

That explains the cold aloofness I picked up from him. As polished as he is, Hlongwane looks like someone who would kill you without blinking.

"There is a swimming pool on the roof of the house if you want us to go and read up there, or we can go to the garden outside," he offers, as he dries the pan before handing it to me to put away.

I choose the pool, I can just imagine how gorgeous it is up on the roof. As I turn from putting the pan in its place, I find Daniel all up in my space, caging me in. I can't retreat any further, my back is now against the handle-less, off-cream cabinet. His nearness and cologne are intoxicating.

"I missed you in my bed last night." He's talking so close to my face that our breaths are mingling and I can't help the hum of appreciation that ripples through my body.

"We are not sleeping together," I manage to force the words out, while my body is begging for him to lay me on the cool kitchen counter and have his way with me.

"Why? Besides, we wouldn't have done much sleep." He sounds and looks like Oyinqaba when he asks 'Why?', but then he packed the heat with the last sentence. It's hard to fragment my thoughts.

"Know why… Broken up…" There has to be a way I can get out of here, because he has me where he wants me and I can't think with him licking my neck like that. It makes my body crave for him to lick elsewhere. Everywhere
.

"I don't remember us breaking up. When did that happen?"

The devil is a liar! I am stronger than this. But then, why are my legs giving in and turning into a weak puddle of nerves? I inhale deeply, trying to calm my nerves. Big mistake, because now, it feels like he's inside of my nostrils and all I can smell is him.

"I left. I can't keep doing this to myself, to my children. Denise was crying because the other children don't believe that you are her father. You can't keep hurting us like this." I see him close his eyes and clench his teeth as if he is in physical pain.

"Denise was hurting, and you didn't tell me?" The words are a harsh whisper and I close my eyes, not because I'm weak in the knees, but because I can see my daughter crying hysterically.

"When was I supposed to tell you? Between your job and your show family, you haven't been around much lately. You didn't even notice that we moved out, until you heard of the book."

He steps away from me as if he is trying to ward off my words. When he takes another step back, I start breathing normally again. Glad that I stood my ground but I also feel bad for him, he looks like he's about to retch in the kitchen sink.

"I will see you in the pool in thirty minutes, I need to make a call." His voice is crisp, with none of the boyish, devilish charm that he was laying on me during breakfast and none of the seductive timbres that it had before I mentioned Denise's meltdown.

I let out a sigh of relief when he promptly leaves the kitchen. That was too close. I almost spread my legs for him wide on that kitchen counter.

"You can do this, Candice. Read a book with him this week and go back to building your life with your children. This is the closure that you need before you fully let go. That's why you agreed to come here, for closure." My words of encouragement sound empty to my ears and I'm glad that I'm alone in this huge kitchen.

I know I am lying to myself, but I'm determined to try. My therapist says there are stages to leaving and I shouldn't be so hard on myself when I fail the first couple of times. I just need to not fall for the magic of this mansion plus Daniel's carefree charm.

Also, don't open your legs! That's what got us here! My subconscious is extremely pissed with me.

Read book. No sex. Easy enough, isn't it? I square my shoulders and head towards the staircase, resigning myself to my fate.

Chapter 16

Dry - January 1998

The day Daniel drove me to Houston House in Randburg was a sunny Monday yet, inside his car, it was so frosty, barely a word was said. I complimented him on getting a car and he only grunted his response, and I got the memo.

I watched the scenery outside and the people who walked about with purpose. It was the New Year, after all, and they weren't as banged up as I or shivering from the need of a bottle of Savanna. I hadn't touched alcohol in the two weeks I was conscious in the hospital and my body was making this little fact known to me.

As we drove to the more affluent neighbourhoods, the only black people we saw were mostly in uniform; it felt like Apartheid hadn't ended, the demarcation was still there, as loud as the silence in the car. Daniel was still mad at my imaginary boyfriend and I let him be. I was dealing with a lot of flashbacks to nurse his ego.

'The place we are going to is highly recommended. They are professional and discreet,' he finally said, as we were driving into what looked like a small estate with rolling lawns, pretty trees, and bungalows.

The magic word was 'discreet'. Daniel was on his way to parliament and he couldn't afford to be tainted by me in any way. I got the unsaid rule: I wasn't to speak of him or our

involvement.
A kind white lady greeted us as we parked, she towered over Daniel slightly and had wide-set shoulders and a surprisingly tiny voice for one so large. 'Welcome to Houston House, we've been expecting you, Mr Sisulu. This must be Candy. Hello, Dearie.'
All I could offer was a wan smile and I flinched slightly when she embraced me. My body hadn't totally healed, with my face still slightly swollen.
Daniel stayed long enough to have me registered and taken to one of those bungalow-looking houses which was their detox facility, then he was gone with a promise to come and see me during the weekend. I was the youngest and only black girl in the detox house, but everyone was too cranky to care. The staff were friendly and welcoming, I also had a therapist for the first time in my life. Her name was Mercy, and not only was she tiny but she was also very kind.
'There is nothing to be ashamed of, Candy. I just need you to be open with me about what led you here, what led you to your first bottle of alcohol.' It was hard to talk, from the shivers that had taken over my body and Mercy handed me a bucket.
I was about to ask what the bucket was for, when I hurled up everything that I had eaten for breakfast that day. I retched and retched, until all that came out was just some gooey water. Mercy was patting my back gently the whole time, and that small touch helped me not feel as alone as I had grown accustomed to feeling.
'It has been our experience that very often, people with addictions present symptoms of underlying psychiatric disorders. That's why I am here to offer you psychiatric assessment. I am highly qualified in addiction medicine to ascertain if there is an underlying psychiatric or other disorder,' she went on after I was done being sick and she had helped me clean up.
At first, it was hard to open up to Mercy but when I began telling her about the first Savanna I drank after my mother's burial, everything came tumbling out. As the days went by, I even forgot that I was supposed to be discreet, and I even told her about Daniel and Kungentando; I couldn't bring myself to call her 'Oyama'.
'When did he find out that you had lied about your age?' Mercy asked one day when we were outside, having our session next to the pool.

The sun was a pleasant change, even though the shivers and vomiting had gradually eased off with the medicine they gave me. I turned my face towards the sun, enjoying its warm caress before I responded.

'When I was already pregnant. I couldn't hide the pregnancy past four months; my mother caught on and demanded to know who was responsible. She dragged me crying to his apartment. When we got there, she was fuming at Daniel for sleeping with a fifteen-year-old child. He was blindsided, as I hadn't even told him I was pregnant yet.'

'Blindsided' was an understatement, it was the first time I saw Daniel open and close his mouth like a gaping fish. From then, things cooled down a fraction between us, and even when we had sex, which I initiated, he was a bit cold and distant. I was hurt. Yet, I couldn't really voice it because he took care of my every other need--from doctor's appointments to cravings, I didn't lack for anything, and he would listen to me cry about something nasty that my mother had said to me.

'You talk a lot about your grandmother, Makhulu. Did you ever tell Daniel about her?'

I hadn't. I realised that with Daniel I, for the longest time, played a part--the flirty, sophisticated young lady from the East Rand, not the young, lost girl from Limpopo. I learnt a lot about addiction from Mercy in the weeks that I spent at the Houston House.

'Our brains are designed to seek out experiences that derive pleasure, and repeat these experiences. The purpose of this is to promote survival by rewarding life-sustaining behaviours, such as eating and procreation. In an area where food is scarce, when food is eventually found and consumed, this triggers the pleasure reward system in the brain, releasing dopamine.' She then went on to explain what dopamine was, as we took our walk around the estate.

'This pleasurable experience becomes associated with the behaviour that led to that experience. This reward system facilitates future endeavours to find food and ensure survival. This very same system that facilitates human survival also rewards drug use and alcohol consumption. Drugs and alcohol target the brain's pleasure centre, saturating the brain with dopamine and making us feel good. How did you feel every time you had a bottle of Savanna, Candy?'

'I felt less alone. For a few hours, I could forget, laugh, and not be the orphan who gave up her baby, dropped out of school and was a disappointment to her grandmother.' Mercy let me blow out some air through my nose until I had my emotions under control before she continued.

'That relief that you got and that escape provide motivation in repeated substance abuse, despite the harmful cost. That euphoria initiates a snowball effect in the brain, manifested by intense craving and loss of control. Once addicted, seeking drugs and alcohol become the primary focus. Once you were hooked on Savanna, drinking it and using drugs were no longer a choice. Addicted people are compelled to continue using, despite the negative effects and their best intentions. Addiction is a disease, Candy. A disease characterised by the psychological and physical inability to stop using and drinking substances despite the accompanied chaos.'

I also learnt a lot about myself, my need for love, and how self-destructive I was and maybe Mercy would have helped me overcome that as well as the addiction, if I didn't have to cut my stay at Houston House short before I finished treatment. If I hadn't discharged myself and fled to Limpopo without even saying goodbye to Mercy.

The reason I left came one weekend. Instead of Daniel's usual weekend visits, which had grown less terse with the progress I was making, that time was taken by Phindiwe and she wasn't happy with me. I learnt an important lesson about her on that visit: She had liked me because she didn't like his wife, and she had liked me until I threatened the financial hold that she had over her brother.

'You are here, eating eggs and sausages every morning, rubbing shoulders with white people, while the money that was supposed to build a home for me and my boys is covering your bill!' she hissed at me, and only lowered her voice when some of the patrons cast a glance her way.

I had never seen that menacing side of her before and it scared me.

'Now, listen here, girlie. Daniel is raising his daughter and you are not his responsibility. Unless you can pay for your stay here, you'd better disappear from his life, and if you know what is good for you, you will go as far away as possible. Otherwise, next time, I won't be this nice to you.'

I got the message, loud and clear. Makhulu's words ringing in my ears, as well as Phindi's threat, I packed up and managed to slip away from Houston House without anyone noticing.

At first, I went back to my mother's house. By some stroke of luck, the briefcase was still there, with most of the money I initially got from Daniel. With my neighbour's reluctant help--I had been a bitch to them during my downward spiral, so I was sort of persona non grata to them--I managed to find a tenant. I opened a bank account where he could deposit the rent money and within three days, I was on a bus to Maebani.

I clutched the photo album that Daniel had given me; also armed with the knowledge that Mercy had imparted on me, I was determined to make something of myself. There was nothing left for me in Gauteng. I had no one else in my corner but me, and I was determined to make something of myself. For me, for Kungentando, for Makhulu, and even for my mother.

Chapter 17

Candice

"You could have come to me." I steel myself against the anguish in his voice. I avoid looking at his accusing eyes and focus instead on the way the skin on his forehead is pleated in a frustrated scowl.

"You could have asked to call me and told me what Phindi said, instead of just disappearing. I looked for you, Candice, and I almost sued Houston House for negligence."

Daniel has slid into the Minister role, scolding me with such passion, it feels like I ran off yesterday, not over two decades ago.

"Why didn't you?" My question makes the wedge between his eyebrows deepen in confusion. "I mean, why didn't you sue them then, since you never found me?"

For a moment, my question has him stumped or maybe it's the fact that I am not cowering under his blatant displeasure. He finally collects himself and splutters an indignant response.

"I went to your mother's house, and they told me that you had come over and left with your bags after putting a tenant."

"Mmmmh…" I take my feet out of the cool pool water, to find that they have turned a bit pink and are wrinkled.

"Don't evade the question. Why didn't you come to me with Phindiwe's threats instead of running away?" I release a long-suffering sigh and wipe my feet until Daniel drags the towel from my hands. He's angry, maybe at his sister or my impudence but I think he's angry at himself, too.

"Coming to you wouldn't have helped or changed anything. I was young, a recovering junkie but even then, I knew she led your nose by her apron strings. What Sis' Phindi said went—even now."

His nose flares and I know that he's using all his inner strength to rein in his temper.

"That is not true!" His voice quivers with emotion, and a wry smile touches the corners of my lips because I think he actually believes that.

"Isn't it? Then tell me why you allowed her to talk you into aborting Mpumi's unborn baby. It was bad enough that Mpumi would have claim over your money, which Phindiwe feels entitled to, but for another man's child to dip into the wealth meant for her boys? She wouldn't have it." He makes to cut in, but I hold up my hand to silence him. I'm far from done.

"You didn't protect your precious Mpumi from your sister's vindictiveness. You never protected me, and even Mandisa has to dance to your sister's tune. Phindiwe might as well be your first wife because you still report everything to her and you put the welfare of her children above that of your own. So, tell me, Daniel, what would you have done had I come to you?" My voice is now shaking with emotion, and I stare down Daniel, who opens and closes his mouth before muttering belligerently.

"I would have done something. You were my responsibility as much as Oyama was."

Suddenly, I feel weary to my bones; like someone just sucked all of the energy out of my body. I stand up, and the world tilts on its axis and I sway a bit. Daniel is quickly on his feet and he's holding my back, steadying me until the dizzy spell passes. He holds a glass of juice up for me to drink.

"I think I just need water, I'm going to get it downstairs."

He tries to argue but I just need to be away from him right now, so I end up downstairs alone. My hand is shaking so much that it takes all my effort to open the fridge. I hate confrontation; no, I am afraid of confrontation, so I always avoid it, preferring to just go along with what a person says than speak up.

I'm feeling raw from reading, remembering, and finally addressing the issue of Phindiwe, who is always looming like a third wheel in this relationship. Her last-born goes to the same school as Denise and, you guessed it, Daniel is footing the bill.

For the first time in a really long time, I need a drink, something strong. I check the cupboards but there's nothing, which is just as well. I take two bottles of water and steel my nerves before going back up. I find Daniel with his head bowed and he's massaging his temple; something he does when a migraine hits him.

"Maybe we should go inside the house? Before the nose-bleeding starts."

He makes no effort to stand up or even lift his head, just continues kneading his temple.

"Phindiwe made me… She made me into the man I am today, and I can never repay her—not enough." His voice is strained, and I resist the urge to comfort him with my touch.

"I guess that makes me feel indebted to her, but reading about what she said to you makes me want to snap her neck. You were a kid, Candice, you had spiralled partly because of me, my actions. I was going to build her that house, I just asked for time to get into parliament first. I thought she understood. She helped me search for you; she saw me worried out of my mind and she pretended to care.

I look up and blink back my tears. Maybe reading this manuscript is a big mistake. After I finished writing it, I didn't read it again. I started writing the book I published because writing became therapeutic to me, like I was meeting parts of myself that I had forgotten along the way and some that I didn't even know existed.

"I think we've read enough for today. Let's just go back inside, and sleep it off." I could use a little mid-morning nap.

"No, let's read one more chapter. Please."

I sigh and put my sunglasses on, then open the umbrella next to the chaise that I'm sprawled on. Daniel finally lifts his head up and his eyes are bloodshot and I feel sorry for him. He picks up the manuscript as if he has the whole world on his shoulders.

'I found a distant cousin...'

Chapter 18

Home - May 1998

I found a distant cousin staying in my grandmother's homestead and even though she wasn't particularly welcoming, she didn't throw me out either. Being back home reminded me of Makhulu, sitting under the shade of her favourite mango tree as she shelled peanuts or peas. Makhulu's bangles shimmering in the sunlight as she pounded something in the wooden mortar with that heavy pestle that she used to lift as if it weighed nothing.

I felt lighter than I had felt in a while, feeling her embrace in every corner of the yard. I locked myself in her room, which had her presence the most, and I just sobbed out the whole story of my life to the empty room. I spilt my guts and I felt her presence saturating the room.

'Ndi khou humbela pfarelo, Makhulu, please forgive me for not listening. I just thought I could forget everything but now I need you more than ever, to help me pick up the pieces.'

I must have finally drifted off to sleep, exhausted, and I dreamt of my grandmother again and this time, she wasn't threatening or menacing but she was telling me her favourite folklore, 'Mutshavona', about an orphan boy whose sister would transform into a bird and sit on the horn of a single-horned cow and warn him of impending danger when he was being poisoned.

The story often changed when Makhulu told it; some evenings, it told of the boy being poisoned by their stepmother to other evening being about him being poisoned by a chief who wanted to marry his sister but couldn't because the boy was a cripple. In the dream, Makhulu sang on cue as she did my hair under her favourite mango tree.

Tswi tswi tswi tswi Doli Mutshavhona
dada,
Mutshavhona, Mutshavhona.
Kholomo ya lunanga luthihi
Mutshavhona dada...

Makhulu kept repeating the song as if it was a warning. Her voice grew more distant, until I woke up to the steady rapping on the door. For a moment, I was disoriented and then I remembered that I had left Gauteng and come back home. The knocking on the door was insistent and so, rubbing the sleep from my eyes, I opened the door to the angry face of my mother's eldest sister.

'You do not come and go as you please in my mother's house, do you hear ?me" Her voice was shaking with anger and I saw the distant cousin smirking from behind her.

I tried to gather my bearings as my aunt went on and on about how disrespectful I was, just like my mother; how my grandmother had spoiled me; how they waited for me after my mother's funeral, until they gave up. I let her talk and when she finally paused to catch her breath, that was when I got a word in edgewise.

'I'm sorry that I didn't come back, I was dealing with the pain of being a complete orphan in the only way I knew how, but Makhulu came to me in a dream and told me to come back, and I'm here to go back to school.'

The anger on my aunt's face softened and after some more scolding, she promised to help me get back to school and finish my high school diploma. I was glad that she didn't ask me about where my child was, especially in front of the distant cousin whom I was sure Makhulu had been warning me about in my dream. I was ready to be a child again and that meant I had to listen to my aunt, because, under all that resentment, she meant well.

***

Chapter 18

Doing my Matric at Luvhivhini Secondary School was both a blessing and a challenge. My aunt was the headmistress there, so it meant that I had to always be at the top of my game. The teachers reported everything back to my aunt because they wanted to be on her good books, which made life a bit harder for me, but it paid off in the end.

I didn't have a lot of friends either, as they would whisper whenever I came into a room. A lot of wild stories about me were flying around, but none of them came close to the real reason why I ended up back in Maebani.

At first, the distant cousin wanted to bully me into doing all the chores before going to school, but I reported her to my aunt. Let's just say it ended with an egg on her face, and whatever resentment she harboured for me intensified. I developed a system: I woke up at the crack of dawn, went to collect water, then, as it heated on the fire, I would quickly clean my grandmother's room where I slept. After my bath, I would make some tea for myself then revise as I walked, alone, to school. My aunt tried to get me to come and stay with her, she stayed inside the school, but I hated the way her husband would leer at me when she wasn't looking, so I refused. I enjoyed my walks in the morning, I got to think and admire the Mopane trees and other vegetation. The sun started dancing over the trees way before I got to school, warming the red soil and sending the little animals running for cover in the foliage.

I would greet the neighbours who were late for the marketplace and some coming back and that often earned me gifts or a walking companion. Everyone had loved Makhulu, and they always shared stories about her whenever they met me.

'Your grandmother was so proud of you,' Mme a Avhadali said one morning, as she gave me some boiled maize cob from the pile that she was going to sell to passing cars and buses at the shops.

'Your grandmother always said how intelligent you are,' this was from Mme a Vhutshilo, after I helped her with the forms that she needed to take to the municipal offices.

I would get waves and friendly greetings that made the journey seem shorter than it really was. There was a very strong sense of community in Maebani, which I had forgotten of when my system acclimatised to the loneliness of Gauteng.

What was hard was walking back home in the evenings when I still had to study late for exams. I was forced to make a compromise during exams, and slept over at my aunt's place. I made sure to study in her office while she worked and only leave with her when she was going back home. Her children didn't like me much either, so I kept to myself or followed my aunt around.
Life was simple and cheaper, I barely touched the money that I'd come with, keeping it locked away in my grandmother's wardrobe. I couldn't drink, even when I craved it, because Maebani bottle stores weren't places for a teenage girl. There were no drugs easily accessible, so I led a clean life.
My mother's other siblings never came around or checked up on me; it was just my strict aunt and with time, our relationship got better. We weren't best friends but she did her best to mother me for that year. It made me miss Makhulu even more.
The memories of my grandmother's robust personality seeped through from every spot in Maebani and at times, I would find myself wiping away unexpected tears. Through it all, thoughts of my grandmother spurred me to work even harder.

***

By the time I wrote the last paper, I was confident that I had passed most, if not all, of the subjects. I decided to go out and celebrate. My options were limited back then, so I settled for KFC in Nzhelele Valley Shopping Centre. I missed the more advanced Gauteng with its hangout spots, movie theatres, and theme parks. After receiving my order, I walked out, checking if they'd added my ketchup, and I walked straight into a hard chest. Large hands steadied me before I fell.
From the start, Vhutuhawe was a gentle giant. He had an almost-shy smile that revealed perfectly-aligned white teeth, and it made me smile apologetically back at him.
'Forgive me, Murunwa, I wasn't looking where I was going.' I frowned up at him, thinking that he probably mistook me for

someone else.
'I am Ca... Masase. I do not know any person by that name.'
'Candice' was at the tip of my tongue, but I decided that Candice had remained behind in Gauteng and only Masase could fit in Limpopo. He smiled wider, showing off his shallow dimples.
'You look like an angel but I see why your parents named you after the morning star.'
He was charming in a corny way, which made him all the more sweeter. We ended up eating together on a bench outside, and he gave me the lowdown of his family. He was the first-born child in a family of eighteen children. His father had three wives, and they all gave him six children each. Vhuti loved all his siblings and he had my insides heaving when he talked of their escapades. It felt good to laugh so freely again.
He drove me back home, and so started our relationship. We met often at parks, in shopping centres, and wherever else we could sneak off to to get in some us-time. I remember our first kiss, it started off shy, a little awkward, and as Vhutuhawe became more sure of himself, it blossomed into a ball of heat. We would kiss often and grope each other, that's far as it went. He thought I was still a virgin and I didn't have the heart to tell him that I had a child; I was afraid that he would judge me or break it off.
My days were lighter, with Vhutuhawe spending as much time with me as possible after work and whenever he had time. Until the dreadful day of the eve of my mother's death came. I can not explain it perfectly but it felt like every hurt dredged itself up and pinned my legs to the bed; I couldn't get up or see beyond the black ball of pain consuming me. There were knocks on my door and I think even my aunt came and her voice was softer, cajoling. She knew what day it was, and she let me wallow in pain for those two days.
When I finally emerged from the claws of sorrow, it felt like I had gone through the wringers; I had lost weight and my eyes were sunken. Vhuti sent a child from one of the neighbouring homesteads to come and get me. I wasn't up for company but he had been looking for me for two days, so the least I could do was go out and see him.
'Never scare me like that again! I was this close to entering and causing a scene.' His hug felt different, he was quivering with

emotion.
'It was the anniversary of my mother's death.' He understood and took me shopping to clear my head. He was sweet, thoughtful, and kind, too; just what I needed then.
Time went by and I spent the festivals on Vhutuhawe's arms, being shown off. Even though he ticked off all the right boxes, after Daniel, I was holding off, and I kept on expecting the other shoe to drop. We transitioned smoothly into 1999, the year when the world was supposed to come to an end. Spoiler alert: We are still here.
The day to collect results came and Vhutuhawe was there, holding my hand. I had passed really well, especially for Mathematics and Chemistry, but my aunt only had enough money to help me get into a polytechnic. I didn't tell her that I had enough money to afford any university of my choice. Things were finally looking up for me, my aunt was proud of me, and I didn't want to ruin it by bringing up my child and the money I got after giving her away. Vhuti helped me apply for Graphic Design at Polokwane Technic Institute and my life seemed set.
Sometimes, I wonder what my life would have been like had I gone to Polokwane Technic Institute and married Vhutuhawe. Would I have been happy? How many kids would we have had? Most of those questions hurt too much, so I try not to dwell on them or on the day I got summoned with all the other villagers to the wedding of Vhamusanda Mulela's daughter in Ha-Mulela.
It was a long way from our village, but my aunt came to collect me; she was happy with my doing well at school, and she even bought me a beautiful blue minwenda and white sneakers. Everyone was excited about the wedding because it was uniting two great families, and people were hoping it would lead to the restoration of chieftaincies in Makhado. My aunt and her husband talked about it, but I wasn't interested in village politics. I wish I had listened closely, then maybe I would have asked them to leave me behind...

Chapter 19

Daniel

I slam shut the manuscript with more force than necessary, my heart heaving at the thought of the nameless man with his hands all over my Candy. I realise that Candice has fallen asleep and use that as an excuse to stop reading but honestly, I can't stomach reading about her with another man. It makes me angry but in a different way than when I was reading of the man who assaulted her and the creeps who preyed on her. I could be disgusted by the latter, but with this one from Maebani, it's different; for one, she wrote his name and she describes him fondly. I don't want Wami thinking fondly of another man, even if their relationship was in the last millennium. That's what Candice is to me: mine, and no one else's.

With my first wife, Nompumelelo, I was embarrassed when she gave her virginity to another man after the pedestal I'd put her on, I felt slighted that she called out his name while I was inside her. But that feeling of a bruised ego pales in comparison to what I feel at the thought of Candice being touched by anyone else. It's like someone has lit an inferno inside me that blackens the edges of my vision. With Mandisa, our relationship has always been transactional and cold, I don't care who she fucks on the side and fuck she does, even though she likes acting holier-than-thou. I know everyone she's fucked, and I've never once confronted her.

After I've managed to get my emotions in order, I pick up Candice; she's gained a bit of weight and it makes her look softer in sleep. She snuggles up against me, hand against my heart, burrowing her face into my neck as she usually does and it makes the ache around my heart recede a bit. Carefully, I walk down to the room that she chose and put her on the bed. I want to get behind her and spoon her but I have people to track, favours to call in, and so, reluctantly, I walk away after putting a throw over her and allowing myself a lingering kiss on her pouty lips.

I take my burner phone and pick one of the few numbers that are programmed into the phone. As the dial tone hums in my ear, I glance out the window, the grey skies matching the tension swirling in my mind. The line clicks, and I hear his voice on the other end-steady, familiar.

"James, it's me," I say, keeping my tone casual, though my heart races. I use the code name that we always use on this line to indicate the nature of my call.

"Henry! To what do I owe the pleasure?" he replies, a hint of amusement in his voice. 'Henry' is the name that tells me that his assistant and some of his team are around, so he cannot speak freely.

I clear my throat, pushing aside the pleasantries. "I need to discuss something important. Can we meet?"

"Of course. What's on your mind?"

I lean back against the counter, glancing at the clock. "Let's just say our friends across Limpopo find their current golf tournament administration to be... underwhelming. They think it's time for a change, and have tasked me to ask for your help to make it happen."

There's a pause on the other end, the air thick with unspoken understanding. "A golf tournament, you say? That sounds rather ambitious with both our schedules, Henry. What do you have in mind?"

"Let's just say I have some golf ideas that could benefit us both," I reply, my voice lowering slightly. "We need to talk strategy... logistics. I'm thinking we could set up a series of holes with our friends- those who are tired of the current golf tournament status quo."

"A round of golf sounds exciting," he chuckles, but I can hear the shift in his tone, the seriousness creeping in. "Where and when?"

"It needs to be discreet, we can never be seen playing a round with these friends. I was thinking somewhere secure, like your game reserve."

"Next Saturday sounds perfect. I'll be sure to email you my schedule. I know your friend has the eye of a Hawk," he warns me that his game reserve is being watched, given his recent investigation, and I should find a way to get in undetected.

"Trust me, James, our friends are very capable. They're as committed as we are." I pause, letting the weight of my words sink in. "This is our chance to aim for the gold trophy in the league." I dangle the promised gold mines and I know that has his attention.

"Very well. I'll see you then," he says, his voice steady now, infused with greed for power and wealth.

"Good. I'll bring the woods, irons, hybrids, wedges, and putters; our friends have their own golf clubs," I reply, feeling a rush of adrenaline. "We'll make history, my friend."

As I hang up, I dial Joshua's number and, as previously, he answers and doesn't say anything.

'I've set up the wild drive for Saturday on our friend's private game reserve. I heard a hawk was spotted there, so our entrance must be very discreet so as not to startle the bird," I say, almost conversationally, as I load the espresso machine. Joshua grunts his acknowledgement and then hangs up. I then send Shefu the good news on one of the dummy email accounts that he set up for our communication. It's much in the same vein-a blasé invitation to a game drive, and I don't state the location. Planning a coup has made me hungry, so I decide to make some lunch as I drink my coffee.

I check in with my team. Candice's interview is still trending, so my PR is going ballistic but I couldn't be bothered; I have bigger fish to fry. Something that Joshua said in our first meeting has been niggling at the back of my mind. I've sacrificed so much to rise through the political ranks and stick it to the Sisulus, but what if there's a better way to crush them from the shadows, when they least expect it?

I hum as I let the thought fester and after concluding all the urgent business, I call Hlongwane.

"S'khulu," his voice rumbles in my ear, as I turn the steak on the pan and it sizzles.

"I need you to hunt someone for me. I don't have his name, I just know a club that he used to frequent in the late 90s, and I have a rough description but not much else to go on." Hlongwane whistles at my request.

"With so little to go on, it's going to cost you," he warns me, and I shrug as if he can see me.

"Money is not an issue, this is highly personal to me."

I only end the call after I'm satisfied that he understands the importance of my request. I'm switching off the stove plate with the mushroom sauce simmering when Candice comes in sniffing. She looks so young and adorable as she scrunches her nose and in her bedraggled state. She comes and squeezes between me and the pots, sniffing as if I didn't make her breakfast a couple of hours ago. No wonder she's gained weight, her appetite is through the roof. She doesn't say anything when I cage her in as I stir the sauce for the last time, I then reluctantly let her go to dish up. After she's polished off her plate, she settles on the couch, tucking her feet beneath her, and points at the manuscript. I drag in some air; it feels like she's asked me to pick up a cobra, what with the dread that pools around my gut as I begin to read.

Chapter 20

A Royal Pain

When we arrived at the residency of the Ha-Mulela headman, we were directed by the throbbing drums. The celebration was already underway. My aunt's husband had had a hard time finding parking, so they urged us to get off first and go secure our seats. I didn't get along with my aunt's children, so they went ahead and I lost them somewhere in the throng of people, and found myself drifting to where all the dancing was.

The dancers were situated just in front of the husband's family, as the wife's side wasn't full yet. There was a lull in the drums and shortly after, a shrill note from a pipe rang out. The tshikona. Makhulu had told me of the royal dance but I had never had the privilege to see it, and the way each player timeously belted out their notes and the harmony even as they danced was mesmerising.

Not to be outdone, the women came in a semi-circle, shuffling and stomping their bangled feet while waving the white pieces of cloth in their hands in rhythm with their drums and whistles. It then became a competition of who could dance better--the tshikona or the tshigombela.

I was fascinated by the dancers but curiosity over who the Mulela princess was marrying won and I craned my neck trying to catch a glimpse. It was hard because all of them were decked out in their royal splendour, so it was hard telling who the husband was. I formulated a little game of trying to determine who was the husband from the posture of the princes sitting behind the elevated podium. It was hard, as I didn't know which prince was from which house but I must admit, they were all very fine to look at.

I kept on eyeing them one by one, until my eyes collided with a familiar set of warm, brown eyes. My eyes widened in shock while his dulled at his deception, and then he wouldn't meet my eyes. My heart in my dry mouth, I felt queasy all of a sudden. I must have appeared pale because one old lady offered me her cloth and she directed me to sit under the shade of a tree, otherwise my fair skin would be damaged by the unrelenting sun. I sat in a daze, still trying to get my head around the fact that my Vhuti was a whole prince. In all our talks, he had never brought it up. Was he the one getting married?

It would explain why he refused to meet my eyes. My heart was thumping just as loudly as the drums. I tried to blink away the moisture in my eyes; news travelled fast in the villages and I didn't want the label of being the maiden who was crying at the princess' wedding. Assumptions would run wild.

The drums morphed into an upbeat tempo as the young boys and girls took over the dancefloor. The bare-chested girls and boys danced fluidly, like a python, to the beat of a drum, forming a chain by holding the forearm of the person in front. They swayed this way and that way as one of them, a girl I recognised from one of my classes, led them in a Venda love song. All of it was stunningly beautiful, but I was deep in my feelings and I couldn't fully appreciate their fluidity.

A hush fell over the square as the bridal party finally arrived in song. In true Venda royal tradition, the bridal party emerged clad in vibrant red and yellow Venda traditional attire, concealed in blankets. The sound of the Tshikona mouth organs took over and wild ululation erupted. Even concealed, the bride and her entourage managed to move gracefully and in tune with the rhythm of the drums towards the front. People parted to allow them to pass and I followed their procession with stinging eyes.

At the front, the in-laws were treated to the gruelling task of identifying the bride, who was still concealed by a blanket. On three occasions, they failed to locate the bride and they were made to pay a fine, as per tradition. There was a loud applause from the guests when they finally located her and unveiled her for all to see.

She was stunning. In a figure-hugging red gown that hugged her generous and perfectly-shaped bottom, mash lace exposing her glowing melanin tiny waist, and the Venda strips tastefully covering her shoulders, the bride looked like a goddess. The gold around her neck and ears shimmered in the brightness of the sun and she was blush-laughing as she was accompanied by the Makhadzi from her intended's family to her husband-to-be. I couldn't dredge up the strength to watch Vhuti getting married, so I slipped away and walked blindly from the ululations and whistles in the square.

I was almost at the deserted fields when I felt a hand on my elbow gently directing me to a halt under some pawpaw trees.

'Vhuti, what are you doing here? Shouldn't you be getting married?' I couldn't hide the bitterness in my voice and he had the decency to look sheepish.

'I am not the one getting married, it's one of my cousins. We come from the same Singo clan but his grandfather was the younger brother to mine.'

My relief was short-lived as his words registered in my mind.

'Wait, you mean to tell me that you are part of one of the prominent Vhavenda clans in Vhembe?' My mouth was dry again, while Vhutuhawe stood a little taller. He was a direct descendant of King Ramabulana.

'That doesn't mean we can't be together. I've talked to my uncles and they said I can marry you. I just have to first marry my intended when she finishes college in two years.'

He was speaking fast, as if afraid that he would lose his nerve and not say the words he wanted to, while I felt my whole chest heating and tying up in knots. My eyes finally lost the fight and my tears freely flowed.

'No, you can't! Not only am I part of the vhasiwana while you are part of the vhakololo, but I also didn't go through the domba ceremony.'

Not only was I a commoner while he was from royalty but I also hadn't gone through the traditional girl child initiation into womanhood ceremony. It was a mess because, in families that still strictly adhered to traditional practices like his, only a girl that has been through the domba ceremony is eligible for marriage. Vhuti started pacing while I hugged myself, suddenly feeling chilly under the Limpopo sun. He came to a stop in front of me, his face lighting up.

'I've got it! You can still undergo the domba ceremony, I'm sure your aunt can help or I can get one of my aunts to help. I'm willing to do anything to have you in my life, Masase. I love you.' The way he was so happy that he'd come up with a solution made me bite my lip until I tasted the metallic taste of my blood.

'I can't.' My voice came out strangled. 'I have a child, Vhuti. Her father is raising her and she just turned two.'

It was better to say that than to admit that I had given up my child, that she was being raised as my baby daddy's wife's daughter. I drew in a shaky breath as Vhuti recoiled from me as if I had a touch of leprosy.

'You didn't tell me that! All this time, you let me believe that you were a maiden!' His voice quivered and rose slightly as he tossed the accusation.

I hung my head in shame as I watched him walk away, my lies had caught up with me. He didn't even know that my real name was Candice yet.

Chapter 21

Candice

"I'm going to sleep," I break the silence that has stretched between us. Daniel looks up and his eyes are hooded, not revealing how reading about my ex made him feel.

"You could have been his concubine. Royals are known to have official concubines." Whatever I expected him to say, this wasn't it and it leaves my mouth hanging momentarily.

"Eventually, that's what he wanted too, but I couldn't be his concubine. I loved him too much to come second-best to him."

I didn't mean it as a dig to Daniel but he seems to take it that way because the blood drains from his face and I have to hand him some water.

What Vhuti and I had was purely tainted our lies by omission, and maybe I was stupid to walk away from being his concubine because I ended up with Daniel but dynasty wars have been known to be deadly. Or, maybe I didn't love him enough, another topic that my therapist loves circling back to. Whatever the case may be, I did walk away and most nights, when I'm alone in my bed, I regret walking away.

"Goodnight." Daniel doesn't acknowledge me as I kiss him on the cheek and leave him with the manuscript bundled in his hands, staring into nothing.

* * *

I didn't expect to sleep soundly but I did, and I'm only woken up by the heavenly aroma of food: bacon, to be precise. I stretch my arms and crank my neck a little, I was sleeping at an odd angle and my neck is paying for it. I want to soak in a scented bath but my stomach also starts growling.

What to do? What to do?

I sigh when my stomach lets out a low rumble. A quick shower it is, then. I'm about to grab my toiletries bag when there's a soft knock at the bedroom door. My eyes widen when they land on Daniel with a big tray in his hands and a coy smile on his face just outside my door.

"May I come in?"

"Sure. Sorry." I open the door wider and he gets in, then sets the tray on the nightstand.

"Go freshen up while I set up here." I don't need to be told twice, I dash to the bathroom and brush my teeth before washing my face. The shower will have to come after breakfast.

I get back to find Daniel bending over, making the bed, and there is no sight of the breakfast tray anywhere. As if he senses my presence, he straightens and then tips his head towards the French doors. Oh, my! Breakfast is set up on the tiny balcony and I rush over, my mouth already watering. I sink my teeth into the tiny ham-bacon-and-scrambled-eggs cocktail burger that is one of Daniel's specialities. The sun is just peeking out. It looks like it rained during the night and the lazy rays form little dancing rainbows on the droplets hanging from the leaves, about to fall.

I sigh contentedly as I raise my wine glass filled with sparkling non-alcoholic champagne: basically, grape juice, as Nomusa would say. I stare at the river in the full glory of the morning glow. One of the things I envied about Nompumelelo—besides her raising my daughter and being married to Daniel—was her deep friendship with Nomusa; as opinionated and as loud as she is, she's like a sister to her.

Over the years ,they've invited me out to do brunch, luncheons, and a weekend away that one time when it was just us three in Bela Bela. I loved all our outings but they reminded me how alone I am. I've never had a friend like Nomusa; it's hard trusting people with my secrets.

"You didn't enjoy breakfast?" Daniel's worry-laden voice breaks into my musings and I look at him for clarity.

"You are frowning and you looked a little sad; wistful, even."

One thing about Daniel is that he can easily read me but his face is usually harder to read, unless he's at his most vulnerable. Which rarely happens.

"I was thinking that Denise would love being in a place like this." That is true. Plus, there is no need to sour the mood by bringing up Nomusa, not when Daniel hates her guts; or mention his ex-wife, whom I'm not sure he will ever get over her walking away, even though it's been close to a decade.

He's smiling widely at the mention of Denise, that one has him in the crook of her little finger.

"Maybe I should buy her a beach house in Cape Town or maybe Durban. I know she loves the ocean. I've drawn you a bath, if you are done here."

"Oh." The casual flip from the beach house purchase to drawing me a bath has me flummoxed. Daniel sure knows how to keep me on my feet. I go in to get out of my pyjamas while he gathers the breakfast tray.

After the dejected mood that I left him in last night, I wasn't expecting this five-star treatment, which makes it all the more sweeter. If I didn't know better, I would think he was trying to woo me. My nose prickles when I get into the bathroom: I'm picking up jojoba oil mixed with lavender, chamomile, and frankincense. I carefully lower myself into the piping-hot water, the foam clinging on to me like a second skin. I sigh again in contentment and lean back, closing my eyes as the oils work their magic soothing and relaxing my muscles.

I startle when Daniel walks into the bathroom and I look at him with narrowed eyes; I'm too relaxed to properly scowl at him. He raises both hands in a sign of innocence.

"I come in peace. I just came in to wash your back; I know you get frustrated when you can't reach the middle of your lower back. Why the frown?"

I feel bad because he's being so nice and I'm frowning suspiciously at him, so I smile at him apologetically.

"It's just that it's been a while since you've offered to wash my back." Or brought me breakfast in bed, or run me a relaxing bath—all which I leave that unsaid and rush instead to add, "I believe the last time was when I was heavily pregnant with Oyinqaba."

He scratches the back of his neck , refusing to meet my eyes, which tells me that he's feeling vulnerable, exposed.

"I guess this is my way of apologising. After reading some of that, I realised that I haven't been the best lover to you and if I hadn't impregnated you and selfishly decided to raise Oyama away from you, then maybe you wouldn't have spiralled out of control. You would have finished your Matric and fulfilled your grandmother's dreams. I don't appreciate enough how much you had to give up for me, for our children." I wipe my leaking eyes with the back of my hand, grateful that he's busy scrubbing my back.

Silence, only broken by the sounds of water splashing down my back and my uneven breathing as I try to rein in my emotions, drags for a minute or two. He stands up and turns to go but I hold his hand.

"Thank you, but there's no way you could have known some of that. When it comes to our pasts, we both tend to be closed off. I wouldn't trade my... our children for anything, even after everything I've gone through. I'm grateful that we made them, especially Oyama."

He grunts and looks suspiciously over my head at the wall before he tells me that I will meet him on the roof in thirty minutes. He gets out of the bathroom as if hell's fire is snapping at his heels, about to consume him. I close my eyes and immerse myself in the still-hot bath.

Chapter 22

Run

Two weeks of radio silence passed after the wedding before Vhuti made any contact with me. I had made peace with our relationship ending. It hurt, it stung, but I had gone through worse; or so I comforted myself. In those two weeks, I was accepted at Polokwane Technic Institute and I was so excited, even though I couldn't share the news with Vhuti, my aunt was excited with me. I was turning my life around.

I was sitting under Makhulu's favourite tree, shelling some peanuts and groundnuts for the samp that I intended to make, when a little boy from one of the neighbouring homesteads came rushing in.

'There's a man in a big car asking for you near the stream.'

Vhutshilo darted out before I could question him on the description of the man.

It was Vhuti. I wondered why I hadn't noticed before then that the guy was a prince. He dressed in understated yet expensive labels and he had two cars that I knew of. That day, he came in another one that looked and smelt new.

After the awkward greetings, he drove off for a while, until we reached Leshiba Lodge, which was about twelve to fifteen kilometres from our village. It was the first time that Vhuti took us anywhere private, we usually went out to malls. When he

parked, I turned to look at him and he was ready to alight.
'What are we doing here?' My voice was suspicious and nervously high.
'I wanted us to talk someplace private.' Vhuti had never roughly treated me but the last time before then when I was in a room alone with a man, I wound up naked, raped, and assaulted to near an inch of my life and I was never going back there again.
'We can talk here.' I remember folding my hands over my chest in a bid to calm my anxiety.
'Come on, Masase, I won't do anything that you don't want or haven't done before.' The way he said it stung; he didn't raise his voice but it dripped with disdain.
'Take me home,' I demanded, and his nose flared in the first sign of anger.
'What? Some guy can have you, even impregnate you, and I can't even be alone in a lodge room with you? I already paid, and do you know how expensive this place is?'
'Take me home, or I will scream.' I tried to swallow the pain that his words invoked.
He was angry and he drove like a demon-riddled madman, but he did take me home, dropping me off without even touching me. The encounter still left me shaken and I locked myself in Makhulu's bedroom, away from the prying cousin's eyes.
That night, I dreamt of Makhulu again. This time, she sang the 'Mutshavhona' song while she led me by my hand to an abandoned field. There, clear as day, were Vhutuhawe and my distant cousin huddled together. He handed her a small envelope. I saw her open it and it was filled with money.
Vhuti assured her that she would get more after the task. All she had to do was make sure I went to the stream, where there would be people ready to kidnap me. That she wouldn't be doing anything wrong, as such things were known to happen traditionally.

***

Chapter 22

The last time I ignored Makhulu's warning, I almost died, I wasn't going to make the same mistake twice. I jolted upright and realised that it was still in the middle of the night, maybe around 2 a.m., judging by the stars. One thing was clear: I had to leave Maebani that night.

I lit the oil lamp and tore a paper from one of my notebooks then wrote a hasty letter to my aunt, telling her that I had gotten an apprenticeship offer that I couldn't miss out on. I thanked her for helping me get through high school, and wished her well.

I made quick work of packing my clothes while wondering why Vhuti would want to kidnap me, since he couldn't marry me; he was a prince and I was a commoner with a child. I didn't want to stick around and find out, though. O thubiwa or khurumedzwa--forcefully marrying someone by kidnapping them--was only usually done by men who couldn't afford some of the bridal rites, such as mufaro or tshitundwana; Vhutu could afford money to bribe my cousin.

I lugged the briefcase from its hiding place and I was relieved to find the money still there. My clothes weren't that many and I shoved them quickly into the small bag that used to belong to Makhulu that I found in the wardrobe. I had heard tales of men raping the girls into submitting to marry them and the family of the girl would cover the shame of having a daughter who had lost her maidenhead by marrying her off to her rapist. Then another thought brought me up short: What if Vhutu wanted to sacrifice me? Kings and royals had been rumoured to strengthen their dynasties and wealth by offering human sacrifices. I remembered Makhulu's stories around the fire that had suddenly become too real. I felt something cold and clammy slither down my spine.

I was packed in under thirty minutes and since I needed something to remember my grandmother with, I searched through her drawers. I found a worn-out picture of her when she looked young and she was standing with a man in camouflage--that could have been my grandfather. As I was tugging the picture loose, a little metal box on top of it tipped over and my grandmother's bangles fell out. I grabbed the bangles, picture, and her favourite cloth with elephant tusks decorating it and shoved them in my bag.

I looked around for the last time, imprinting the room in my mind. Something told me that I wouldn't be back for the longest time. I would miss this room because it made me feel closer to Makhulu.

With my heart heavy and thudding dully against my ribcage, I looked around to see if there was anyone in the yard before I let myself out. I locked the door and placed the key in the envelope with my aunt's letter. Walking alone in the middle of the night in the village was scary. I should have carried the oil lamp. There weren't any streetlights or people going about their business at all hours like in Gauteng. Ghost and witchcraft stories rang through my mind as I rushed through the wet grass. I tripped on the root of a baobab tree and I would have fallen if I didn't balance on the briefcase.

I tried to will my heart to slow down and not thud so painfully and loudly, but that was impossible. Every shadow made me stop short, every tree swaying looked like a creature with spiky arms. I almost peed on myself along the way but I still managed to reach the school while it was still dark and I slid the envelope addressed to my aunt in the school's letterbox.

Just beyond the school, some villagers had set up a fire and were waiting for the bus. I greeted them and one older lady shifted so that I could sit with her on her reed mat.

'You almost missed the bus, muduhulu.' No sooner had she said those words before we heard the low rumble of the bus.

Everyone began scrambling to gather their belongings; I had only the briefcase and the small bag with me. I was the first to get on the rickety old bus and I chose the remaining window seat, the bus was almost full. I took the money that I'd shoved into my bra and paid for the ticket before taking Makhulu's cloth and wrapping it around me; the window behind me was broken and a large piece of plastic that had holes in it stood in its stead. Once I was warm enough, I drifted off to sleep.

***

I woke up in the glaring sun of early afternoon, I had to blink and look around before I realised that I was on a bus, then I remembered what had made me flee from my home. My stomach felt hollow and it wasn't from the lack of food, although the old lady who sat next to me offered me some steamed maize bread that I gently turned down. I wouldn't have been able to stomach it.

'That's a beautiful cloth you have on. I didn't know that they still made these,' she complimented, and I looked down at Makhulu's cloth.

'It belonged to my grandmother,' I mumbled.

Before she could say anything, the conductor cut her off by stating that we were almost in Johannesburg. I took off the cloth and folded it carefully before putting it in my bag. The bus parked in the old Park Station and the bustling activity there made me forget all the thoughts that had accompanied me on the bus ride. I didn't even get to say goodbye to the old lady, who seemed to have vanished while I was dragging my briefcase from under the seat.

I had to keep my wits about me as I alighted from the bus. The many African dialects poured over me as I clutched my bag and briefcase close to my chest. I ignored some of the catcalls and offers to help as I navigated my way out of the station and through Johannesburg central jungle, and found taxis to my mother's house.

I belatedly remembered that there was a tenant when I got there and the house was locked, no hidden key in sight. I checked all the spots where we used to hide the key. Tired, hungry, and anxious, I went to my neighbour's house and she was kind enough to offer me a place to refresh and said I could stay the night on the floor of her sitting room.

Asking for help from Daniel did cross my mind but I reminded myself that he was married, and Phindiwe was right, I couldn't keep running to him. I also wanted to see Kungentando so bad; she had turned two while I was in Maebani and I could have used more of her pictures. I had to remind myself that I had no claim over her and that she was better off without me. I had to get some direction in my life first.

So, when I went to buy cool drink and bread for my neighbour, I also bought a newspaper. I have never been an overly-religious person, Makhulu never went to church, in the Christian sense, and my mother was usually too tired and only went during Easter and Christmas, but I believe Providence or God and my guides led me to buy that newspaper. There, on the Classified Ads page, in bold red letters it read:-

"Apprentices wanted!
Sorbet, in collaboration with Beauty Therapy Institute, is running a joint apprenticeship and part-time study (at half the price!) collaboration for all aspiring beauticians..."

The apprenticeship ran throughout the country but I knew that if I stayed in Gauteng, I would end up running into Daniel and his sister. I was told that they came looking for me and it would be the first place that Vhutuwe would search for me if he was relentless in his pursuit.

I decided to move to KZN, which was far from both men and my life in Gauteng, where I had spiralled out of control. Plus, my neighbour had a sister in Durban that she went to the payphone to call.

It was all set in a matter of three days. I was going to live with her sister and pay a small amount of money for rent while I looked for a job, in case the apprenticeship didn't pan out. In less than a week, I was back in Park Station--this time, in a Greyhound bus, and bound to the coast.

I was anxious about going to a place where I didn't know anyone but I was also excited about starting on a clean slate in a place where I wasn't Candy, the reformed party girl, or Masase, the reserved girl doing her Matric with her juniors. I could be Candice and decide for myself who I wanted Candice to be.

The prospect was daunting, especially as Thuli, my neighbour's sister--whom I would come to rely on a lot in the coming years--came to collect me from the bus station and took me to her home. She stayed in a cottage at the back of her employer's property in Westville.

It was a pretty cottage with two bedrooms, the other was used by her daughter when she came to visit during school holidays. I fell in love with Durban at first sight; it didn't have the stifling heat of Maebani or the noisy pollution of Johannesburg but its air was moist and had a sea breeze that carried a promise of new beginnings.

Chapter 23

Candice

Nowami,

You looked so peaceful sleeping that I didn't have the heart to wake you up. Something came up and I had to go. I will probably be gone the whole day. I'll think about you every minute that I am away.

Yours,
D.S.

I look at the elegant sweep of his handwriting on the note that he left on the breakfast tray and try to swallow my disappointment.

At least he made you breakfast, my subconscious has suddenly grown kind but even looking at the cold meats arrangement that he made doesn't cheer me up.

This has been the longest time that we have exclusively spent alone, just the two of us, since before Denise was born. He is being attentive, in between reading we laugh and reminisce, and he gives me massages. Daniel's foot massages are orgasmic, toe-curling stuff of legends. We have been intimate without having sex, something that we never did before. We always communicate with our bodies, the reason for us having three kids.

For once he hasn't been the minister, someone else's husband or a father—he has been mine; lulling me into a false sense of dreaming that this could be our reality, this cocoon that we are living in Eswatini. The note, now hanging loosely in between my thumb and forefinger, is a sharp reminder that he will never be fully mine.

You came here for closure, remember?

Snarky subconscious is back.

I gulp down the freshly-squeezed orange juice to help the croissant that seems stuck in my throat go down. I won't spend my day alone, moping around like a love-struck teenager. Nope. I need to explore this beautiful place; move around the yard and the gorgeous garden at least.

If I had my phone, I would check on the kids. I feel guilty going so long without talking to them but I haven't been at my best, my emotions are all over the place. Denise has the uncanny ability to pick up when I'm not okay emotionally. A week apart won't hurt them; they have Amandla to play with and Daniel checks up on them every day.

I'm putting the dishes into the dishwasher when a car engine drones outside and I hate how perky my mood gets. It plummets again when, instead of Daniel walking through the door, there is a knock. Frowning, I tighten the belt around my gown and open the door. Her stomach greets me first and her pearly teeth flash at me, deepening her dimples, and she's even more stunning in person than on canvas. The lady of the house is here, in the flesh.

"Sawubona. I'm sorry to just pop in like this but I have been burning to welcome you. I hope you don't mind." Her sweet smile belies her apologetic hesitancy; she's warm but a bit shy too. I greet her back and open the door wider for her to come in.

"You have a beautiful home, thank you for lending it to us. Should I get you juice?" She waves my thanks aside and gracefully waddles to the refrigerator.

"Ntsikelelo doesn't ask for favours that often and we are rarely here now, the house was probably lonely. Hlongwane didn't want me constantly driving to go about my duties down at the village, especially now that I am in my third trimester. We mostly stay down in the village."

Her voice is a bit muffled by the fridge and she comes out with a tub of mint chocolate ice cream, cheese, peanut butter, and chocolate. I watch, amused, as she scoops generous amounts and puts them in a bowl. She adds some Smarties from the cupboard and chocolate syrup.

"He doesn't know I drove up here today but I had to get away. I had to! His kids are slowly driving me crazy!" She has a mischievous glint in her eyes as she shoves a spoonful of the gooey sugar death into her mouth, which tells me she shouldn't be eating this much sugar either and her husband would flip if he found out.

"Your secret is safe with me. I wanted to explore this place but I was afraid that I would get lost." She's easy to talk to and before long, we are chatting like old friends.

We instantly gel and she offers to show me the village, her village. It's hard to think of her as a chief. She's young and has this motherly aura to her, those people that you instinctively know give great hugs.

She waits for me downstairs as I quickly go and freshen up, and when I get back, I find her with a refilled bowl and she's now in the living room, reclining on the sofa. She struggles to get up and I hold her elbow, hefting her up.

"I swear, this is my last pregnancy," she mutters after her thanks. "But then again, that's what I said last time."

"I've been there, but the three I have is now enough. How many children do you want?" She grins widely and says 'a whole soccer team'.

I wonder how much about me and Daniel she knows but she doesn't pry, and we talk of children as she drives us down. I tell her I'm anaemic and how each pregnancy seems to leave me a little weaker than the last and, unlike her, I really am done having children. She's easy to talk to and she's open, definitely a friend I would like to have.

The green and grey hues are even more beautiful up close. This place is serene, and I wish Denise could see it, she would love it here. Amandla would love the monkeys darting quickly on the trees, my grandchild's love for animals has grown with her. I realise that I haven't travelled much with my children, maybe I should start taking them on trips and one day, we will visit here again. Swazi points to a mountain that is taller than the one on which their house is perched.

"If I wasn't pregnant, I would have taken you up there. You can see the whole village from there ,and there is a waterfall. It's perfect. Babe, my father, used to take me there until he was too sick to make the climb. Even in a wheelchair, he wanted to go up to our spot. Stubborn old man." She laughs a bit at the last line but her voice is choked, and she tries to blink back the tears but some still fall.

"I'm sorry, I didn't mean to dampen the mood but I miss him so much. It's like I lost him last week, not years ago." I put my hand on top of hers on the steering wheel and squeeze lightly.

Now wouldn't be the right time to inquire if her father is the old man who was walking her down the aisle; she needs to be comforted.

"My grandmother died when I was twelve but I still miss her every day." This time around, she squeezes my hand. A comfortable silence hangs over us until we get to the village hall.

"This is where I hold meetings and settle disputes. Hlongwane recently had it renovated."

The fresh paint and sparkling windows bear testimony of the renovations and I wonder if she knows that her husband is an arms robber; it's not my place to ask. We move on to where the cattle are dipped, and lastly, she takes me to her home.

Her homestead is made up of traditional concave beehive huts, which are perfectly thatched with premium dry grass, around a large cattle byre. There is activity all around the homestead: children running and playing around the yard, teenage girls making different artefacts from wood, reed, and grass. Some older ladies are busy with the cooking, while a queue of people waiting to be fed has formed around the biggest tree.

Everyone greets her respectfully but also affectionately, and the twins I saw in the pictures run circles around her before hugging her legs and darting off to play with the other children. A little chubby girl, who could be the replica of her mother, lifts her chubby arms towards me to be lifted.

I take her and she rests her head on my shoulders without saying anything and starts sucking on her thumb serenely.

"You are lucky. Tsandzile doesn't usually take to strangers." I barely acknowledge the words as I gaze into the little girl's huge eyes. She's like a little porcelain doll, with skin made from the smooth dark pebbles, warmed in the sun.

After what feels like many pit stops, we finally step into the largest hut in the homestead. It is a true relic of Swati huts of old but inside, it is surprisingly modern, with heated ceramic flooring and air conditioning. Underneath the thatched grass are sturdy tiled walls. The windows are large and made of shatterproof glass. The interior is modern-meets-rustic, almost similar to the mansion that we are currently staying in. There is a homeliness to the place that is comforting.

"Masomalenhle! Lenhle! I'm back!" she shouts, before slumping gratefully into the largest leather couch that I have ever seen.

I sink into the next one and it feels squishy and comfortable. Tsandzile is now playing with my earlobes, I'm grateful that I didn't put on any earrings; she would be yanking on them by now. The large flat screen mounted on half of the wall is showing some basketball match in America and there's popcorn in a bowl on the small table and a glass half-full of coke. Whoever she's calling must have stepped out recently.

"Swazi, do you want S'bali to kill me? You said you were going out for fresh air for five minutes." The voice sounds eerily familiar...

My eyes widen when they land on the person who is busy reprimanding Nomaswazi to even acknowledge me. It can't be! I feel lightheaded and I try not to clutch at the toddler who is now bouncing on my knees screaming, "Lele, Lele, Lele!" excitedly.

The dizziness intensifies and I rest my head on the back of the couch, closing my eyes a bit to stop the world from spinning. I hear someone calling my name but I'm sliding and tumbling slowly into the darkness.

Chapter 24

Daniel

It was hard leaving Candice sleeping. I snuck into her room to cuddle, just as I've been doing since we got to Eswatini. Apart from a serious case of blue balls, it's the most peaceful sleep I've had in over a year. I hate that I had to go out today, of all days, but I'll make it up to her tonight; Hlongwane already helped me make the arrangements to.

"S'khulu, we found your guy. He was very infamous around the club that you mentioned, so it was easy for my guys to find him. What do you want us to do with him?"

"Keep him hanging, while I conclude today's business." To keep up the appearance of a casual game of golf, I had to leave at around three a.m. and now, at the crack of dawn, we are about to land. Ntsikelelo will be staying behind, he has some business of his own to attend to, I'll text him when my meeting has been concluded. I lug the bag of golf clubs with me as I disembark and quickly get into the waiting Land Cruiser.

The sun is rising lazily over the horizon, casting a golden hue across the sprawling landscape of the president's private game reserve. It's a stunning sight, one that I've seen before but never fail to appreciate. The rolling hills are dotted with acacia trees, their silhouettes stark against the encroaching light, while the distant sounds of wildlife stirring awake create an ambience both serene and electric. As we pull up to the lodge, a grand structure of timbre and stone, I can't help but feel a mix of the thrill of negotiating and dread if any part of this goes sideways. This is not just any meeting; it's a delicate negotiation that could tip the scales of power in the region.

I step out of the car and take a moment to take it all in. The lodge is a masterpiece of rustic elegance, with large windows that offer panoramic views of the Savannah. The air is thick with the scent of earth and grass, mingling with the faint aroma of wood smoke from the fireplace inside. The place feels alive, almost sentient, as if it senses the weight of the discussions that are about to unfold within its walls.

As I walk towards the entrance, the heavy wooden door swings open to reveal a spacious foyer adorned with rich fabrics and warm lighting. The walls are lined with trophies from the hunt—a testament to the president's prowess and the kind of power he wields. I glance at my Vacheron Constantin watch; it's almost time. I move away from the lodge, following the trail that leads to the greens. Joshua suggested we have the meeting outside because then we won't have to search the room for bugs and he has a scrambler, in case anyone is wearing a wire. I never would have thought about listening devices and scramblers, but Joshua seems well-versed in the department of espionage. The morning sun rises steadily over the lush, rolling hills of the private game reserve, casting a warm glow on the vibrant greens of the golf course. I'm the last to arrive, to find Joshua casually chatting to the president as if he's known him his whole life.

"Gentlemen," I greet them, making sure my voice is smooth yet authoritative. "I trust you are well?"

We exchange pleasantries, but it's clear that the air is thick with unspoken agendas.

As I take my stance, I feel the gentle breeze on my face, carrying with it the distant sounds of wildlife. I swing back, the club kissing the ball with a satisfying 'Thwack!', sending it soaring down the fairway. Joshua cheers, a wide grin on his face, while Mr President shakes his head, already plotting his comeback. He's one competitive motherfucker.

"Thank you for meeting with us, Mr President. We have an important matter to discuss." I look him in the eye, gauging his reaction. He leans against his bag, a slight smile playing at the corners of his mouth.

"Let's get to it, then. Shall we?" he replies, his tone inviting yet laced with challenge.

We walk down the fairway, the thick bush lining the course a reminder of the reserve's wild inhabitants. A herd of antelope grazes nearby, seemingly unfazed by our presence. I can't help but steal glances at them, momentarily distracted from the game and the impending discussion.

"We're seeking your cooperation regarding the situation in Zimbabwe," I begin, choosing my words carefully. "The current regime is… unstable. We believe a change in leadership is imminent, and we would like your assurance that the transition will be smooth."

The president raises an eyebrow, intrigued but cautious. "And? What's in it for me?" he asks, his gaze unwavering.

I sense the tension building, and I take a deep breath, ready to present our offer. "In exchange for your support, and if you can ensure that the new government is welcomed into the Southern African Development Community without sanctions, we will open our network to you. Additionally, we have access to significant resources—namely, gold."

His interest piques at the mention of gold, a glimmer of calculation crossing his features. "Gold, you say? How significant are we talking?"

Joshua leans forward, as if checking his golf clubs, tilting the bag to show the gold bars at the bottom of his bag and states casually: "We're prepared to present a substantial amount today, as a gesture of good faith. And there's more: should you agree to support us, we can guarantee the rights to a lucrative gold mine once the new regime is in place."

At the second hole, I line up my putt, the green rolling smooth beneath my feet. The sound of a bird's call echoes through the trees as I sink the ball into the cup with a satisfying plop. "Nice one!" Mr President exclaims, clapping me on the back. I can see his competitive spirit igniting; he's determined to match my score.

The president's expression shifts, the weight of our proposition settling in. "You believe this will go unnoticed by the international community?"

Joshua interjects, his voice steady, "With your influence, Mr President, we can orchestrate a narrative that keeps the focus elsewhere. You will be seen as a stabilising force in the region, ensuring peace and prosperity."

"If this goes sideways, nothing comes back to me, or you risk a personal attack from me. Understand?" It's to be expected that the president should want his name not to be dragged into this treacherous attempt.

The sun climbs higher, and as we reach the seventh hole, we find ourselves surrounded by the beauty of the reserve. A majestic giraffe ambles into view, its long neck stretching gracefully toward the treetops. We pause, clubs in hand, captivated by the beautiful moment. It's not every day you get to play golf alongside such magnificent wildlife.

I wish I'd brought Candice, the thought pops up unbidden, making me falter. Joshua's side-eye asks if I'm okay and I offer an almost imperceptible nod 'Yes'.

"I propose we toast to our partnership," I say, wanting to finish the deal and get on with my day. "We have brought some of the finest whiskey for this occasion."

The president chuckles, a sound that eases the tension slightly. "Very well. Let's see what you've brought."

As I retrieve the bottle from my golf clubs' bag, I can feel the weight of the moment pressing down. I uncork it with a flourish, the sound echoing in the field, and pour three generous measures into plastic tumblers. I hand one to the president, who takes it with an approving nod, and pass another to Joshua.

"To new beginnings," I declare, raising my tumbler.

"To new beginnings," they echo, the president's eyes sparkling with a mix of ambition and cunning as he clinks his tumbler against ours. The president takes a sip, savouring the rich flavour, and I can see the gears turning in his mind. I grit my teeth and follow suit, hating this part of the negotiations, but then again, not drinking would be akin to sabotage.

"Very well," he says, hands his tumbler back to me. "Let's discuss the details of this arrangement."

When I'm sure the president is focused on his hole, I discreetly spit out the whiskey, hating that the smell and taste lingers in my mouth. The conversation flows more freely now, each of us contributing to the strategy we need to implement. We outline the steps, the timing, and the necessary assurances to maintain stability during the transition. The president nods along, his expression shifting from scepticism to interest as we delve deeper into our plans.

With our minds now aligned, we continue. Joshua takes the lead on the eighth hole, expertly navigating the tricky dogleg. He's been playing for long, and it shows. "Beginner's luck!" he jokes, his confidence infectious. I can't help but feel a twinge of envy as he makes a near-perfect shot.

I watch as the president's demeanour softens; he is not just a leader but a man who enjoys the thrill of the game.

"Tell me, Daniel," he says, an amused glint in his eye. "What would you do if you were in my position?"

It feels like a dig, since I've never hidden my ambition to be in his position. I smile, I'm in my element as I spin a tale of power dominoes, embellishing the risks and rewards of the president's role in our mission. He listens intently, clearly taking note of everything I say. As we approach the final hole, most of our plan has been hashed out. Each of us is keen to finish strong, what with the stakes much higher than ever. The air is thick with anticipation as I line up my final putt. I take a deep breath, block out the noise of the reserve, and let the world fade away. The ball rolls, teetering on the edge of the hole before dropping in.

Mr President and Joshua erupt in cheers, and we all share a laugh—the camaraderie and competition blending seamlessly against the breath-taking backdrop of nature. As we walk off the course, the sun climbing higher from behind the hills, I can't help but think about what has been set in motion today and how my name will not go down in history books for my part in it and strangely, I'm okay with that. I do not have the familiar craving of flaunting this moment to the mighty Sisulus and that's saying something. The president leans forward, his eyes alight with ambition.

"You have my assurance," he says, extending his hand across his golf club. "Let's make this happen."

I grasp his hand firmly, sealing our pact. A sense of relief washes over me; we have navigated the treacherous waters of diplomacy and emerged victorious, and all I want is to get out of here and deal with the rat who thought he could lay hands on my Candice.

We leave the private game reserve around noon. Joshua raised an eyebrow when I refused the president's generous offer to sleep overnight. But, I have a man to torture.

Chapter 25

Candice

When I come to, it feels like my whole body has been dragged into a grinder then spit out. My eyes are heavy, my vision hazy and when it finally settles, I almost jump out of my skin.

There is an old man with wrinkled, leathery skin with tiny moles conglomerating on his cheeks, and hair coiled like tiny Mopane worms. He has beads crisscrossing his chest, one with a tiny horn is dangling from his chest and brushing against my arm as he pushes a smoking pipe around me and mutters some words that I don't quite get.

I want to scream but even opening my mouth is a struggle, I am so tired. He carries on until I feel some of the lethargy leave my body and when I lift my head, I see Nomaswazi standing at the edge of the bed, worriedly chewing on her lower lip. She doesn't speak until the old man is done grunting and belching, her apologetic voice laced with worry.

"You gave us such a fright. You just switched off with Tsandzile in your arms after my brother came into the room. Then as we were calling your husband, Mkhulu came in and commanded us to bring you here."

I try to remember the last thing I was doing before I blacked out. The door opens, and then I remember as I see the tall man with a frown coming in.

"Sipho?" I have to be sure it's not my son-in-law living a double life, and his frown only deepens as he and Nomaswazi share a look.

Mkhulu starts grunting and belching again, Swazi and her brother kneel and clap their hands. He starts shaking, and his eyes bulge and he starts chanting totems.

"Nine boNkhosi, Sidlubula Dledle sikaNobamba, Lokothwayo, Ludvonga lukaMavuso, Sidvwaba Siluthuli, Mlangeni, Mntungwa, Kunene. Ndlovu ezidl'ekhaya ngokuswela abelusi, Sibhahuza sikaMawawa, Mlangeni, Sobhuza. Khulumani bo!" This time, his eyes roll to the back of his head, with only the whites showing, and I want to get off the bed and run but my feet feel like lead.

"There is a son that has to be brought home; the ancestors have been patient but now they are angry. There is a child that is yet to be born with powers beyond us, he is a child of the ancestors, but if the son is not brought home and properly introduced, there will be blood spilt—innocent blood and bad blood. Bring the son home." Our mouths are hanging all the way to the floor but he's not done. He turns and looks me directly in the eyes and I feel this chill deep in my bones.

"Your grandmother wants to speak to you." I'm still trying to gather the strength to talk when the most shocking thing happens: Makhulu's voice comes out of this man's mouth. My tears well up at the voice's hoarse timbre.

"Naledzi ya Masase. Lukanda lutete lu no nga naledzi ya mutsho. Muduhulu wanga, listen very carefully, I do not have enough time. I failed you, my child. Yes, I raised you, but I failed you." Tears stream down the old man's face as he speaks and I feel it, the pain that she's carrying. My heart is suddenly heavy and tears also find their path down my face.

Makhulu continues speaking, "There is a family gift that will be explained to you later, I was supposed to leave it with you. The gift always skips a generation, but your mother would hear none of it. I couldn't pass on the gift to you and now it has to be passed on to your grandchild. You need to get my cloth and my bangles, and do what needs to be done before this child is born. Do not fail him the way that I failed you. Take care of the little one that you are carrying. I am always looking out for you."

The old man grunts and his eyes bulge out again and I feel the exact moment that Makhulu leaves his body—leaves me, because her presence is no longer tightly-coiled around me. My head starts spinning and the old man pushes the smoking pipe towards me and the heady smell of burning sage revives me. He has stopped belching and grunting but there is still an intensity around him as he points at me with the smoking pipe.

"You recognised the late chief because your son-in-law is the spitting image of his father. You collapsed because he," he points the smoking pipe at Nomaswazi's brother, "is almost identical to your son-in-law. He is the son of this homestead and the ancestors are using you to bring him home."

"I don't understand. This gift that Makhulu was talking about, what is it?" He looks almost bored by my question but he still responds.

"The bangles that your grandmother wore, Tshotswane, are worn by traditional healers, an indicator that the healing gift is inherited from a female ancestor. Your grandmother was a healer but because some in the family wanted the gift, she had to hide who she was and didn't openly heal people. Your grandmother died without passing on the gift to you because your mother was afraid that the same people who were fighting your grandmother would come for you. Your grandmother couldn't go against your mother's wishes but managed to make sure that the bangles and cloth are in your possession." It's all so hard to digest and I feel a bit light-headed again.

"I have another brother." I had forgotten that Nomaswazi and her brother are still with us. He helps her up and she sits on the bed next to me.

"You called me 'Sipho'. Is that his name?" Lenhle asks, and he also looks just as emotional as his sister.

"Yes, he is married to my daughter. Her name is Oyama."

"How is he like?" Swazi asks, while holding my hand.

"He's tall and he looks just like Lenhle; the resemblance is uncanny. He talks exactly like him, too. He has a spiritual gift, and he's a loving husband and father. He doesn't talk much but when he does, he talks with wisdom."

She's crying and I'm beginning to be alarmed. Lenhle is also blinking back tears and when I look for the old man to ask him why our family gift didn't pass to Amandla instead, I find that he's disappeared and it's now just us.

"I'm so sorry, I'm just so happy. He sounds just like *Babe*, I can't wait to meet him. I have a brother, and your daughter is going to be my sister!"

I'm still a bit overwhelmed at all these revelations and having heard Makhulu's voice. Something she said keeps niggling me at the back of my mind but I can't quite make it out. A small world it is, I wonder how Sipho is going to take it and how Oyama is going to handle the revelation that her unborn baby is going to be a spiritual child. I know how she struggled until she finally came to accept her husband's gift.

'Take care of the little one that you are carrying.'

The words ring in my head, their meaning explicit and I want to pull out my hair. No! It can't be! Nomaswazi notices how pale I've grown and I ask her to take me to a pharmacy. Masomalenhle insists on driving us because it is some distance away.

I can't be pregnant, I keep repeating to myself. I can't be pregnant.

Oyama will be so disappointed in me, again. Daniel will kick up even more of a fight over my leaving. I'm on contraception, for crying out loud! This time, I took the shot to avoid any more mistakes. I should have just taken out my womb.

We drive to the mall with little Tsandzile nestled against my chest and Nomaswazi asking me about Sipho; she's excited, and that makes me happy for him. He deserves a family that will love him unconditionally, unlike that mother of his. She was so dramatic at their wedding, crying as if her son was dying instead of marrying the girl he's been in love with since he was 19.

Sipho and Swazi are almost the same age but he's younger, no one knows how the chief met his mother and if he was aware that he had another son elsewhere.

My hands are shaking as we wait for the three minutes to be over. I'm glad that Swazi insisted on coming to the toilet with me. This is a mess. How do I keep on going around in circles? I feel my heart constricting and I blink back the tears.

"Hey, it's going to be okay." I try to return her smile but fail miserably. It's not going to be okay. This time spent in Eswatini was supposed to be about me finding closure and moving on, not finding out that I am about to have a fourth baby!

"Thirteen weeks, thirteen weeks! Oh, my God!" I bow my head, hiding my face in my hands, and sob.

It's all so overwhelming, just as I was beginning a new life for myself. I feel the resentment rush through me, I sob even harder because this little human being that Makhulu insisted I take care of doesn't deserve this resentment. I sob because I see all my plans going down the drain and I'm back to where I started.

Chapter 26

Daniel

"I don't see why you two had to join me," I mutter, as my driver turns into a seedy street in Yeoville.

Joshua ignores me while Shefu, my contact for our current mission, smiles widely, enjoying my displeasure. I've known Shefu for decades but we only got closer when I took over from that bastard, Mhlanguli, and Shefu was one of the first to unreservedly show his support. I saw the same greed for power and domination in him, but that almost surpassed my own, and we forged an unlikely alliance.

It helped that we weren't in direct competition; plus, his gifts aren't half bad. Each of my kids now has a registered farm and Candice even has a mine in Zimbabwe, unbeknownst to them, courtesy of their bamkuru Shefu, whom they've never met.

"I'm bored, and I figured you might need my old gnarly hands in case punches are needed. We wouldn't want to ruin your dainty hands so soon after your manicure appointment." Shefu guffaws at his own joke while I scoff and that only makes him laugh even louder. The bastard has always loved the sound of his own voice.

"I see Camilla is rubbing off on you," mutters Joshua, and Shefu immediately bristles. Interesting.

The rest of the drive passes in blessed silence. Shefu keeps throwing sharp gazes at Joshua and I'm brimming with carefully concealed rage. I keep seeing Candice's pale face when I was reading that chapter, how her hands were clawing at my thighs without her even noticing. She drew blood and still, it wasn't enough to atone for my sins. I left her to fend for herself. I saw that she was spiralling, and I threw a bag of money at her and walked away with our child. I'm not one to dwell on alternatives but these past few days have unleashed a vortex of regret and 'what-ifs' on me.

What if I hadn't been so hell-bent on power, and given Nompumelelo the out she asked for when she came back, and started a family with Candice? She was smart, even back then; with a little guidance, she would have been unstoppable. I couldn't see that, beyond my own need for domineering the family that shunned us. There was also the issue of her age, but if I could forge Oyama's birth certificate, I could have done the same with Candice's. Why didn't I see how broken she was in the hospital? I saw it in her eyes, but I was too triggered by the thought of Candice with another man who was giving her drugs to allow myself to question that broken look in her eyes.

The questions swirl around my head, and by the time Hlongwane meets us outside a butchery on the outskirts of Yeoville, I'm a shuddering mass of anger. I'm angry at the pig who dared violate my woman; she was just a child, dammit! Mostly though, I'm angry at myself, angry at all the choices I made. For what? An office I've spent decades trying to reach and yet, it still eludes me, approval from a family that still holds me in disdain even after I've proven myself to them time and time again. It makes me want to scream, but instead, I turn to ice as I follow Hlongwane past the store front, past the fridges, to a hidden basement, where Candice's tormentor is currently hung like the flayed carcass of a beast about to be cut in pieces.

"The boys warmed him up for you." Hlongwane makes a sweeping gesture towards my son-in-law's brother, Sibusiso, and his friends, and I give them a nod of approval.

This feels like the time when they caught Mhlanguli stalking my daughter. I'd told him what would happen should he return to South Africa after I threw him out for taking advantage of my drunk teenage daughter, taking her virginity, threatening her—and impregnating her, to boot. Killing him when I found out would have brought too much heat, considering his position back then, I thought beating him up and banishing him would be enough. But the bastard crawled out of whatever gutter five years ago and that time, I was able to kill him without any heat, and with the help of Sibusiso and his crew, his corpse was fed to pigs, and Mhlanguli was never heard from again. Then I linked Sibusiso and Hlongwane, the rest is history.

"What's his name?" I ask in my normal monotone, the iciness of my voice camouflaging the anger coursing through my blood stream.

"He goes by many names, but the one he's infamous for is 'S'khova'. He used to be a terror in the late 90s and the turn of the 2000s. We found him cornering a young girl." Sibusiso spits at the snivelling man when he says the last part.

I imagine that the young girl was a drugged Candice and instantly, my sight starts sporting at the corners, black spots that I try to reel in because I need to know for sure that this scumbag put his hands on my woman.

"Do you remember a young girl with pale almond skin, big eyes, high forehead?" He shakes his head quickly, making gabbled sounds around the gag in his mouth. No recognition showing on his face, just shitfaced fear.

"No? Pity. She was a bit wild in the early 2000s. She was willing to do anything you wanted, as long as you used a condom, but that was too much for your fragile ego. So, you drugged her, hit her to within an inch of her life, and you still proceeded to have your way with her without the condom that she'd begged you to use." His eyes widen slightly and that's all the confirmation I need, and the black spots move from the edged of my line of sight and they cover everything.

When the darkness clears, blood is seeping from my second-favourite suit, my Antonio Vietri shoes are surrounded by a sticky blood clots, and I have testicles in my hand. I can hear someone retching in the background and I try to slow my thundering heartbeat before I lean over and check the scum's pulse. Faint, but still there.

"Get him patched up, blood transfusion and the works. When he's healed,

I want him sent to the worst prison you can find and gift him as somebody's bitch." Hlongwane is looking at me with the same cold glean and he nods at my instructions.

I turn after dropping the testicles in a bowl next to the dangling body of Candice's tormentor. The blood clinging to my skin feels sticky and I have skin beneath my fingernails. The cold shower dampens some of the ire that still lingers. One less person who has hurt what's mine gets to roam the streets free from tonight onwards.

What about you?

My subconscious bitches at me and I grip the towel at the thought. If I was a better man, I'd let her go, but I'd rather be the monster that slays all her demons for her.

"You blacked out," Hlongwane states matter-of-factly when we're alone in the back of the car that's taking us back to the airstrip we left from the other day with Candice.

I don't respond; partly because I never acknowledge those blackouts and partly because the clothes that I'm in are itchy against my skin. Not the material per se, but their quality reminds me of days when I had just met Candice, working as an apprentice whose whole salary went to my sister for the upkeep of my siblings, and Phindiwe, in turn, dug up all my clothes from charity thrift stores. The Levi jeans I'm wearing are a far cry from those clothes but still, the itch won't leave my mind. I scramble my mind trying to find a distraction.

"Is everything set up for tonight? It has to be perfect." Hlongwane looks at me like he wants to say more but thinks better of it and responds to my question instead.

"Everything is set. Our wife distracted her while it was being set up." I nod my appreciation at him.

"When are you getting your own wife? I know your brother is tired of you third-wheeling in his marriage," I tease him, using a term I remember from Oyama's teenage years, before she started loathing me.

"I thought I'd found someone better than our wife, but it ended rather badly. I'm torn between letting her go and finding her. Besides, my demons want to gobble the poor woman up. I also experience blackouts like yours, but mine are often triggered by sex. If I ever took her as my wife, I will break her." His words hang heavy in the space between us. I wasn't expecting his show of vulnerability and it chafes my mind.

"You are a better man than I." He's not getting a wife because he fears breaking her and I can't let the love of my life go, even though it's becoming clearer to me how much I've broken her.

"Don't knight me yet, I haven't found the woman who consumes me enough to want to break her, because I let her slip away. I will find her and I will enjoy breaking her will," he tells me, with a twisted smile that reveals the maniac that lives just beneath his surface.

The car stops and we get off, we start talking about arms and transport routes. There's been some heat coming from the police lately and I note down that I need to pay the Police Commissioner a visit soon, remind him who owns him.

Chapter 27

Candice

Nomaswazi finally manages to calm me down and helps me drink water. When the panic and despair ebb away, tongues of anger—red and hot—coil around me. Daniel knew! He knew about this pregnancy, that's why he has been making me breakfast in bed, all those feet massages and back scrubs. That son of a...

"I know you are shocked right now, but babies are a blessing." I know she means well, so I swallow the bitter retort that springs to the tip of my tongue. It's not Swazi's fault that I got myself into this mess.

"It's just a lot. My daughter is also pregnant and I'm old now. I don't think that I have the energy for another baby."

She doesn't push the matter, thankfully, and we go back to the car. I ask them to drive me straight home. I just want to be alone for a while.

As if sensing my inner turmoil, Tsandzile is nestled against me, her one hand over my thudding heart while she suckles on the other one. I lean in a bit and I smell some of her pure baby fragrance, that uniquely baby-elixir of talcum, sweet milk, baby shampoo, and coconuts. The smell calms me, reminding me of holding Denise and Oyinqaba.

Feeling their sensations against my cheek or chest, paired with the sweet 'newborn smell', was one of the greatest sensations that I was addicted to.

There is no use rejecting this baby because I know I'm going to love him or her with the same fierceness that I love my other children with. Fortunately, Swazi and Lenhle aren't saying much, Jazz plays softly in the background as I stare outside the darkening landscape. Life is so simple here; maybe I should just move this side and become a hermit. My children can play with Nomaswazi's brood and I won't have to be afraid of them being hurt by other children's words.

As we drive up the winding driveway, my anger starts to simmer again when I see a big SUV parked outside. Daniel is back and so is my fiery anger. Tsandzile starts stirring against me and I have to put a lid on my anger. I kiss her gently and hand her to her mother.

Swazi and Lenhle also alight with me and I don't have the nice words to tell them to go, so I don't say anything but walk in front of them. I fumble in my purse for the keys and when my hands bump against the pregnancy stick that we saved, I feel my anger bubbling to the surface again.

The lounge and downstairs area is bathed in darkness, even though the rooms upstairs have their lights on. I feel the wall until I locate the switch and when I turn on the lights, a short string of "Surprise!" that is mostly bass and Swazi's lone falsetto rings out.

I blink in surprise, my hand over my roaring heart as I take in the huge golden balloons in the shapes of numbers four and three, other balloons—gold, black, and colourless filled with silver confetti. The whole lounge area has been transformed into an elegant soirée venue. There is even a gorgeous two-tier fancy luggage cake.

Daniel is beaming, clearly proud of himself for pulling this off, while all I want to do is claw out his eyes. Instead, I focus on Hlongwane... Wait a minute... I blink and blink again but I still see two of him. The other one has his hand around Nomaswazi, Tsandzile is now nestled against him, while the other one is grinning widely, standing next to Daniel.

"Careful, you will make her faint again," Lenhle warns as he moves towards the chaffing dishes lined on the table against the wall.

"You fainted?" Daniel's smile has slid away and he's fussing over me and I have to dig my nails into my hands before I scratch his eyes out.

"My iron levels were down," I murmur, trying to see if that will elicit any reaction, specifically guilt, from him but his frown remains the same.

"I thought you didn't need the iron tablets anymore. I will get them for you tomorrow. For now, happy birthday, Nowami." He kisses me softly on the lips and I close my eyes to blink back the tears.

This is the first time that Daniel has ever thrown me a party and invited anyone outside of our children and his sister. This is exactly what I longed for but now it feels so empty and I just want to storm upstairs and curl up in my bed. But Lenhle and Swazi are demanding a toast, Daniel has his arm around me possessively as he accepts a glass of non-alcoholic champagne from Lenhle and I accept another one from him as well.

"To the love of my youth, my wife, the mother of my children. At times, I wonder how you are still here, standing next to me, after all that I have put you through; I marvel at how you love me through all my imperfections. I love the fierce love that you have for our children and I know I've always made promises to you and didn't follow through. At this point, I sound like a broken record but I promise to give you all that your heart wishes for."

There are cheers from everyone and he embraces me before kissing me deeply, I accept the kiss out of habit and I go through the motions of smiling and playing the perfect hostess. It helps that our guests are keeping a lively back and forth banter.

"I can't believe that you roped my wife into this. You know how I feel about her driving now." It's still eerie how alike they are, they even sound like the same person.

"Our wife. Besides, you worry too much. She's made of stern stuff." Now that I'm assessing them, I realise that the one wearing a ring is Nomaswazi's husband, while Daniel's friend doesn't have one and he's barring his teeth at his lookalike.

"*Mine*." A kiss and a squeeze to emphasise his stake, "Go out there and look for your wife. Oh, I forget, the wife you wanted to marry nearly stabbed you to death."

"Hlongwane!" Swazi looks as if she's about to explode and Ntsikelelo hisses angrily while his hand tightens on the glass that he is holding.

Hlongwane grins widely at his brother after throwing an apologetic look at his wife.

"She did stab him," he mumbles, and Swazi throws him a withering look.

"Where is Nompindiselo? Have you found her yet?" Lenhle pipes up, before shoving a chicken thigh into his mouth.

"No, I'm still searching for her." A chill runs down my spine at the murderous glint in his eyes as he says this.

"Ntsikelelo, you promised me that you had let this go. Can we stop talking about this and spoiling Candy's birthday celebration?" Swazi shoots all these huge men towering over her a withering glance and they mumble their apologies like belligerent children.

The dinner continues and I avoid Daniel as much as I can until the men go to the study, with Tsandzile fast asleep in one of her fathers' chest. Nomaswazi helps me carry the dishes to the kitchen. The catering company will come clean up tomorrow but I need something to keep me busy.

"Are you feeling better now?" she asks, as she takes out some ice cream and I hand her two bowls.

"I am. Thank you for tonight, I had even forgotten that it's my birthday." She smiles, and tells me that it was her pleasure.

"That girl you were talking about, she really stabbed him?" A dark look passes over her eyes and her lips thin into a straight line, I regret asking.

"Right in the gut; two shallow thrusts and a deep thrust, too. It was a miracle that most of his vital organs where missed, and Ntsika managed to find him before he bled out." I can tell that she is still affected by the incident.

"Why would she do that to him?" I know there are times that I wish to scratch out Daniel's eyes, like today, but I don't think I would ever intentionally stab him.

"Their past is very dark," she says cryptically, and then changes the subject. We chat for a while before the men come back and they all say their goodbyes, and they leave me alone with this man whose sight I can't stand right now.

"You've been avoiding me the whole evening, what did I do? Did you not like the surprise?" He sounds scared and I almost laugh but then I remember why I've been avoiding him.

"This has been your plan all along, hasn't it? You knew! That's why you've been so nice to me, why you are doing all these sweet things for me?" I'm breathing heavily when I'm done talking, and Daniel looks perplexed. He's a good actor, I give him that, but I'm mad as a hippo with a hernia.

"Nowami, I've been trying to right my wrongs. Give you some of the things that you wanted, that you deserve, and I'm sorry that I have been such an ass to you that you are suspicious of me when I am doing the bare minimum of what I owe you." He's saying the right words and that makes me angrier, so I storm off with Daniel hot on my heels.

"Tell me what I need to do to fix this." He's pleading, and it's unlike the in-control man that I have known most of my life and that infuriates me.

"How about you undo making me pregnant all the time or ever meeting me?" I throw back at him, and he's about to respond when the shrill tone of his phone goes off. He fishes it out of his pocket and stops when he sees who is calling, it must be his precious wife.

Whoever is on the other side of the line doesn't give him a chance to say anything and I see Daniel blanch before ending the call. He looks at me with stark fear in his eyes and I forget that I was angry at him, then move towards him to comfort him.

"It's Oyama. She's been rushed to the hospital." I feel all the blood leave my body and I sway against Daniel. Not my baby. No!

Chapter 28

Candice

I am bundled up in the lounge with a huge blanket and some hot chocolate as Daniel runs around the house like a headless chicken. I'm in a daze after all the revelations from my birthday.

I am forty-three years old now, with a baby on the way and a grandchild who could be in danger right now because I need to pass my gift, which I only discovered today, down to him. I spoke to Makhulu or rather, she spoke to me. Daniel is trying to right his wrongs and I feel nothing.

Daniel comes down with my bags and his all packed; he's on the phone with Ntsikelelo.

"Thank you, man, for everything. I owe you big time. She's taking it badly. Yeah, I am done. You can come to get us."

I watch him blankly as he mops his face and I realise that his hands are shaking. I want to wrap my hands around him and shield him; at times, I don't understand myself either. I just know that my anger has been deflated and I realise that I played a role in where I am today. If I hadn't wanted to say goodbye to him with my body, the only way we were effectively communicating three months ago, we wouldn't be here.

He sits at the edge of the sofa that I am sitting on, not facing me. He starts talking and his voice is hoarse with emotion and fatigue.

"My mother. Her name was Chaonaine, a Ngoni woman from a tiny village called Devende not that far from the Mozambican-South African border." I sit up straighter, holding my breath because this is the first time, since I have known this man from the late 90s, that he is mentioning his mother. He's always prickly and sparse about his past but he's never mentioned her, ever.

"She had smooth, rich skin; the colour of tumbled onyx stones on the bed of a clear stream. It glowed in the sunlight and its lustre wasn't eroded even by the dire poverty that we sunk into. I remember how, when I was still very young, she used to bounce me in the air and when she laughed, her white teeth flashed against her dark gums. Everything about her was generous—from her hips, her bosom to her heart." There is something hauntingly sad about the way he recalls her, his voice thick with unshed tears.

I give in to my urges and take his icy hands into mine. He briefly looks at me, his eyes bloodshot, and it's like he's looking through me. All he can see is his mother.

"She was hardworking, she held down two to four jobs at a time and worked herself to the bone. She worked until the day she died, to take care of us, of our father, and it makes me so bitter that even though I managed to remove him from her life, I didn't have the power to preserve her life until she could eat some of the fruits of all her hard work." He sniffs and roughly wipes his nose with the back of his shaking hand before returning it to mine.

"She was a beautiful, humble, and hardworking woman but it didn't matter to the mighty Sisulus because to them, she was an outsider. It didn't matter that the Ngoni people are descendants of Zwangendaba and broke away from the Zulus; to them, she was a Shangaan, unworthy of that piece of shit that they called a son. When he chose her, which is the only good thing he ever did, they ostracised not only him and her but also us—their offspring. I was often made fun of growing up; what with a family as well-known as mine but with holes even in my underwear, ashy feet, and cracked soles." Now his whole body is shaking and I throw my arms around him, trying to broker some of my warmth to him.

"I swore that I would make them eat their sneers and their disdain, that this son of a Ngoni woman would one day lord over all of them. I had a plan from when I was in Standard 5. I studied under the strict tutelage of Phindiwe and my mother, whenever she was home. I passed and managed to get sponsorship to go to college and do not one but two degrees. When my mother died, Tat' Xhamela finally reached out to us. I had only seen him when they came to collect our father's body to go and bury him with their own. We buried our mother alone, Phindiwe and I. We had to ask one of our neighbours to act as her relative so that we could get her a death record."

His body is shaking in earnest now and his voice has become so roughened that the only reason I can hear him is that his body is moulded into mine. He gulps down saliva, desperately trying to wet his parched throat.

"When I met Nompumelelo, she reminded me of her—my mother. The same humble and hardworking persona, she wasn't as dark as Chaonaine but her skin was just as smooth, and she was Xhosa. I took her to meet Tat' Xhamela, her family was held in high esteem by the mighty Sisulus and so I knew, from that day, that she was the woman I was going to marry. Then I met you and, for once, I wasn't doing anything for the plan or for revenge—I just met a girl and fell in love. It was supposed to be about me indulging myself until Mpumi came back and the plan continued."

His body has stopped shaking and I should let go now but now I need his heat because my heart has suddenly turned icy. I don't want him to continue but he's offloading and talking so quickly now, like he can't wait to get it off his chest.

"At some point, I even thought that maybe the plan could change, be altered ,but then your mother came and I discovered that not only were you pregnant but also underage. That wouldn't have altered the plan, that would have derailed it completely. My siblings and I would have gone back to the outskirts of the Sisulu family, shunned. I didn't want my child to be ostracised like we were and I didn't want you to end up like my mother. I would have resented you, just like he resented her. I didn't want to be anything like him. So, selfishly, I went on with the plan, even though Mpumi betrayed me, and though I couldn't get over that betrayal but for the plan, I forged ahead. Even when she left me, Mandisa fit into the plan, and elevated me politically and impressed the shit out of my family."

I have to close my eyes tightly and bite down my lips hard to stop myself from crying out. His hands hesitantly brush against my shoulders but luckily, he pulls them down.

"Reading through the manuscript made me realise how much I've hurt you with my baggage. Loving you was never part of the plan, but I didn't mean to hurt you either. I know nothing I can do and say now can make up for it, a less selfish man would let you go but I'm much more selfish, and I foolishly thought giving you some of the things that you've always wanted would fix the hurt."

He chuckles mirthlessly, and then the silence stretches between us; he, trying to regain his composure while I am trying to compartmentalise all of the revelations that I have had today. I just want to curl up and give in to the growing pull of the dark hole that I fell into after my mother's death. I want to crawl into it and be held by my grandmother.

"Say something, Wami, please…" He tilts my face so that I can look at him. This proud, gorgeous narcissist that has torn apart and at the same time, mended my life.

"Denise and Oyinqaba get to be just like you, longing for a family that doesn't even know or acknowledge them. At least your father chose you; even when it meant that he was castigated to poverty, he chose you. What do my children get, Daniel? Beyond the trappings of wealth and whatever time you get outside of your plan, what do my children get? I chose you, time and again, even though I was never enough but that's on me because I chose you. But my children, who chooses them? How long do they have to wait until you see and choose them?"

He flounders, his mouth opening and closing. There is a hoot outside and we stare at each other for a moment before he gets up and takes our bags outside. I look around the house with its family pictures proudly displayed and I say a silent goodbye before I leave.

The ride to the airstrip passes in a quiet conversation between the two men in front while I pretend to be sleeping. I finally fall asleep and wake up to Daniel carrying me into the private jet. I close my eyes and feel him settling me down on the leather seat, then putting on my seatbelt.

His footsteps are measured and heavy as he moves across me, and I hear him sink into his seat. He lets out a sigh that ends in a choked breath and then he is sobbing. I keep my eyes tightly shut and force my hands to be still as I listen to his wretched sobs. He cries for what feels like an eternity, then there is silence. I hear some papers being shuffled before Daniel's gruff voice starts reading out loud, picking up from where we left off in another lifetime: My new beginnings in Durban.

Chapter 29

Durban and New Beginnings - 2000

Having grown up in landlocked provinces, I was quickly seduced by the allure of Durban, with its sandy beaches stretching endlessly along the coastline and the ocean sparkling under the sun. My life was a whirlwind of school and work at Sorbet, leaving little time for leisure. However, every chance I got, I would escape to the beach, where I often found solace. There, I would lay out my towel, open a book, and settle myself cross-legged, letting the rhythmic crashing of the waves serve as my soothing background soundtrack.

The months leading up to my attaining my Cosmetology qualification were among the most peaceful and joyous of my life. The weather in Durban was a perfect blend of clear skies, damp humidity, and mild winters, occasionally punctuated by dramatic storms, which only added to my love for the city. My only connection to my past life was through letters to my aunt, to whom I selectively shared my experiences--careful not to reveal my exact whereabouts, in case my words were intercepted. This distance allowed me to fully immerse myself in the idyllic surroundings without the burden of constantly looking over my shoulder.

Sis' Thuli, who adamantly insisted that I refrain from calling her 'Mam' Thuli', became my confidante during this transformative period. She refused to allow me to wallow in self-pity during my initial months in Durban. 'Everything happens for a reason,' she would say, her voice a mix of warmth and wisdom. 'You are young, and life hasn't dealt you the best hand. Yet here you are, standing tall. You are healthy, beautiful, and you have your entire life ahead of you. So, give it your best shot.'

Those words resonated deeply with me, especially when I confided in her about some of the challenges I had faced. I couldn't share everything, as she was still my neighbour's sister, and I was uncertain of what she might relay back. Thus, I channelled my energy into my studies, work, and living as quietly as possible, determined to make the most of my new life.

Among the modules I studied, I found the Cosmetic Science module to be the most enjoyable. However, I faced challenges in Anatomy and Physiology for Beauty Specialists and Business Administration, while the other modules felt more manageable, thanks to the practical experience I had gained at Sorbet.

Aanya, the owner of the Sorbet branch where I worked in Pavilion Shopping Centre, was a delightful and petite spitfire. Her sweetness contrasted sharply with her fiery temperament; it was often difficult to ascertain her exact age, but when someone crossed her, she would erupt with a passion that left nothing in its path unscathed.

I successfully passed all my modules, though graduation was bittersweet, with only Sis' Thuli in attendance. I wished that my grandmother and mother could witness my efforts to forge a better life for myself. 'This one is for you, Kungentando. Giving you up wasn't in vain, and I hope one day you will understand,' my heart whispered, as I held my certificate of completion tightly in my hands.

Aanya took a special liking to me, often playfully suggesting that she would marry off her youngest son to me; while he was indeed cute, that proposal never materialised. Instead, once my temporary position ended, she offered me a permanent role at the salon, along with a well-deserved raise.

Working at Sorbet was a joy; I developed a loyal clientele who would share their lives with me as I worked my magic on their faces. Aanya encouraged me to specialise in facials, prompting me to dedicate another year to studying my craft. Balancing work and study kept me afloat, allowing me to think less and less about

Kungentando, Makhulu, and my mother.
During storms, however, memories would surge back, and my tears would flow in tandem with the rain.
By 2005, restlessness began to settle in. While Durban felt like a dream, I sensed a disconnect within myself. When I confided my feelings to Sis' Thuli, she understood completely and encouraged me to consider working on a cruise ship. She also suggested that I start dating and stop living like a hermit. Ultimately, I opted for the cruise ship. Although Aanya was saddened by my departure, she graciously referred me to her husband's friend, who owned several ships.
Not only did she secure me a job, but Aanya also organised a small farewell party in my honour. The gesture filled me with bittersweet joy; I was leaving behind the security of a stable job, a consistent and safe life, and the people who had become like family to me. Yet, deep down, I knew I needed to spread my wings. The world was mine for the taking, and I was ready to embrace it.

Chapter 30

Daniel

I know exactly when Candice falls asleep instead of the pretence she kept up when we got on Hlongwane's private jet. I was grateful that she didn't get up and offer me any comfort when I broke down, I wouldn't have known how to accept it. I haven't cried like that since my mother died and when Oyama tried to take her life. I thought no pain would ever get to me like those two gut-wrenching moments but Candice's words stuck a chord, they cut me deep.

'...At least your father chose you, even when it meant that he was castigated to poverty, he chose you.'

My father has always been the villain in my story. He was a weak man who failed to provide for his family, but even drunk out of his mind, he always found his way to our mother, to us. That makes him a better father and husband than I am. I was so consumed with proving a point that even when Denise clung to me a little harder each time I left, I thought that with time, she'd grow up and understand. I thought they knew how much I love them, how I'm doing all this for them, for our legacy.

'What do my children get, Daniel? Beyond the trappings of wealth and whatever time you get outside of your plan. What do my children get? I chose you, time and again, even though I was never enough but that's on me because I chose you. But

my children, who chooses them? How long do they have to wait until you see and choose them?'

I couldn't answer her back Eswatini and even now, her questions glare at me, making me feel; oh, how I hate feeling. Running from my emotions, I pick up the manuscript from my lap and I continue reading silently. The next part in the manuscript is one I remember as vividly as if it happened yesterday.

It was 2009, I was sent to wine and dine some of our unofficial sponsors for the upcoming World Cup. The pricks had chosen a cruise ship for our meeting, because it was the biggest prick, Harold's wedding anniversary and his wife was dead-set on the cruise. He booked us tickets as well and it wouldn't have been so bad if it hadn't been soon after another one of my then-wife's miscarriages. The guilt of knowing that whatever Phindiwe had given me to give Mpumi might have damaged her womb was gnawing on me; but, instead of facing it, I ran to the Caribbean Sea.

The sun hung low over the horizon, casting a golden hue across the waves as the cruise ship floated serenely through the Caribbean Sea. I stood on the deck, a glass of something far too fruity for a man of my age in hand, I had discreetly asked for virgin servings from the bartender, attempting to seem impressed by the big prick's tales of the oil trade. Yet, my focus was fractured; the gentle sway of the ship seemed to echo the disquiet in my heart.

"Daniel, you with me?" Harold, waving a hand in front of my face, pulling me back from the trenches of my thoughts.

"Right, yes. Sorry, just... admiring the view," I muttered, forcing a smile. The truth was, I was lost in my misgivings and there's nothing more that aggravated me than regret.

As I turned to glance at the horizon again, my breath caught in my throat. There, in the distance, was a woman who made my heart stop. Candice. I blinked twice, to make sure my imagination hadn't conjured her. She was standing by a small booth filled with beauty products, her hands deftly arranging the items as she spoke to a couple of eager guests. The years had been kind to her; gone was the pale young woman I had left at the rehabilitation centre and in her place was a vibrant woman, whose peals of laughter seemed to draw everyone to her.

"Daniel?" Harold's voice broke through my reverie, but I barely heard him. I was too busy wrestling with the emotions that surged within me: Shock, longing, and a tinge of anger. I hadn't seen Candice since she assured me that she was doing good at the rehabilitation centre and then she disappeared from the face of the Earth without so much as a note goodbye.

"Excuse me for a moment," I said abruptly, setting my drink down before making my way toward her. It was reckless, but nothing mattered at that moment except getting to my heart's desire.

The closer I got, the more the world around me faded. Candice sparkled—that's the only way I could describe her, her skin glowing as if kissed by the sun, her hair long and curls straightened into a bun. She caught sight of me, and for a brief moment, her expression mirrored my own shock.

"Daniel?" she breathed, as if saying my name was a spell that could reverse my presence.

"Candice." The word slipped from my lips, heavy with years of unspoken feelings. I felt awkward standing there, the past crashing into the present in front of strangers on board.

"What are you doing here?" she asked, her voice a mix of surprise and alarm.

"Work, unfortunately." I gestured vaguely behind me, where Harold was busy chatting up the rest of the delegates. "What are you doing here?"

A faint smile grazed her lips, but it didn't reach her eyes. "I'm a beautician on board. It's not exactly where I thought I'd end up, but..." she trailed off, her gaze drifting away from me. She looked uncomfortably at the nosy cruise members who were looking back and forth between us as we spoke.

I made a split-second decision and I dragged her away from her table, past the throng of tourists lazying around in their swimwear on the deck, and brought her to a secluded corner, and I caged her against the hardwood wall of the massive ship.

"Why did you leave me like that? You didn't even say goodbye," I demanded to know, the words slipping out before I could stop myself. The tension between us thickened, an unspoken history hanging heavily in the air.

Candice crossed her arms, a defensive gesture I recognised all too well. "What do you want, Daniel? To reminisce about old times?"

Her tone was sharp, and I felt the sting of her words, so I lashed out in the only way that I knew would hurt her like she hurt me. "No, not exactly. I wanted to know how you just disappeared without even a single thought about our daughter. You never even wrote to ask how she's doing."

The air became charged with resentment, and for a moment, neither of us spoke. Her eyes darkened, the hurt of the past reflected in their depths. "You think you can just stroll back into my life and use her against me, like it's nothing?"

"I didn't mean it like that," I said, my voice steady, though my heart raced. I knew this was the moment I had been both dreading and longing for. "You disappeared, Candice, even after I was trying to get you help. You left without a word, and I was left to pick up the pieces. I've had to live with that every single day. How could you just... walk away?"

"I walked away?" she shot back, hissing quietly so that no one else could overhear us. "You were the one who made me give her up! You were the one who insisted it was for the best! Don't you dare put this on me. I spiralled because of you, don't act like you were some bleeding hero."

I felt the heat rise in my cheeks, not from embarrassment but from the weight of my own guilt. "I know. I know I made the decision... but I thought it was what was best for everyone. You were so scared, Candice, you were still a child yourself."

"Scared?" She laughed, but it was hollow, devoid of joy. "I was terrified, yes! But I was also in love, Daniel. I wanted to keep her. I wanted us to be a family. But you..." She paused, her voice trembling. "You didn't even fight for me, for us."

"I didn't know how," I admitted, the truth spilling from my lips. "I thought I was doing the right thing. I thought it would be easier... for all of us."

"Easier?" She shook her head, disbelief etched across her features. "You think it's easier to pretend that I was happy that our daughter was being raised by your wife because I am unworthy of the mighty Daniel Sisulu? To live with the knowledge that I've lost her forever?"

The weight of her words hung in the air, suffocating. I took a step closer, driven by the longing I felt—a longing for reconciliation, for understanding. "I never stopped thinking about you. I've missed you every day since—"

"Since you sent your bulldog to make me leave," she finished, her voice bristling just a fraction. I frowned and before I could even question what she meant by that, she continued, "Do you even know how I've managed? How I've survived without you both?"

"I can only imagine," I said, my heart aching. "But I've tried to move forward. I've tried to build a life, but there's always been this void. I needed to know how you were doing, Candice. I need to know that you were okay. I hired so many different investigators to find you."

Her eyes softened, and for the first time, I saw a flicker of the girl I used to know—the one who would smile at me across a crowded streetwalk, who would hold my hand as we walked through the park, who shared dreams of a future that never came to be. "I was okay, Daniel," she replied, her voice barely above a whisper. "I finally got my act together, I went back to school and I got my diploma. I've been doing well. Everything is going well for me."

"Everything?" I echoed, a sense of bitterness creeping into my voice. "And what about us? What about the life we could have had?"

Candice looked away, her gaze lost in the distance. "We can't change the past, Daniel. We can't go back to what might have been. All we can do is accept what is."

"But I can't accept it," I said, desperation creeping into my tone. "It's not fair. We were supposed to be the endgame, Candice."

"Were we?" she challenged, her eyes flashing with defiance. "Because it felt like I was the only one who was blindsided. You were the one who turned your back on us. You are the one who got married. I see your ring, go back to your wife, Daniel."

"I didn't turn my back," I insisted, desperate for her to understand why I had to stick to the plan. "I thought I was doing what was best—"

"Best for who?" she interrupted, her voice rising again. "For you? For your career? Because it certainly wasn't for me or our daughter. You made a choice, Daniel, and now you have to live with it."

"I've had a lot of time to think, to reflect on my choices. I've realised how wrong I was in taking our daughter from you. I should have come up with a better solution, one that didn't cost you everything."

Candice nodded slowly, her eyes searching mine. "I want to believe you, I really do. But rebuilding broken trust takes time, Daniel. It's not something that can be rebuilt overnight."

"I know," I said, my heart twisting with hope, for what? I wasn't sure myself back then, but I knew that having found Candice, I was never going to let her go. "But I'm willing to wait. Maybe there's a way you can be in Oyama's life again... whatever it takes."

She looked down, her fingers fiddling with the edge of her immaculate scrubs. I took a calculated gamble, hoping that Candice was still desperate enough to be in our daughter's life to let me back into her life. I wasn't even sure of the promises that I was making, I was just a slave of the pull that was between us and I was willing to lie, steal, and even kill to be by her side. Whatever it took.

"I need time, Daniel. Time to think about whether I want to open the door of our past again. It's a lot to process."

"I understand," I said. I didn't understand but I knew her weaknesses and I wasn't letting her go, no matter what she thought. There was no way in hell. "But just know that I'm here. I'm not going anywhere."

As we stood there, the world around us faded into a soft blur. The sounds of laughter and music from the ship faded away, leaving only the two of us suspended in this moment, caught between the past and the future.

"Maybe we can start with coffee tomorrow?" I suggested hesitantly, deploying the smile that was ever only reserved for her, my Candy. "Just to talk?"

A surge of hope filled me, when she nodded hesitantly. "I will bring Oyama's picture album," I brazenly used our child to reel her in and from the way she enthusiastically nodded, I knew that I had found my in. I thanked my lucky stars that I had taken to travelling with the album, it kept me grounded.

As she turned to go back to her booth, I felt a rush of emotions—excitement, apprehension, and above all, a longing to bridge the chasm that had opened between us all those years ago.

"Candice," I called after her, my voice firm but gentle. "I'm glad to have found you again."

She paused, glancing back at me with a faint smile that spoke of the past we'd shared and she disappeared into the crowd, leaving me standing on the deck, my heart both heavy and light. That was my second chance with Candice and by the time the cruise ended, Candice was back in my arms, where she's always belonged.

Chapter 31

Candice

I wake up with a start, realising that the plane has landed and Daniel is scooping me up from my seat. I must have fallen asleep while he was reading. I try to wriggle out of his arms but he holds me tightly in place and I relax against his arms. I realise that the past two days have been emotionally taxing and I am exhausted—physically and mentally. My emotions have settled in dull acceptance and now I have to put my problems aside and focus on Oyama and my grandson.

"Please take us straight to the hospital." Daniel's only acknowledgement of my words are a gentle squeeze and he continues down the stairway with me snuggled against him.

It's still dark, it must be the early hours of the morning but I can see the morning stars converging to chase away the darkness. We get into the car and Daniel doesn't put me down on the leather seat but he puts me on his lap and I snuggle against him. He rests his chin on top of my head, not saying anything, but I understand his clinginess and his need to have me close.

The drive passes in a blur of silence and when we stop outside Netcare Mulbarton Hospital almost thirty minutes later, the sky is lighter. Daniel still doesn't let go of me, and I don't say a word as he leads me into the hospital with my hands tightly clasped in his.

"We are here for Oyama Sisulu, she was brought in last night." I feel for the receptionist who is at the receiving end of his angry words.

She quickly types into the system and tells us to head up to the ICU, I feel my blood growing cold and I sway a bit. Daniel lets out a soft curse before he swoops me up in his arms again. I'm feeling faint, my blood levels tend to trouble me a lot during pregnancy and with all the stress that I've been under, I need to go and see my gynae today.

Many heads turn as we get up to the ICU department, it looks like the whole family—minus the children, Lola, and Pacou—is here. MaNtuli, who is Mpumi's mother, Nomusa and Sipho's grandmother are sitting on the comfy-looking black chairs. Jarred is standing behind Mpumi's chair; his head was bowed over her but now he is also staring at us in open curiosity.

The only person who didn't look up when we got here is Sipho; his head is bowed and his shoulders are heaving as he circles his beads. His brother is standing some distance next to him like a bodyguard, with his buff tattooed arms folded and his eyes bloodshot.

"What happened?" Daniel demands, not bothering to put me down nor caring about the speculative looks that we are getting.

"One minute she was fine, playing with the kids and the next, she just collapsed, only she was barely breathing. We rushed her to the hospital and they've put her on the ventilator while they are running tests. So far, nothing has come up," Jarred fills us in, and Mpumi breaks into a sob.

For once, I don't have any tears and I signal for Daniel to put me down. He does but the room swims and I have to hold onto him until the room stops moving.

"Is she alright?" I hear Nomusa's voice as though it's coming from a distance.

"Anaemia and the shock of everything." I'm surprised that Daniel actually responds to her and doesn't just ignore her like he usually does.

When the world stops moving sickeningly, I let go of Daniel's sweater and I move slowly towards Sipho. What I have to say will be better understood by him. He doesn't look up when I place my hands on his shoulders and I take a deep breath, trying to structure the news that I'm about to deliver as gently as possible.

"She won't get any help from the hospital, Sipho." Only then does he look up and the torn look behind his tear-soaked face chips at my heart.

"You have to go back home, your paternal home, and be welcomed into your true home, and I have to do right by my grandson as well. He carries the spiritual gift that was handed down from my grandmother's lineage, as well as your father's lineage and he won't make it if we do not fix everything. I have to get my grandmother's bangles and cloth. You have to go to your home, Eswatini, you are the son of the late Chief Sobhuza."

There is now deathly silence, even Daniel is looking at me in shock. I didn't fill him in about any of the revelations.

"Is it not enough that I have had to carry all the family's burdens my whole life, now my son has to suffer for sins that he didn't commit before he is even born?"

The rancid bitterness in his voice cuts deep and he makes to tear off his beads but his grandmother stops him. She gently touches his chest and softly cajoles him until his shoulders stop heaving and we all listen to his soft sobs.

Daniel is at my side before I collapse to the floor and he holds me, leading me to the seat that Nomusa just vacated for me. I just hope that I have the strength to see this through—for Oyama, for her baby, and for my unborn baby.

Chapter 32

Daniel

Candice is pulling away from me and the thought makes me weak at the knees. I hate this feeling that's clawing at my chest, demanding that I lock her up in some tower so that she never leaves me.

She's going to leave you just before your biggest break, just like your mother did.

I shove my sneering subconscious' voice to the far recesses of my mind, I can't afford to crash out now, not in the middle of the hospital where my daughter is lying in a coma and I am powerless to do something. I listen, in shock, as everyone else, while Candice explains that she fainted when she saw Hlongwane's brother-in-law, who is the spitting image of our son-in-law. That when she woke up, there was a diviner who told her that the Dlamini clan were Sipho's paternal family.

It all sounds like a bunch of poppycock, but that's not what has left me in disbelief. All of this happened, and Candice didn't, once, confide in me. Not at the surprise party I threw together, during which she spent glaring at me as if I killed her favourite soapy character. Not when I relayed to her that Oyama had been rushed to the hospital. Not on the flight over here. Hell, even on the car ride from the airstrip would have been nice. But, not once did this woman who overshares everything with me, tell me of all these revelations that affect our daughter.

Alarm bells have been going off in my mind since that revelation, her fainting episodes and her pale face, could Candice be sick? What if it's terminal? Like cancer. My knees threaten to give out at that thought and I take out my phone to tell my assistant to look up hospitals with the best cancer centres in the world.

"You look determined," my ex-wife says, trying and failing to hide her knowing smirk.

Being with Jarred led Mpumi to the fountain of youth; she's glowing and has none of the stress lines that used to plague her in the terminal stages of our marriage. I debate whether I should share with her my growing panic over Candice pulling away but Mpumi leans over and speaks quietly, for my ears only.

"I was worried when Oyama mentioned that Candice suddenly disappeared, especially after that interview she gave, I thought maybe you did something to silence her." Her words sting and surprise me at the same time because I've forgotten all about the media circus that Candice's book started.

"I'd never hurt her. Well, I'd never intentionally seek out to hurt her," I respond in the same vein, making sure my words reach only her. Mpumi looks at me as if I've grown three heads and I don't blame her; I blacked out a lot towards the end of our marriage, I'm surprised she's even cordial still.

"You don't care that the media probably saw your little display?" Mpumi asks, curiosity colouring her voice. I walked in here proudly carrying her in my arms, the gossip rags would have had a field day if they had pictures that basically confirm the allegations flying around. That might have been my sole concern a week ago, but now, all that's consuming me is thoughts of Candice leaving me.

"All of that won't matter if she leaves me," I admit, hating the defeat in my voice.

"What do you mean—?" Mpumi is cut off by Candice.

"Please take me home, I need to get some stuff before we head back

Eswatini." Candice doesn't look at me, just smiles briefly at Mpumi and starts walking away, not waiting to hear if I'll take her or not.

I sigh and, without another word, I go after her. I want to shake her and beg her to look at me at the same time, but then she sways a bit on her feet and every other thought falls away. I take stock of the lines etched on the edges of her pinched mouth and forehead when I steady her in my arms. There's no sign of the soft glow that had begun to encase her skin while we were hiding out Eswatini.

"You need to get checked for all these dizzy spells first, and then you can rest before…" She pushes me off her mid-sentence, and she whirls around to poke my chest like a tiny whirl storm.

"Oyama needs me more and for once, I can actually do something for my baby girl. I won't be useless to her anymore." Her voice breaks and I hold her fists to my chest just as the elevator stops. Some people come out, giving us speculative looks, but all I can see is the anguish on Candice's face. I pull her into the elevator, away from prying eyes who don't deserve to see her vulnerable and breaking.

"Stop beating yourself up. You are not and have never been useless to Oyama, even when she was angry and suicidal as a teen. You were torn-up and feeling helpless then, but you prayed for her day and night. I tried to get you off your knees because you were heavily pregnant with Denise, but you kept praying. You've fought to be in her life, you've withstood being shamed; her anger, her pain—you've taken it all just to be a part of her life. You didn't throw her away, if anyone needs to atone to our daughter, to you, it's me." Mentioning Oyama's suicide attempt triggered her tears and I hold her as she cries, the pitifully-soft sobs making my heart crack wide open.

In the end, against my wishes, we end up back in that hellhole that Candice has decided to call home. I make some calls while she opens the windows and she moves to her bedroom. I get reports on Mbuso and Mandisa, then I call Joshua to ask for the jet again and inform Ntsikelelo that we're coming back after apprising him of the bombs that Candice dropped on us at the hospital. His brother's wife is with him, I can hear her concerned questions as we talk.

I find Candice kneeling besides the bed with a white cloth with elephants drawn on it and bangles clasped tightly in her hands. Her face is red and streaked with her tears, yet I have never seen a more beautiful woman in my life. I hate that she's always so hard on herself when it comes to Oyama; I wish I could carry her guilt for her because it doesn't belong to her, it's mine to carry. I'm the one who forged that birth certificate, I'm the one who decided that Mpumi would raise our child, convincing myself that I was also doing it all for Candice to have a chance at a brighter future.

I walk out and make more calls and set up an appointment with her doctor and her therapist; she'll need to see both after we come back. I call Denise, and my babies are subdued today, probably fearful about what's happening with Oyama. I assure them as much as I can, and I even talk to my granddaughter. It's hard getting past how she came into this world. Because of my failure as a father, I didn't protect my little girl from the predator that was part of my circle and Amandla will always be a reminder of my failure. Though, right now, talking to her on FaceTime, after the initial shyness passes, it's like talking to a younger and shrewder version of Oyama—the version that hero-worshipped me.

By the time Candice comes out of the tiny bedroom, I've been talked into buying a large Barbie playhouse for Amandla and taking the whole crew to the biggest obstacle course in South Africa. We make our way to the airport and even though I'm clutching Candice's hand throughout the journey, I know she's slipping further and further away from me.

Chapter 33

Candice

I shiver as I go into the cold water and brace myself before I wade deeper into it, clutching two of the last mementoes that I have of Makhulu. Just as she showed me in the dream, I keep on walking into the water until I am fully submerged. I feel a bit apprehensive with the spirits all around me, even though Sipho and his grandmother spoke to them and asked them to let us do what needs to be done for our little angel.

I fight against my fear of drowning and when I am in the deepest part of the stream, I float belly-up, feeling all the power surrounding me and flowing inside me. I let the bangles fall from my hands, one at a time, until I am only left with the cloth. In my heart, I am letting go of the gift and asking our guides to bless and anoint the boy on whose shoulders this gift is going to fall. I plead with them to protect him and allow him a happy and normal childhood.

Once my veneration is done, I let go of the cloth and without looking back, I swim back to land. When I break out into the surface, my whole body is covered in goosebumps and I can't help the shivers that bombard my body.

Sipho's grandmother wraps me in a large white cotton cloth and I hug my arms around my stomach something fierce. I feel some slight cramps and I silently beg my baby to keep it together; we have to do this for Oyama who is still in a coma.

Sipho's grandmother's hands linger a bit on my stomach and I see her face split into a smile. The cramps also subdue into tiny flutters.

"They are your biggest blessings, my child. Chin up."

I feel my eyes fill up with tears and I nod. Now, for the hard part: Introducing Sipho to his family. After I delivered the message yesterday, we waited for the test results to come back and when the doctor told us that they are inconclusive, Sipho, his grandmother, Daniel, and I prepared to come back to Eswatini.

I miss my children but there wasn't even time for me to drop in and see them. Nomaswazi and Masomalenhle were waiting for us at the airstrip with the two-in-one brothers, they still freak me out with their likeliness. Nomaswazi burst into tears when she saw Sipho; I could see him and Lenhle also blinking back their tears. It was beautiful to watch. Sipho's grandmother kept muttering something under her breath, I was close enough to hear that she was talking to her late husband, thanking him for helping bring her boy home and telling him that she will be able to join him soon, seeing that Sipho was now with his family.

"Are you still feeling cold?" Sipho's gentle question snaps me out of my thoughts and I realise that I am still shivering.

"A little, yeah. How are you feeling about today?" Daniel and the Hlongwane brothers went to fetch Swazi's great-uncle, who stays in Hosea in the Shiselwani District. He has to do the welcoming ceremony.

"Once I got here, most of my anger just ebbed away; I felt this rush in my blood that I can't quite explain. Seeing my siblings so happy and so welcoming, it filled a hole that I wasn't even aware that I had. I've always wondered about my father, you know. Khulu and Sibusiso did a great job raising me but there was a gap. Now I have a sister who is a chief, a brother who looks just like me, and a lot of nieces and nephews. My children have cousins from my side of the family now. I'm happy, but I will be at peace once Nokwindla wakes up from that coma. I don't want to think about my mother right now because it will only burden my unborn baby and my wife.

I can't afford to lose either of them."

I get it now. Oyama always says that Sipho has an old man in him and I see it in his wisdom and in the way he is in tune with his spiritual side. It shows without him saying it; the way he carries himself speaks of the chiefs who came before him, but we didn't know that. I'm grateful that my daughter found such a husband.

We are now sitting on the peak that Nomaswazi told me about and she was right, I can see the whole of Maphalaleni from up here as it lazily stirs to life. The warm, early sunrise bathes the entire forest in shards of golden light sifting through the grey mist that blanketed the forest at night.

The scenery is beautiful, but not as beautiful as Lenhle in all his traditional regalia: A red cloth with the face of a lion and the pendant on his neck—knee and head bent and one hand looped around Sipho's neck as he tells his father about the arrival of his son. I know Swazi would have been a crying mess, seeing her brothers look like two halves of her father. Due to her advanced pregnancy, she couldn't climb up here with us, but she's busy with preparations for the welcoming ceremony.

"Nkhosi, Sidlubula Dledle sikaNobamba, Lokothwayo, Ludvonga luka-Mavuso, Sidvwaba Siluthuli, Mlangeni, Mntungwa, Kunene. Ndlovu ezidl'ekhaya ngokuswela abelusi, Sibhahuza sikaMawawa, Mlangeni, Sobhuza. Babe, ngiletse indvodzana yakho. Mamukele. Usite nangemsebenti wakhe ube imphumelelo."

Lenhle's voice—as he recites their clan names and asks for their father to accept Sipho, his son, and make sure his ceremony is a success—is filled with quiet authority. Sipho's grandmother seeks my hand and I hold her shaking hand in mine, this is a great moment for her as well.

The sun peeks out from the fluffy clouds and its beams dance on the two brothers, warming Lenhle's shoulders and covering Sipho's bareback. I'm suddenly overcome by the need to cry, my tears cold because of the light breeze up here.

We trail slowly down the mountain as Sipho fills Lenhle in on his life, family, and franchise. I notice the Sipho is walking taller, his shoulders straightened as if knowing his father has given him that extra confidence.

It makes me think of my own sweet little Oyinqaba. Would moving them away from Daniel do more harm than good or would staying hurt him just as it seems to be hurting Denise?

No answers or revelations flood me, only bile rises in my throat and I discreetly vomit behind a shrub. When I rejoin everyone, only Sipho's grandmother noticed that I was gone and she hands me a stick of ginger to chew on. I accept it gratefully and listen to the brothers' conversation.

"If *Babe* had known about you, I know that he would have done everything to find you and he would have sent you to college, like me." There is a hint of apologetic sadness in Lenhle's voice and I can tell that he feels guilty. Sipho clasps his shoulder and squeezes it lightly.

"Then I wouldn't have met the love of my life. Everything happens as it should; even our trials and tribulations. I am here now and I have a beautiful life, even though the beginning wasn't as easy as it should have been."

When we get to the homestead of Chief Nomaswazi, we find the whole village gathered. There is a man who must have been tall in his youth but is now stooped and his skin is hanging over his bones in age.

"You must be the reason why boDlamini have kept me alive this long." His face is writhed in a wide toothless smile and I let out an internal sigh of relief.

"Where is his mother? She must atone for depriving our Inkhundla of its rightful son and possible heir for this long," a thin man with the long face of a donkey and a scowl permanently etched on his face speaks, and I see some of the villagers agree with him. I rejoiced too soon.

"I am his mother. I birthed his wife, and that is his other mother, she raised him as her own son, not grandchild." The long-faced scowl is now fully turned on me but I do not blink nor flinch.

"That's not the same—" the bully starts, but Nomaswazi cuts in. It is my first time seeing her in her Chief regalia, sitting on her throne, and she looks resplendent.

"This does not concern you, Maloyi. This is a Dlamini matter and you are only here in the capacity of a guest. Let us handle this. Am I clear?" She throws him a withering stare and doesn't blink at the animosity in his answering glare.

"Yebo, Nkhosi," he mutters insolently.

The ceremony continues, despite his sour disposition. A cow is slaughtered, bile is smeared on Sipho's head, shoulders, and back. Just like that, the Dlamini's have welcomed their long-lost son and we have completed what needed to be done for my grandson.

Chapter 34

Candice

All I want to do is get to my tiny flat, soak myself in hot water… Crap! Now I can't do that. Okay, new plan: Get home, get a long hot shower, eat whatever takeout I get at the airport, and fall asleep. I will get my babies tomorrow. I miss them, but I need to be at my best around them, so I have today to mop around all I want, then tomorrow be the best version of myself for my babies. But I never get what I want. Do I?

"I just got a call from the hospital. Oyama just woke up, so we will pass by the hospital first."

I feel like groaning because I feel like I am sleeping on my feet, but my baby just woke up and that alleviates some of the burdens on my shoulders. Sipho's grandmother gives me a soft squeeze on the shoulders; she understands how tired I am, and I smile sleepily back at her. Daniel and Sipho are having a quiet discussion that we can't quite get, so I close my eyes, bracing myself for the landing.

When the plane starts dropping, it feels like the little food that I had is coming up. I grab the nearest container and feebly throw up in it, when I finish and raise my head, a bottle of water and one of those magical ginger sticks are thrust at me. I gurgle the water and spit, chew on the ginger, and then drink the remaining water.

I really need that long shower. I'm too old for pregnancy and it feels like each pregnancy is worse on my body than the last one. Ironically, before I knew that I was pregnant, I was perfectly fine.

"Are you okay? You look pasty." I grimace at Daniel's choice of words, no woman wants to be told that she looks pasty.

"I'm just exhausted, I will be fine." I don't know if he knows I'm pregnant or not but a part of me doesn't want him to know until I figure out my next move.

He looks dubiously at me but doesn't push the matter. I sink into the plush seats of his car and close my eyes as the car starts moving. Great, now I have motion sickness. When my eyes fly open, Sipho's grandmother hands me a little bag with all the magic sticks and I chew on one gratefully. Tomorrow, before I go and take the kids, I have to pass by my gynae first.

Oyama looks just how I feel, pale, with heavy bags under her eyes and her stomach looks like it's too big for her to carry. But she's alive, so I hug her shoulders fiercely and she hugs me back just as tightly. The tears of fear that I have been banking up come rushing and a sob escapes my lips. I don't know what I would have done if she hadn't made it.

"Thank you, for finding Sipho's family and connecting them with him." She's wiping my eyes as she talks, and I'm grateful that she no longer scoffs at my tears as she did when I first met her and the many years after that disastrous meeting that made me go into labour.

"What were you doing Eswatini, anyways?" *with Tata,* I read the unspoken words in the frown that is clouding her face.

"I will tell you all about it when you get out of here, okay?" She smiles, a smile just like her father's, and then hugs me briefly before kissing me and then turning her attention to Sipho.

I manage to slip away without anyone noticing me. Well, *almost.* I bump into Nompumelelo getting out of the elevator with some food. My stomach growls loudly and we laugh before embracing and then she leads me to the waiting room, to feed me.

Daniel's former wife is ageing backwards; she has this soft glow that she never had when she was with Daniel. Apart from the greying hair on her temples, she looks like she's in her thirties rather than in her fifties. She hasn't lost much weight but she looks fitter, bubblier, and youthful. She looks like a woman who is loved well. I sink my teeth gratefully into the still-warm toasted bagel with bacon, egg, avocado, and cheese. It tastes like an orgasm just bursting in my mouth.

"You are totally making out with that bagel." There is laughter lacing her words, and her kind eyes are dancing with life.

"I've been dying to grab a bite." I carry on eating as she tells me about her children and her Centre; I can tell that both are very fulfilling to her.

"How did you manage to walk away?" The question slips from me and she smiles at me in understanding, not needing any clarity as to what I am referring to.

"I left in bits and pieces. At first, it was my spirit that left—with each transgression, the infidelities, the fighting, his family. Next, my heart left and reunited with the love of my life, Jarred. Even after my heart had left, though, I still came back, and I don't know how much longer I would have stayed if my affair hadn't been brought to light. You want to know why I still went back?" I nod, because I have seen her with Jarred and it blows my mind how she could have still walked away from the man who holds her heart and soul, to be with Daniel.

"I was afraid, afraid of the unknown, and comfortable in the façade that I modelled to the world, of the minister's wife who was at the peak of her corporate career. Leaving meant diving out without a parachute or safety net. It meant I had failed—failed Oyama, failed my mother—but now, I know that I had been failing myself in all those years that I stayed when I was no longer happy. I wasn't living then, just existing, and once I trusted my heart and spirit, my physical body then also followed them. It was the best decision for me, for Oyama, and my mother eventually took down our wedding pictures."

Her words ring in my mind even long after she has requested an Uber ride for me. She left when she found her heart, but how do I leave my stupid heart behind? Because, even after everything, my heart beats only for Daniel and our children. Mpumi wanted to drive me home but I didn't want to take her away from her family or for them to know that I had left. My phone is still with Daniel and I know Sibo must be going crazy, trying to get ahold of me. I sigh, standing outside the dingy flat, thinking of the flight of stairs going up.

I make it up in one piece and I let myself in, opening the windows, again, to take away the musty smell of an apartment that had been empty and locked up for a week. So much has happened in the space of that one week, the events dart through my mind as I take off my clothes and step into the shower. I moderate the temperature and bathe with water a degree lower than my normal temperature.

I am brushing my teeth when there is an insistent knock on my door. Great, there goes my plan to sleep the whole day away. If it's Daniel, I will simply take my phone and chase him out, there is no way I am listening to him read right now.

I tighten the belt around my fluffy robe with hearts and bears that Denise got me for Mother's Day and open the door before whoever it is that is banging on it breaks it down. I pause before unlocking the burglar gate as I take in who is standing primly outside my door.

"Aren't you going to let me in?"

I snap out of my frozen state of incredulous gawking and open the gate, and, as she brushes past me, a soft, flowery scent tickles my nose. I take a deep fortifying breath before I lock the door and turn to her. I see her looking up and down my shabby apartment with open curiosity and a hint of… disdain? I'm not sure, it is hard to read her facial expressions. I just want this over and done with so that I can go back to sleep.

"Mandisa?"

Daniel's wife turns and this time, I am sure it is disdain in her eyes as she sizes me up. Yay, me! Someone should have warned me that today is Meet Daniel's Wives Day; maybe I would have gotten a little pampering, a deep facial, and not look "pasty", as Daniel put it.

"I never could understand his fascination with you. I mean, I get that you are yellow, but beyond that, I really can't see the appeal." Her voice bellies all the private schools that she graced, probably from infancy and her years abroad—cultured, even when its icy tone is like a whiplash. This will take a while, I let out a long breath before heading to the kitchen to grab some Cheerios and coming back to settle on the couch without any finesse.

"I am talking to you. Or do you not understand English? Ufuna ndithethe?" Even the way she raises her eyebrow, in a perfect arch, is classy. Right, I should stop studying her face and respond out loud.

"Have a seat, Mandisa. Talking while standing with your hands folded like that, is no way to speak to your husband's first wife." I see the blood drain behind her face and all of the disdainful composure that she had falls away, and that gives me a little satisfaction.

II

Part Two

Dancing with Demons.

Chapter 35

Daniel

My shoulders are heavy with exhaustion as I pull up to the estate, or maybe it's just the weight of what I am about to do. Instead of driving up to the home I bought for my children, I pull up in front of the identical house that I bought for my sister. I step out of the car, the gravel crunching underfoot, and I can't shake the tension coiling in my stomach.

As I walk towards the front door, I recall the day I bought the townhouse for Phindiwe—Candice had moved in with Denise, who had just turned one, and suddenly, the home in Killarney that I had gotten for Phindiwe wasn't cutting it anymore. I didn't mind; I simply sold the other house and it covered the purchase of this one and the estate rates.

I put in the code and push the door open, steeling myself against what's to come. Phindiwe is inside, as I knew she would be, her presence filling the space with a robust energy. Like me, my sister dresses to the nines, even when she's alone at home, and I have never begrudged her that, footing her account expenses at Catherine Gaeyla Fashion boutique.

Phindiwe is arranging flowers in a vase, and for a moment, I watch her, the way her hands move with a practised grace. But the sight does nothing to soften the hard edges of my heart; instead, it reminds me of all the times she's manipulated, twisted, and turned my life into something I barely recognise.

"Daniel," she says, glancing up with a smile that doesn't quite reach her eyes. "Mandisa has been blowing up my phone looking for you and you're here. How lovely."

"It is lovely, isn't it?" I retort, my voice sharper than I intend. "Do you think it's as lovely as how you chased Candice away when she was at her most vulnerable?"

The smile falters, and I see the flicker of defiance in her gaze. "I see she told you."

I close my eyes at the flippant way she acknowledges running Candice off, no remorse—but a hint of annoyance.

"It happened decades ago, and she still found her way to get you back in her clutches. Candice was a distraction that you couldn't afford; not at that point of your career. You know that."

"A distraction?" My voice rises, echoing off the walls. "She was the mother of my child! I put her at the rehabilitation village to get help. You had no right to interfere."

Phindiwe places the flowers down, crossing her arms. "I had every right to protect you, to protect the legacy that we were building. I've done everything for you, Daniel. Raised you, nurtured you. You owe me."

The resentment bubbles up, hot and furious. "Bullshit!" I hiss, and see Phindiwe cower at the face of my anger, good. "You were just concerned that I wouldn't finish building your house, even though I spoke to you and you said you understood."

"She lied. I never sai—" I don't give her the chance to bullshit me further.

"Owes you? Is that what you think? You think you can take my life and twist it into something that fits your narrative?"

"I made you who you are. I got you out of that shanty town, where your potential would have been buried under alcohol and prostitutes," she counters, her voice steady, though I can see the cracks forming. "You wouldn't even be here without my sacrifices."

"Sacrifices?" I scoff, the bitterness spilling over. "You think I've forgotten? You think I owe you gratitude for what you did to me? What you let them do to me?"

"What I did?" She steps closer, her eyes narrowing. "You were a child, and I did what I had to do to ensure you survived."

I can't hold back any longer; the years of pent-up anger surge forth like a tidal wave. "Survived? You think what you did was survival? You were my sister, Phindiwe; you were supposed to protect me, not trade me for sexual favours! You pimped me out when I was just fourteen, goddamnit!"

The air around us becomes still, the accusation hanging heavy between us. Her face pales, and for a moment, I think I see a flicker of remorse, but it's quickly stifled by her defensive posture. "You don't understand the choices I had to make! You think I didn't also spread my legs to make sure you and all your siblings were fed? Do you know how many dicks I had to suck off? Big dicks, small dicks, smelly dicks, and limp dicks. I don't even know who the fathers of half my children are! Do you hear me complaining? I did it for us!"

"For us?" I laugh, a harsh, bitter sound. "You think dragging me into that life was for us? You shattered me, Phindiwe. You destroyed any chance I had at a *normal life*!"

"*I did what I had to do to keep us alive*!" she yells back, her voice cracking. "You don't know what it was like—the desperation, the choices! You were just a boy!"

"*A boy who trusted you*!" I shout, the words cutting through the air like a sharp chef's knife. "A boy who thought you loved him! But all you cared about was yourself!"

The silence that follows the slap Phindiwe throws at me is deafening. She is breathing heavily and even though my cheek is throbbing and my eyes are smarting, I can't rein in and hold back all the anger and resentment that I've been holding on to for years.

"I did everything you asked of me, even when I was chained like a dog, and those depraved women made me their sex slave that they could pass around and desecrate. You told me I had to do it for the family, for my future—and I did it without question." My voice cracks as my heart races.

"Everything you wanted, I gave you, and you knew… you knew what Candice meant to me! When you said I should give her up and make Mpumi raise our child, you knew it nearly broke me but I still did it. I asked for your patience, so that I could take care of her. You looked me in the eye and you said you understood. You helped me look for her!" All I see is Candice in that hospital bed, I remember the metallic taste of fear that gripped me when I learnt there were drugs in her system. What I had to do to get her into that facility that only helped white people back then. I black out at that point and when I come to, the vase that Phindiwe was arranging flowers in has disintegrated to pieces, as has her precious glass dining table; the flowers are strewn across the room and she has a cut on her cheek.

My sister's eyes well up with tears, and for a moment, I almost feel pity. But then I remember the years of manipulation, the lies, and the cold reality of her choices.

"You don't get to play the victim now," I say, my voice low, filled with an intensity that shocks even me. "You chose this path. You chose to throw out Oyama's mother, and use me."

"I did what I thought was best," she pleads, her voice trembling and when that doesn't get any response from me, it turns nasty, "You were supposed to be grateful. I sacrificed everything for you!"

"Sacrificed everything?" I shake my head, the anger still swirling within me. "You sacrificed me. You sacrificed my childhood. You sacrificed the family I could have had. You sacrificed my marriage to Nompumelelo. Do you even see that?"

"I was trying to make your dream come true," she cries, her façade cracking. "I wanted you to have a better life than I did."

I want to scream at her that she instead gave me a life filled with shame and resentment. That she taught me to survive, yes, but at what cost? I want to tell her that I carry the scars of her efforts but I know that I'm trying to push all of my sins onto her. Phindiwe has always been cutthroat and conniving, and that got us out of the gutter. She might have told me to take Candice's baby, to give Nompumelelo those abortion pills, but I wasn't fourteen-years-old then; I was old enough to know better. I went ahead with her plans and that's on me.

Her shoulders slump, and for a fleeting moment, I see the woman I once idolised. "I thought I was protecting you," she whispers, her voice breaking. "I thought I was making you strong."

"I can forgive it all, but I will never… never ever forgive you for chasing Candice away. Ever. I acknowledge all that you did to get me out of the gutter, all that you did for my career, right or wrong. I raised all your children, found them well-paying jobs. Consider me signing over this house to you as your severance pay for all that you've done for me. We're through. I'm done. I'm now focusing on my family."

I take one last look at the woman who raised me, at her hardened stare, as flawless as she looks, all I can see is the girl who made us clothes from the sacks of flour that our neighbours threw out. Then I remind myself of all that I've done for her, that debt has been repaid. I turn around and leave her standing in the rubble caused by my blackout.

In the car, Candice's phone starts ringing. Phindiwe. I reject the call, block, and delete Phindiwe's number. I have to convince Wami to get a new sim card, but knowing my little spitfire, that is not a fight I will win. Maybe her favourite takeaway will make her more pliable. As I drive out, I'm on the speakerphone with my lawyer, ordering him to cut off all of Phindiwe's accounts, and handle the deed transfer. When I end the call, I realise something: My shoulders are no longer burdened with any weight.

Chapter 36

Candice

I'm impressed by the speed at which Mandisa's mask of condescending confidence slips back into place. She scoffs, then walks around my tiny flat, perfectly-manicured nails trailing on the pictures of Daniel with mostly Denise and at times, Oyinqaba, that Denise insisted I frame. She scowls fleetingly but then schools her features again, it must be considered an art to always manage to appear unaffected.

I'm halfway through the bag of Veggie Crisps when she comes back and stands in front of me again with her hands folded, her nose upturned. Her façade of sophisticated elegance is stunning but her eyes are wary as she sizes me up.

She hasn't changed much from the pictures that I used to stalk online when Daniel told me that he was going to marry her. Her figure is still that of African Barbie, even after giving birth to that adorable boy, Monwabisi. No hair is out of place in her sophisticated French twisted Grade A weave. The long lapels of her jacket reach just above her knees, in her elaborate Fuchsia three-piece pantsuit and pearl neck piece that would give any First Lady a run for her money.

She looks chic and poised but the longer the stare-off drags, the more I notice the subtle changes. The lack of laughter lines around her face, when almost every picture of her back then was of her laughing or grinning broadly, the pinched and sour look that she's spotting on, and the dull lustre of her eyes that make-up cannot hide.

"It's funny that you have given yourself that title when all you are is his longest standing piece of skirt, who keeps popping out babies just to stay relevant in his life. You are using those children to secure the bag. Shame on you." Her voice is dripping with venom and I pop a sea-salted sweet potato crisp into my mouth, loudly chewing it to grit her tits and also to collect myself.

Her confidence reminds me of when I was nine months pregnant with Denise and I went to Mpumi's flat, only I was begging her to let me see my child but, like Mandisa, I was so certain of my place in Daniel's life. The irony makes me laugh out loud, the short tinkle makes Mandisa frown.

"I think that's what you tell yourself to justify all those nights that you spend rolling around that huge four-poster bed alone. Or when he calls you 'nagging' for daring to question him about his lack of attention in your marriage. That is how you console yourself when he hits you; you tell yourself that, at least, you are his wife—the one who took his surname and the one he parades in front of the whole world." The way that she's digging her nails into her left hand would have drawn blood if she had on natural nails, not the blunt French tips.

"What Oyama saw was a once-off thing. He—"

"Oyama never discusses you with me," I cut in, before she accuses my child of something that she never did and before she catches these hands for accusing my child. "I know, because you and I are a lot more alike than you would care to admit. So, you thinking of yourself as superior to me is a coping mechanism. You are the wife and I am just his glorified baby-making machine."

"That's because you are nothing more than a glorified baby-making machine. Tell me, Candice." The sneer in her voice would have hurt me if I still had fucks to give but she chose the worst day to come at me. "What is it that keeps you hanging around him, sniffing after my husband like a bitch in heat? Is it the money? I can write you out a cheque right now, that will set you up for life."

My laugh stalls her hand from reaching into her pocket. I laugh until I have tears streaming down my cheecks, only stopping when my tummy starts aching.

"When Daniel told me that you paid off his secretary, I didn't quite believe him but now, I do. The baby wasn't his, by the way; he never slept with her. The secretary caught on to your paying-off ways." I can see the shock almost dismantling her mask of arrogance but it quickly slips right back.

"You can't pay me off, Sister-wife, not from the estate that I also have a share in." This time, the mask slides off completely and she charges at me but I push the coffee table and she collides into it, hurting her knees.

"Stop calling me your sister-wife!" Her cry of frustration strikes a chord in my heart.

Warily, I get up and head to the cabinet in my bedroom. I take out the documents locked in the secret compartment, before heading back to her. I find Mandisa still pacing and muttering only God-knows-what.

"You should sit down for this one. Unfortunately, I don't have any alcohol." She eyes the manila file that I'm carrying as if it is a hissing snake.

Stubbornly, she remains standing as I look through the file until I take out three documents and I proffer them to her, she frowns before unfolding her arms and suspiciously moving forward to accept them.

"What is this?" Her voice has lost all of its contempt and is now filled with uncertainty.

"Doesn't it look familiar? The first cream document is our unabridged customary marriage certificate; I think you signed one similar to it. The second white paper is the lobola agreement record, and the third is a court order regulating the matrimonial property system. Daniel had to take that before he married you."

As she reads, her eyes quickly darting through the pages, I see the exact moment all blood drains from her face, and she starts swaying. I help her onto the couch without any protest from her. I go into my tiny kitchen and make her sugar water. Her hands tremble as they accept the glass, and I take away the documents before she spills any water on them.

"What is Xhamela's signature doing there? When? HOW?" She looks and sounds bewildered, her Bambi eyes wide.

"This is a conversation that you should be having with Daniel—"

"Tell me *now*!" I fight the juvenile instinct to roll my eyes at her.

"After I had Denise, when his divorce with Nompumelelo was finalised. My family gave him an ultimatum: He would either do right by me or they would take me and Denise, he would have no claim to either of us—ever. The very next week, he came with his uncle and Phindiwe, lobola was paid in full, and we had a celebration where he gave me the name 'Nowami'—the bride that he chose for himself. My uncle and aunt and his uncle and sister accompanied us to register the marriage at Home Affairs."

When I finish explaining, tears are already trickling from the corners of her tightly-shut eyes. I feel sorry for her and I wish that I knew how to comfort her without adding salt to injury.

"Then how did he marry me? Why?"

Her dejection should bring me joy after how she belittled me but all I can feel is her pain. There is no use telling her that she was part of the three candidates that Daniel showed me when he explained how our marriage couldn't be public, because then everyone would question how Oyama looks like me. I did walk away then but he got my aunt to send me back.

"Your father knew about me before your marriage was agreed upon. It was also a customary marriage but you got the ring, the lavish wedding, and the whole country as your audience." Her eyes fly open in righteous indignation. The regal bitch is back.

"Daddy wouldn't! My marriage is a civil marriage." Whatever sympathy I had for her goes flying out of the window at her petulance.

"Oh, Darling, all that fancy English, and you didn't even take the time to read what is written on top of your marriage certificate. I have a copy of it here." I'm fumbling through the file, thumbing past a copy of Daniel's latest will and testament when my door is burst open.

Daniel enters with some Indian takeaway that immediately makes me salivate. He stops short when he sees his wife with a tear-stricken face and red-rimmed eyes. He closes the door, crosses past her, and comes to stand in front of me, his eyes searching mine—for what? I also don't know.

"You just slipped away from the hospital. I brought you food, and your phone back." He places both on the coffee table next to me, completely ignoring Mandisa, who starts sobbing softly. My heart breaks for her once more and when Daniel leans over to kiss me, I turn my face away.

"Take her home and explain the truth to her. You owe her that much." He opens his mouth to argue, but I put up my hand. "Take your son's mother home and tell her the truth, Ta' kaOyama, I need some time to myself." The steely tone in my voice tells him that I am fed up with both of them.

He kisses my forehead before walking up to Mandisa, who hasn't stopped crying.

"Let's go home." I'm glad that his voice is gentle, because she's still in shock.

I know how hard it was for me. It took me weeks to accept that I, alone, wasn't enough for him. It didn't make sense then, because I didn't know of his grand "plan", but I chose this whereas she had no idea. She gets up dazedly and doesn't look my way or say goodbye. Daniel picks up her latest Chanel handbag that is probably more expensive than buying this flat, and follows her.

I pick up the tandoori chicken and I almost squeal in glee. I hadn't even realised that I was craving it. Now, to get back to my plan of eating then sleeping the whole day. I will check my phone and process everything—tomorrow.

Chapter 37

Daniel

The silence in the car is oppressive and I'm already over the confrontation that's about to unfold. Going toe to toe with Phindiwe left me flayed wide open. It was close-up there with the death of my mother, because my sister who has been my counsel, my partner in crime, is essentially dead to me yet she's still alive. All I wanted was to kick back, eat some Indian takeaway with Wami, and let being close to her soothe me; even if it meant sleeping in that ghastly apartment of hers. The thought reminds me to shoot off a text to Joshua, requesting a guard placed outside Candice's apartment, in case Mbuso tries something again.

"You're just going to ignore me, after the bombs that your slut dropped on me?" Mandisa asks, as I drive through the gate of my house.

"Choose your words carefully, Mandisa, I'm not above cutting off your tongue for insulting her." My voice is dead even to my ears, and it's effective in getting Mandisa to shut up.

Not too effective, though, as she starts yapping the moment we get inside the house. God, I need a stiff drink and I detest alcohol.

"She was lying, right? There's no way those documents were real. No way. You tricked her into believing that you went along with what her family wanted." Mandisa is spiralling, and it's strange watching her become emotional instead of the perfect porcelain doll that I've been married to for the past decade.

"It's real, Mandisa; Candice is my wife. I did, however, make her family demand that we marry or she walks. I knew that was the only way to spook Tat' Xhamela to sanction our union. It wasn't that hard, her uncle would do anything for money." I watch as my words sink in and for a moment, Mandisa flounders with her thoughts.

"Why? Why would you do that?"

"Because Candice is mine, Mandisa; she slipped away from me once, and I wasn't going to risk losing her again. I had to convince everyone that she didn't mean much to me so as not to put a target on her back. This was the only way to keep her close and ensure that if anything happened to me, she and my children would be taken care of." My words force a sob out of my wife but it doesn't move me, even a little.

"Then why did you choose and marry me?" Her voice is breaking and I know what I'm going to tell her will break her further but it has to be said.

"You were the best of three candidates, taking into account your political connections, and Candice said she likes you." The last part quickly dries her tears.

"You bastard!" Mandisa tries to slap me but I hold her hand before it gets anywhere near my face.

"I wouldn't do that, if I were you; your days of slapping me around, punching me, throwing stuff at me… are over. That one slap I once gave you will feel like a pat, compared to what you'll unleash right now if you dare lay a finger on me." My words are quiet and I see the hesitancy before she defaults to her usual ice bitch façade.

"You wouldn't. Daddy—" Anticipating her threat makes me laugh out loud when she mentions her father; the heinous laugh of a man with zero fucks left to give.

"I wonder if your father would still think you shit unicorn gumdrops when he learns who the real father of your son is." I watch as my words land and Mandisa pales. I savour the fleeting look of panic and tremor that passes through her, before she quickly puts on a mask showing that she's unaffected. Only, the mask is skewed by the wild look in her eyes, the look of a mouse that finds itself cornered by a lion.

"I don't know what you're trying to insinuate. Monwabisi is a Sisulu," she says it with full conviction that I admire, moving from mouse to rattlesnake right before my eyes.

"I never said he wasn't, but it's not my Sisulu blood that runs in his veins. Is it, Mandisa? What I want to know is, did Mbuso get to you before or after our marriage?" Mandisa's eyes widen and now, real fear shines bright as day in her eyes.

"I don't know what you're talking about, Daniel. You're just trying to move away from the fact that you tricked me into marrying you when you knew you were already married to that..." I level one look at Mandisa and she trails off, not daring to finish her insult.

"Your first mistake was assuming that I wouldn't do a DNA test on Monwabisi when he was born. You were cold and frigid when we got married and then, one night, you were all over me like white on rice, wearing that lingerie set, and Monwabisi was born seven months later, at a bouncing eight kilos—a healthy, full-term boy. When I discovered that we did share some DNA, albeit not direct, I had to do some digging. Your little monthly spa days are not very creative, Mandisa."

Mandisa flounders, her mouth gaping like a trout that's been caught on a hook. She starts to say something, changes her mind, and then she tries to hold my face, but I shrug her off and then those crocodile tears swim in her eyes. When she sees that I'm unmoved, she wrings her hands, genuine perplexity shining all over her face.

"You love Monwabisi, you dote on him, how? If you've known since he was born?" Her voice shakes a bit.

"He's innocent of your duplicity. He's a smart kid, warm, and lovable, too, and that's a miracle, considering who his parents are. I didn't expose you because you are a means to an end, Mandisa; you always were."

I watch as she swallows a lump and shudders, before uttering the next words: "We can go back to how we were, now that all our cards are out in the open. You can use me and my family contacts as much as you want. I will stop pestering you about your… Candice. Just, please, don't tell Daddy about Monwabisi."

Two weeks ago, her words would have given me satisfaction, but now, they land on a hollow part of me.

"No."

"What do you mean 'No'? You still need me for your plan to get into Office some day; as you said, I'm the best candidate for First Lady." Mandisa pouts petulantly when she says that, looking every inch of the spoilt heiress that she is.

"I don't care. I'm done with whatever dance this is between us. I'm exhausted, and I don't need you anymore." Now that I have Joshua and his team on my corner, I add silently. Plus, I'm not sure what the plan is anymore. I just know that I'm done with living this façade, it comes at too great a cost.

"Where does that leave me and Monwabisi?" Mandisa asks gently, her voice resigned.

"Our divorce will be amicable. You keep your favourite car and the SUV that takes Monwabisi to school. I know you love my Sandton townhouse, so you can keep that, as well as your spa facility. I'll have my lawyer draft an education fund for Monwabisi; he'll get a car and an apartment when he turns twenty-one. You do not say anything of what you know to anyone; violate that, and you lose everything, and I will come for you with everything that I have. Fight this, and you walk away with nothing."

"If you're waiting for me to fall at your feet and thank you, you can go fuck yourself. Fuck you very much." The venom in her voice makes me smile but I know she will take my terms. She doesn't have a choice, and she knows it.

"What do I tell my father? He has a lot riding on this union," she asks, her shoulders drooping a bit.

"I don't know, and frankly, I don't care. You're a big girl, Mandisa, I'm sure you can cook up some lie; maybe your tears will move him," I offer with a shrug.

"So, what? You and Candice get to ride off into the sunset?" The venom is back in her voice. "You know that she'll never be First Lady material, she doesn't have what it takes—the poise, the connections, and neither does she know how to work a room."

Instead of niggling me, her words make me smile, because seeing Candice and I riding off into the sunset shifts and settles something in me—the part that's been afloat since I was fourteen years old.

"She doesn't have to be anything other than what she is."

Chapter 38

Candice

I take a deep breath before I press the dial, half-hoping that it rings to voicemail. She picks up on the second ring, going on a tangent about my disappearing acts, and I suck my breath, preparing myself for the backlash of what I am about to tell her.

"Sibo, I'm sorry. I just wasn't in the right frame of mind, and I had some family emergencies to deal with," I finally manage to get a word in edgewise, and even though she sucks her teeth at me, she still asks how I am doing.

"I've been better." I don't tell her that I've spent the last half-hour hugging the toilet bowl. The magic ginger sticks didn't help this time. I feel and look green.

"Listen, I went through your emails and I… I don't think I can go through with the interviews or the book tour right now. I'm not sure what my next move is but I need to figure it out and fast."

I expect her angry words to rush like a wild torrent down the line but I wince when she lets out a high-pitched squeal. I have to remove the phone from my ears for a bit, until she calms down.

"That's just the thing! You didn't read my last email. It seems the more you cancel interviews, the more speculation arises around your book and it has been selling like hotcakes. We need another print run soon…" I zone out when she starts talking about all the technicalities. Who knew people wanting to be all up in my business would someday make me rich?

"This works out better because you say nothing, so there can be no suits of defamation following you and we can plant some scandals in a few gossip rags. People will eat it up. Especially surrounding a minister as prominent and as sexy as Minister Sisulu. It really is a pity that you aren't his scorned mistress. Do you know the millions a memoir from his scorned lover would rake in? But we can play around that angle!"

Sibo goes on and on, and I don't correct her or interject. The kind of secrets that I have on Daniel would buy me a small island in the Seychelles. I listen to Sibo droning on and on about how sexy, dark, and dangerous Daniel is, until I put her on loudspeaker as I navigate through my cupboard. The only edible thing left is oatmeal and my stomach isn't impressed, until I add the ginger to the oatmeal.

As it simmers on the stove, I look for something to wear and conclude my business with Sibo. Our call ends when I'm fully dressed and stuffing my face with my ginger oatmeal. One down, I call my gynae's office next and luckily, she has an opening in about an hour. That gives me enough time to Uber there; I really shouldn't have left my car, because Daniel still found me without it. When I reach the bottom step, I am huffing and puffing; I need to get out of this flat—pronto.

The prospect makes me chew my bottom lip, because this is something that I have been pushing to the back of my mind. What do I do next? Clearly, staying in the dingy apartment in Turffontein hasn't helped me get away from Daniel; instead, I have spent more time with him than I have in years. Mandisa wouldn't have been able to get access into our old complex. But going back there smacks too much of failure—I would have failed myself and I would have failed my children.

The Uber driver isn't chatty, thank God. He quietly gets me to my destination and I head in. I don't have to wait long in the waiting room, before I am ushered in by the receptionist-slash-secretary to the consultation room.

"Candy! Are we having another pap smear in the same year? I know your shot isn't due for another three months." Kendra's smiling face makes mine relax in an answering smile.

"The shot is why I'm here today, I'm pregnant. I took a home pregnancy test and it said I'm thirteen weeks pregnant." Her smile has slid off her face and she's frowning, probably imagining a malpractice suit.

She insists on taking a scan, and the moment the echoing heartbeat fills the room, my walls come down a notch and I can't help the tears. I can't help but wish that Daniel was here, holding my hand and blinking back tears as he has in all of the other foetus scans that I've done before. I'm having another baby. We are now at 14 weeks but Kendra is worried about my high blood pressure; warning that if it hasn't gone down by the next appointment, she might have to put me on bed rest.

"Are you sure you want to keep this baby? I remember how adamant you were the last time you took the shot that you don't want any more children." I might not know what my next move is but I want this child that pushed against all barriers to be here.

Oyama got discharged last night and I find her lounging around the pool in a long black hoodie with Ndebele prints on the sleeves that I saw Sipho wearing Eswatini, while the kids play Marco Polo in the pool. Denise's shriek when she sees me makes my heart melt. Oyinqaba almost knocks me off my feet and I have to hold onto his wet, wiggling body before we both fall. His speech has been slow but now, listening to him talk about Anton, these two have a full bromance going on, I realise that he needed this time with kids around his age to strive. Anton is remarkably patient with Oyinqaba, for a teenager.

After five minutes of fussing over me, with Amandla reminding me of the promise I made to take her to the petting zoo—I did not but apparently, grandmothers are way too forgetful; her words, not mine. After being coerced into taking them all to the petting zoo, I am left alone with my first-born while they resume their games.

"You look worse than you did yesterday," Oyama goes straight for the jugular and I snort before lowering myself down to the lounging chair next to hers. She is back to glowing, as if she was never in a coma.

"I'm pregnant with the worst case of morning sickness that I have ever experienced," I confess, and wait for the recrimination. I don't expect her to throw back her head and laugh.

"What is it with my parents and sex? Yhu! If it's not Mama and Daddy having car sex in their old age, it's you, Mum, getting knocked up by Tata!" She can't stop laughing, even when I hit her shoulder with the balloon giraffe that I picked up. These millennials are so disrespectful.

"Plus, Mandisa came to my flat yesterday." I tell her everything that happened—the revelations, and how I discovered I was pregnant Eswatini.

It feels good to offload to someone. Ever since Oyinqaba's pregnancy, our relationship has gotten to a point where I consider her my closest friend. Before Oyama can respond, Denise comes running to me, spotting some puppy eyes.

"Mummy, can we stay here until after the holidays end? Or, until you find us a better flat? Pleeeeeeeeeaaaaaase! Please, please, Mummy!" To think that I came to fetch them because I was afraid that they would think that I am neglecting them. When I agree, she squeals in happiness and gives me another wet hug before she goes back to the water.

"What's up with the flat? From the way Denise describes it, you guys are now staying in a death trap. Did anything happen to your apartment?" I sigh as Oyama looks at me, waiting for a response.

"The plan was to leave your father and start afresh with my children, and I thought given his aversion to poverty, he wouldn't be caught dead in that flat. But now, I'm pregnant, he's always in my flat, and I just don't know what to do!" She hands me some serviettes and I dab my eyes dry.

"Why did you stay married to him after he married Mandisa? Why did you agree to keep your marriage a secret? Even I wouldn't have known if I hadn't read about it in your manuscript." I sigh, and think about something that I have been avoiding confronting for so long.

"I left as soon as he told me that he was going to take another wife. I went to my aunt who was staying in Pretoria then. When I told her why I packed up and left, she told me that polygamy wasn't new to our people, that I should be grateful that he married me, that, unlike my mother, I would have my children's father in their lives. She said a lot of women were in polygamous relationships that they weren't even aware of. Then she called Daniel to come and get us." I let out some air that is bubbling around my heart at the memory of my aunt's rejection. I needed her to look after Denise while I went back to work but she would hear nothing of that. I had no one to leave my baby with and no one in my corner. Oyama's hand covering mine reminds me that I'm not alone anymore.

"At first, when he said we should keep our marriage a secret, I was relieved. Your mother, Nompumelelo, was a tall order to follow; the media would have dissected me and had me for breakfast. I wasn't a Harvard graduate or a corporate guru, I didn't run any charities nor did I want to. I wasn't minister-wife material, what would I say during those parliament galas? I had no knowledge of current affairs." Oyama squeezes my hands.

"Hey, don't talk about yourself like that. You went back and completed your high school diploma. You put yourself through college and held down two jobs before meeting my father again. How you turned your life around took guts, Candice." I sniff and offer her a watery smile.

"I didn't think about how not being publicly acknowledged would affect Denise. She was just a baby then, she was happy, and we were well taken care of. We got Daniel the man, not the politician."

"I used to envy that, it felt like Denise, Oyinqaba, and even Monwabisi got the best parts of both of you," Oyama confesses quietly, and it makes me even more emotional.

"It was never my intention, nor your father's. The way I saw it, being with Daniel, even in secret, meant I got to be in your life again, even though you hated me. I got to look after you in the shadows." Oyama takes my hand and I immediately stop spiralling, and look into her earnest eyes.

"I owe you an apology," she begins, and I immediately brush her off.

"No, Yaya, I deserved your anger and hatred." I've hated myself for not fighting harder to keep her all my life and I didn't mind paying penance for it.

"No, you didn't. Sure, when I was fifteen, it was all too much and I had to blame someone for how my life was spiralling. I'm sorry I blamed you, because it was easier to blame you. You took it all—my pain, my anger—and never once complained. I'm sorry for always lashing out at you, the names I called you…" Her voice catches and I squeeze her, I never knew I needed to hear this apology until now.

"Reading the story of your life made me see you, and I understand now—why you stayed, and why you love uTata. Yet you let me say you were nothing more than his sperm dish."

"You weren't wrong," I chuckle mirthlessly. "In a way, I was, even when we secretly got married, I had to convince myself that it meant I was more to him than just a sperm dish. I hid the sting of not being enough for him, and I focused on becoming his peace and safe space. Looking back, I was in blissful denial; if I didn't confront the issues, then they didn't exist."

I trail off as I remember how happy I was in those years, I even managed to convince myself that Mandisa wasn't part of our lives. Daniel spent every moment when he didn't have to work with Denise and I. My bubble burst when Monwabisi's birth was announced in all the major news outlets.

"Then we had Oyinqaba. Denise started asking questions that I couldn't answer. Speaking with you and becoming closer to Nompumelelo showed me how much I gave up, and had me yearning for more. Daniel didn't understand my change of heart, and he keeps asking for more time… So, I left, with nothing but a few clothes and documents." I gulp down some air hungrily, because breathing is suddenly hard. Oyama coaches me through breathing until I can speak again, though in a broken voice.

"Only, the kids hate the new flat, and I can't afford better yet; I only get the money from the book sales after two months. I can't go back to work because I'm pregnant again, I need constant medical care. I feel like I'm drowning in a sea of all my wrongdoings."

Chapter 39

Candice

"Are you happy? With uTata?" I accept the glass of pink lemonade from Oyama and I take a long sip as I process her question.

"This past week, we have both been uncovering parts of each other that we'd kept hidden. I realised that, deep down, your father is a broken little boy, thirsty for his family's validation, and I haven't resolved all my issues either, so we have been bleeding on each other. But I was also happy to just be alone with him—with no expectations or the world looking in, just the two of us in a bubble. It also made me realise how unhappy I had grown over the last couple of years."

She doesn't say anything, just lets me talk as she massages her protruding belly.

"I want the Daniel I was with this past week and the Daniel I met again on that cruise ship, who swept me off my feet. I want the Daniel who takes Denise on dates because he's trying to make up for all the lost opportunities with you. I want the Daniel who goes with Oyinqaba for his speech therapy sessions and holds family game nights with me and the kids." I chew on my bottom lip as a wave of emotions washes over me. "I don't want the Daniel that is power-hungry, callous to the next person's feelings—cold, harsh, and abusive. But how do I get the one without the other?"

"You don't, not until he is willing to put in the work to actively get rid of all his toxic traits. And you will keep allowing those traits because the broken part of you thrives on being a victim of his toxic traits. I hate therapy, but it does help. You should continue with yours, and maybe do joint sessions? Because I didn't hear you say that you want to leave him."

Oyama has always been very perceptive and I know Daniel is not her favourite person, so I'm grateful that she is being so objective.

"Whatever choice you make, just know that the children are only as happy as you are. If you are happy, it translates into the household you run. Mama stayed for so long with uTata because of me but in the end, the whole thing blew up in their faces and it left me suicidal." I close my eyes as I remember how beside myself I was when I learnt that my baby had slit her wrists. If Daniel hadn't knocked down that door in time, she would have died.

The kids have left the pool and are now in their playroom. We are still sitting outside, watching the sun's last golden dance before it gives way to the stars.

"Let's forget about Daniel, Denise, Oyinqaba, the coming baby or even me for a moment. What is the one thing that you want to do the most in the world right now? Only think of your wants and needs." I look at my younger reflection. My girls are me in different stages in my life; it's amazing, and makes me nostalgic at the same time. When I don't say anything but just look at her, she keeps talking.

"I realised while reading your book that you stopped being Masase, the little girl with big dreams, the moment that you found out that you were pregnant with me. Even when I was being raised by Mama, all that you ever did was either to make me proud or as an atonement for abandoning me. Then when Denise and Oyinqaba came, you had to leave behind a career that not only excited you but you threw yourself into being their mother, neglecting your wants and needs. Even leaving uTata now is based more on Denise's need to be acknowledged publicly by him, rather than it is about what you want. So, I want you to close your eyes and tell me where you see yourself." I feel silly as I close my eyes, but I acknowledge the truth and wisdom in her words.

"Remember, you don't have kids, grandbabies nor a husband; you are just your Makhulu's morning star." Oyama's words drone on and I take a deep breath; once I relax my muscles, the picture pops up almost immediately.

"White sandy beaches, I can almost feel the grit of the sand under my bare feet. I can hear the crushing of distant waves in the startlingly-blue waters. The wind caresses my skin as I walk towards the wet edges of the beach. I can almost taste the salty air, and the water is, at first, icy cold, and then it gets warmer as I venture deeper into it. I come out with the cloth of my wrap plastered on me and I make my way to the tiny open bar that I own. I'm well-liked; everyone waves or shouts a greeting as I pass. I'm at peace and my laughter rings out true and loud."

When I open my eyes, I can taste the bitter tinge of palpable disappointment in the back of my mouth. Oyama's gentle smile chases away the disappointment. I'm here, baring my soul to Kungentando and she's not scoffing or looking at me with disdain. That is a major win in my cards. My heart almost bursts when she takes my hand and puts it on the little foot on the side of her belly. The baby wriggles and kicks against my hand and I feel the same peace that I felt in my imaginary beachfront.

* * *

I should have taken up Oyama on her offer to stay the night, I just didn't want to cramp their style. Besides, they are already looking after Denise and Oyinqaba, plus the twins. She also gave me a lot to think about; once I get into my flat and take a shower, I will sit down and draft a plan of action. I thank the Uber driver and brace myself for the long climb up the stairs.

"Nowami." I jump in fright because I hadn't noticed Daniel lounging against his car in the diminishing light post-sunset. I watch as he moves his lithe limbs in quick strides that eat up the distance between us until he is so close, our breaths mingle as he looks down at me.

"Shouldn't you be with your wife?" The man has the timing of a baby when you are trying to sneak in some sex after months of deprivation.

"I am looking at her right now. I've been waiting for her for close to an hour." I roll my eyes at him and I hear him chuckle.

"Don't be smart. You know I mean Mandisa." He shrugs, and then wraps his hands around me, bringing my head to his chest.

"She went home after our talk last night. I was called by her father today, and after that meeting, I came here."

His long fingers curl under my chin, tilting my face up to welcome his kiss. It's a slow, tentative kiss that has me sighing and melting into his arms. That gives him room to deepen the kiss, until I feel my panties getting drenched and tiny sparks are flying behind my eyes.

"What was that for?" My voice is sultry and breathless.

"I miss you," he says, before nuzzling my neck with his warm lips; I gasp when he sharply nips at my weak spot.

Then it hits me that we are outside, in full view of the flats on De Villiers Street. The sun has set but it's still light enough for people to see us making out, if the catcalls coming from the top window on the flat next to ours are anything to go by. It will only take a moment for someone to recognise him; if they hadn't already, during his numerous visits.

"Daniel, people can see us!" I try to move away but he only buries his head deeper onto the side of my neck, sniffing me before he nips at me again.

"Daniel!"

This time, he does look up but only to smooch me again.

"The only thing I'm afraid of right now is losing you, Wami. I feel like you are slipping right through my fingers."

He doesn't give me a chance to respond, when I open my mouth, he descends on it again and this time, his kiss is hungry and potent with desperation. By now, we are also getting wolf whistles.

"I'm right here. I asked for space to figure out where I want to take this next. This conversation isn't one that we should be having on the side of the road."

He sighs and steps away but my hands are still held captive by his.

"I can give you space, even though it will kill me, if you'll give me one night and day. Just give me tonight, Nowami."

"Go with him!" An Afrikaans accent rings from the flat above us, and Daniel laughs while I'm staring at him, mortified, as if he has grown two heads.

Daniel has never been a PDA guy; well, not since after Oyama's birth, and, for obvious reasons. Seeing him so relaxed about us having an audience is mind-boggling.

"Okay, then. One night and day," I offer, and laugh when he all but drags me to his car amid cheers from our rapt audience.

This is how you conceived Denise and the one currently in your belly, my subconscious sneers, and I shove her to the corner of my mind kicking and screaming. I'm already pregnant, so, that ship has sailed. I'm going to have this one night for me. Probably not what Oyama had in mind when she gave me that pep talk, but this is how I'm taking it.

Chapter 40

Daniel

After the night and day I've had, I'm surprised how relaxed and happy I feel as I steal a look at Candice. 'Stimela' by Bra Hugh thumping from the discreetly-placed speakers all around my car. I catch Candice watching my hands as they drum on the steering wheel as I play on an imaginary trumpet.

"My father didn't have much, but he had a gramophone that used to be his father's, that he got when his father died. Whenever he was lucid and happy, he would put on Hugh Masekela's records." The surprise I feel at the revelation is mirrored in Candice's face. What's more shocking to me is how nostalgic my voice sounds. Watching Candice face her old demons and ghosts head-on has woken up my own, and for once, I let them fester instead of pushing them into the recesses of my mind.

"I remember him and my mother loved 'Stimela', and I didn't understand why because it was sombre, while Bra Hugh's other songs were groovy and catchy. It reminded them of how they met, when my mother came to South Africa on a train to look for her father who had come to work in the coal mines. Her mother was sick and she set out, alone, to find her father and bring him home because he was all that her mother talked about." For once, I can admire my mother's bravery and my father's devotion to her beyond the pain of how they royally fucked up my childhood.

"She didn't find our grandfather; no one would help or even talk to her at the train station. My father saw a gorgeous girl crying and set out to be her hero. His family had all the connections, they could have found my grandfather but they flat-out refused. My father used most of his money going with my mother from coal mine to coal mine but they didn't find her father; only one man had a vague memory of him getting tuberculosis and never returning to work."

'Chileshe' comes on and I hum the first few lines. I'm back in our little shack, watching my father twirl my mother around. Mama lived for those moments, when the boyish man who had been her hero resurrected from the throes of poverty and resentment that led him to drink, steal from her, and treat her like shit. I can hear Mama's laugh tinkling as her husband dipped her... When he was in that mood, we—my siblings and I—ceased to exist. Such moments became rarer as we grew older and yet, I know Mama longed for them; I saw it in the way she lovingly cleaned that gramophone, while my academic trophies gathered dust in the shack.

"What did they do, then?" Candice's softly-voiced question brings me back to the present, before responding, I take her hand and kiss the soft flesh inside her wrist to chase away the bitterness those memories drudged up.

"My father had spent all his money on the search and my mother asked him to give up. They came to Johannesburg hoping to find a job. My father could only find menial work that barely covered their boarding and food, let alone a ticket back to Mozambique. My mother was pregnant with her first child, a girl she lost to kwashiorkor before she turned two. She always said my father was never the same after that. She then had Phindiwe and never went home again. I know her wish was to die and be buried among her people."

The rest of the journey passes in comfortable silence between us, Bra Hugh's trumpet keeping us company. I don't tell Candice how, after seeing the way love ravaged my parents and stripped them of their dignity and drove my mother to her death, I swore to never fall in love. Love was a gamble I couldn't risk, until her. I'm not sure she would even believe me if I told her, but I do hope I can show it with my actions.

I drive towards our destination and when I see Candice look around, trying to place where we are, it elicits one of my rare wide, childlike smiles.

"Remember the first time I took you out for a sleepover? I didn't have much but I wanted to impress you, so I took you to this guesthouse. I was so nervous but you didn't care where we were, as long as we were together." I see the moment she softens and then she blesses me with a bashful smile. I was banking on the sentiment behind this guesthouse being a thousand times better than taking her to some fancy Sandton hotel. There was no way I was letting us sleep in that dump again. I'm also uneasy because Mbuso hasn't shown his hand and I'm sure Mandisa has told him everything I said to her.

When we get to the reception area, I had already booked ahead, so we are given the key and shown to room 5. It's still a small establishment and they have managed to keep it similar to how it used to be—artsy and warm. Candice grins at me as I insert the key, and I have to suck in my breath at how beautiful she is when she's this laid back and without her guard up.

"I think Oyama was conceived in this room." I laugh when she calls out my name in admonishment.

"You were so shy, nervously pleating your fingers while your toe almost dug a hole in the poor carpet." The memory brings heat to Candice's cheeks. Candice looks down just as she did back then, and I lift her face with the same gentleness and the same heated look that I gave her over two decades ago.

"You are still the most beautiful jewel in the world. Just don't tell Denise that I said that." The heat has now travelled to Candice's neck. She's flushed, and looks like the love-struck girl I fell for again. These were the same words I told her before she gave me her virginity.

"The way you're looking at me from underneath your lashes is going to make me rush this and I don't want that, I want to remake all the memories that we did on that first night. I want to take off your dress and feel your hot flesh that is softer than silk. I want to trail kisses from your toes, while you wiggle with pent-up need." I slowly undo each button as I speak, and I can see that Candice is just as affected as I am because her skin is peppered with goosebumps.

I want to bury myself inside her and drown the crippling fear of her leaving me, I want to be lost in her in the very room where I fell in love with her. I was lost and bewitched by her big, wide eyes then, and the feeling hasn't faded since. She became my sanctuary back then and she didn't even know it. When the scarecrow and her crew were on their degradation orgies rampage, it became more bearable, because all I had to think of was that night when Candice gave herself to me so freely, so lovingly. I wasn't lying about Oyama being conceived here, it was the first time I had ever been inside a woman without protection and I like to pretend that it was also my first time.

Though, to be fair, it was the first time that I had any sexual relations that didn't make me want to crawl out of my skin. I was able to wait for Nompumelelo till marriage because kissing her didn't quite flush out the scarecrow's taste from my mouth. I was worried that if I ventured further with her, I would black out as I had begun to with those old disgusting croons. I never had to worry about that with Candice, though, one kiss from her, and I'd forget to breathe, let alone all the vile things done to me since I was fourteen. Candice quietened my demons without even trying to. I hope the awe I feel for her is shining through my eyes as she tilts her head up, waiting for my kiss.

Chapter 41

Candice

The look in his eyes has my panties drenched.

No one has ever looked at me the way Daniel looks at me; as if no one else in this world matters and he is burning up with the need to consume me. I was low-key worried that after meeting with Mandisa's father and reminiscing about his parents, he would be moody but he seems to still be in the seductive, happy mood that he was in when he kissed me in the street. His fingers linger on the hook of my bra and I groan when, instead of unhooking it, he trails my breasts. When he rubs my overly-sensitive nipples, I swallow the whimper that almost escapes, before he moves his hand down-south, partially invading my underwear.

I let out a cry when he replaces his fingers with the wet warmth of his mouth. The friction from the bra's lace against his rough tongue lapping on me has me crying out loud as a wave of pleasure unexpectedly washes over me, leaving my whole body humming with a need for more.

"So receptive. Even before it tasted me, your sweet little cunt was already weeping with need for me and I took care of it, just as I'm going to take care of it now. Look at how greedily your lips grip at my finger. The heat is almost making me combust in my pants, Wami..." I hiss when he adds another long finger while his thumb circles my clit. My head falls back when he increases the tempo but he brings my eyes back to look at his fingers as they disappear into my lace panties. I want to feel him, all of him, without the barrier of his clothes and my underwear.

"What do you want, Nowami? Tell me how you want me to take care of you." His voice is even and in control, even though the tent around his crotch area tells me that he is as affected as I am.

"Naked… Ummm… yeah, right there… I need to feel your naked skin… mmmmmm…," My body hums as he keeps teasing my G-spot.

I whimper when he drags out his fingers just before I come undone and I watch as he licks his fingers clean, making my walls clench with need.

"You taste salty, but with a hint of pineapple, strawberries, and cream. Undress me, Nowami. I am yours to do with as you please."

My shaky hands are taking forever to peel off his shirt and I grunt my impatient annoyance, and he chuckles but doesn't move to help me. I duck my hand into his pants and he hisses when I circle the sensitive head of his penis. I pump his thick girth and when I feel it pulsing at a crazy rate, I let him go and his groan elicits a satisfied smirk from me.

He takes off his clothes in record time, sweeping of my bra and ripping off my panties with one hand. All thoughts of finesse and seductive torture out the window, his body is burning up for mine, just as I am panting with the need for him.

He lifts me to the bed and just when I think he's going to thrust into me, he goes down and kisses the soles of my feet, making me giggle. Daniel sucks on my toes, the wet warmth of his tongue shooting straight to the throb between my legs, making me moan. My body arcs as he litters tiny kisses from my feet going up, leaving me writhing with need. When his lips pause just a breath away from my heated pink innermost flesh, I shove his head deeper and the vibration of his laugh against my labia almost makes me combust. It's been over a month, and I'm embarrassed when my body is shivering its release after just two long slurps from Daniel.

When he finally impales me, stretching me to the fullest, we both shudder. I buck my hips but he doesn't move, he wipes the wet curls from my face and kisses me slowly before forcing me to open my eyes and look at him.

"Thank you, Nowami, for not only giving your soul to me from that day, but also for staring at the most depraved parts of mine and still loving me as if I deserve your love. You mean the world to me, Candice Nowami Masase Sisulu."

My nails dig into his back as he puts my feet on his shoulders, making him feel impossibly deep as he fills me up completely—mind and soul.

"You're... so beautiful," he grunts as he pumps inside me, each stroke of his penis setting my body on fire. He tells me how being inside me is his haven, that nothing can get to him when he's there. The raw honesty shining in his eyes as he says this makes mine blurry with unshed tears. Daniel has always been the most open during lovemaking, but never like this. It feels like he's baring his soul to me with each stroke, each bite, each shudder, and every groaned word that leaves his mouth.

This might be our last night together or the beginning of our forever, so I cling to him for dear life, crying out as he plays my body as if it's his personal trumpet; letting out the final high note just as he roars his release. Bathed in the afterglow of our lovemaking, we cling to each other, our bodies slick with sweat and our hearts beating in perfect harmony. I close my eyes, shielding my tears because just as I did twenty-seven years ago, I have given Daniel another piece of my heart.

* * *

I can't stop laughing as Daniel keeps making impressions of other ministers in parliament. I hold up my hands for him to stop, as my sides are now aching. I wipe the corners of my eyes and I find him looking at me with a strange look on his face. I quirk my eyebrow at him and he breaks into a sexy smile that makes my breath catch.

"I can't remember the last time I heard you laugh so unreservedly." I catch my breath from all the laughing before I can talk.

"You should have seen me the day Oyinqaba dumped a whole crate of eggs on Denise. Her shriek could be heard in the courtyard, and when she tried charging at him, she kept falling. He was also falling in his attempts to run away, it was all such a gooey mess. It took them the whole afternoon to clean the house but I had a great laugh at both their expense."

He's trailing patterns on my still flat-ish tummy. I had to know that I was pregnant to tell the slight difference. Now would be the perfect time to tell Daniel about the coming baby—this is the happiest and relaxed we have been in ages—yet, something is holding me back. I don't know what or why because he's always been the first person I told when I found out I was pregnant with Denise and Oyinqaba.

It's a little close to 5 a.m. and the sky is already brightening up, and we haven't slept a wink. In between lovemaking, we've eaten snacks, talked, and laughed. I don't even feel sleepy yet. I want this night to go on and on. Daniel really did recreate our first night together; we didn't sleep then either. He talked and made me so relaxed and those guffaws from all those years back re-echoed tonight.

"Thank you." He stops trailing his fingers to give me a baffled look. "For tonight, and reminding me where it all began. So much has happened between us that I sometimes forget the good times."

His smile is almost shy; he moves his hands to cradle my face and then leans in to give me a gentle kiss. My stomach flutters and I sigh as I melt into the kiss.

"I never forget, because you are the one constant bright spot in my life. You and my children." The soft pad of his thumb brushes my slightly-swollen lips.

We are a mash of limbs, it's not clear where I end and where he begins, and I feel content. We don't say anything for a moment, just listening to our heartbeats echoing each other.

"How did the meeting with Mandisa's father go?" Daniel appraises me with slightly-wide eyes. I never ask him about his business with Mandisa; he is the one who always ventures information.

"Not good," he grimaces, and I wait for him to continue. "He was angry that his involvement got mentioned to his daughter. He wanted me to take the fall and he wanted to make sure that this marriage doesn't fall through. He has a lot riding on the Sisulu surname."

"Mandisa? How was she?" I can feel the tension radiating off of him.

"Hurt. Angry. But mostly, her pride was pricked and she was throwing the mother of all tantrums. She's threatening to take Monwabisi and disappear. Can we stop talking about this, please?"

He doesn't give me a chance to say anything, just kisses me until the tension around his shoulders has all moved down to his stiff rod. I sigh in delight at his slow strokes—lazy, sleepy sex is my favourite. My orgasm quietly rips through me but the spasming of my walls brings Daniel down from his wave with a short, loud cry. I fall asleep soon after, with Daniel lightly drawing patterns on my back.

Chapter 42

Candice

The tantalising aroma of food lures me back to full consciousness. My nose twitches as I try to make out what is beckoning me without opening my eyes. Daniel's soft laugh has me opening my eyes. He's in his fluffy Father's Day gown; he goes everywhere with the thing.

"I knew food would do the trick. I've been trying to wake you up for the last thirty minutes."

"What time is it?" I sit up and rub my crusty eyes.

"A little past one." I get out of bed, then paddle to the shower.

When I come back feeling fresh, and thankfully not sick this time, I find the small table on my side of the bed set up with brunch. I'm fed over light conversation but the magic of last night is beginning to fade and the food struggles past the lump in my throat.

"Are you okay? You seem a little subdued." I smile at him, but don't bother lying because I'm very easy for him to read.

"I love you. I was always scared that when my past came to light, just like Vhutuhawe, you would become cold towards me. But instead, you've loved me harder than ever." He's already shaking his head.

"Wami, don't—" I put my finger on his lips. I have to get this off my chest.

"You are amazing, Daniel. You are funny without trying to be. You feel everything so deeply, you love and hate with the same depth. You are the smartest man that I know. You would do anything for our children and that made loving you even easier for me. Denise told me that the whole week we were Eswatini, you were reading them their bedtime stories via video call. How can I not love that about you?"

Tears are pooling up in his eyes and I rapidly blink mine away but my voice is rough with unshed tears.

"You've held me down for the larger part of my life. When I was going through the phase of wanting to know my father, you held my hand through that and cushioned the blow of not being able to find him. I would call you crying, and you would drop everything to come and be with me. We've been through everything, mina nawe, Myeni wami. Remember when I had PTSD after Denise? You were there, getting me a therapist, and that saved my life."

I'm now wiping off his tears and I don't know how the hell I am keeping mine in check.

"I was a mess; you called me your mess and loved me even through our arguments. You've been my light, as well, in my darkest moments. We didn't have to make sense to anyone else but us. The only thing that has crippled me in our relationship is that I never seemed to be enough for you. For the longest time, I thought it meant that I wasn't smart enough or I embarrassed you in some way."

"Nowami, I—" I talk over him because if I lose my nerve now, I may never do this again.

"But these last few days, we got to talk, really talk, and I understand now. I understand your past, your pain, and your need to stick to the plan. The past week has reminded me exactly why I love you. It's been a week of revelations and even though I love this side of you, Ta' kaOyama, it's not enough for me anymore. I want all of you but I know better than to make you choose; I don't want you to end up resenting me the way your father resented your mother. If you love me as much as I think you do, please, let me go. Please."

He has stopped crying and is now pacing the floor, probably trying to come up with a strategy or a way to get me to stay with him.

"Is it because of Mandisa? I asked for a divorce, and even though she and her father are fighting it for now, she'll come around. She won't come at you again or ever threaten you and the children." When I shake my head, the tears spill over and yet, I can still see his panicked face through the moist haze.

"I can publicly announce that you are my wife, anything, but please don't leave me. Don't take my children away from me."

The desperate plea in his voice cuts me up but my mind is made up. I've been struggling with this decision for the last few months and now, I know in the pit of my stomach that this is how things should be.

"I don't want to be known as Minister Sisulu's wife. I've never wanted the spotlight, Daniel. I still don't."

"Then, what do you want, Candice? Fuck!" He punched his hand on the wall and is now holding it gingerly. I get up and go to the little fridge and take out the tray of ice. I fill a towel with the blocks of ice and I gently put it on his fist.

"I want you to deal with your demons, Daniel. I want all of you to be this thoughtful, loving, and considerate. I know that might take years and I don't mind." I see the hope take root in his eyes and I hate that I have to squash it.

"While you work on those demons, I want to be far away from here. I want the sea and sandy beaches. I want to raise my children in peace."

"I can get you a beach house in Durban or Cape Town, whichever you prefer. Anything, as long as I get to see you at least once a month." I shake my head and I see the despair take root in his eyes.

"Then that would still be us, just moved to a different province. I won't keep your children away from you, Daniel. You can see them at any time. Fly them down, video call, and everything, but I don't want to be with you right now. I don't want to see you until you are fully the man that I love. I was thinking of relocating to Mozambique."

Chapter 43

Daniel

No word has been said, just our breathing grating the air. The ice has melted into a puddle at my feet and I couldn't care less about the throbbing of my hand, not when my whole world is falling apart. My head is buried between my legs. Through peripheral vision, I see Candice's hand hover just above my shoulder and I hold my breath, hoping, but she pulls it back to her side.

When I killed my father, it was out of anger, yes, but part of me thought my mother would be relieved that her tormentor was dead; instead, I had to watch as she received the news and broke down. A part of her died that day, and I can't help but blame myself for that death. I've done everything that I thought Candice needed me to do, but she still wants to leave me; to go to Mozambique, of all places.

"Why Mozambique?" My voice is harrowed when I finally break the silence, and I can hear her swallow before she responds.

"When I was working on the cruise ship, it was my favourite place to dock at. When the ship pulled up at the Maputo cruise terminal, it always filled me with this excitement and I had hoped to one day save enough money to build a beach beauty bar there. I've been dreaming about it a lot lately." I hear the hesitation in her voice and I don't need to look up to know that she's biting the corner of her lip; so I wait, head still bowed.

"I'm also afraid that if we are anywhere close, I will come crawling back to you." The confession hangs between us and I feel like something is choking me.

"Am I that horrible as a husband and a father?" I hate the quiver of brokenness in my voice.

"Your obsession with getting back at the Sisulus by having so much power that they grovel at your feet makes you callous to the next person's feelings. We are all pawns in the mighty Sisulu standoff. You say that once you get into the presidency, then you can let it go but I'm afraid that it will never be enough; that you crave this more than you crave your next breath." This brings my head up but she doesn't give me the opportunity to protest, to assure her that the dream has shifted.

"Oyama told me how hard it is living under constant media scrutiny and I don't want that for Denise. Eventually, you won't be able to hide us anymore, I can't go through what I went through with Oyama. I just can't. So, I want to pick up my children and run as far and fast as I can. I know it will be a huge adjustment but they have international schools that side that teach the Cambridge curriculum that the kids are currently learning, and I found a special needs school for Oyinqaba. His speech has already developed a lot and the speech therapist can also do virtual sessions with him to settle him in."

Candice is speaking quickly and only pauses to catch her breath, and then she worries her lower lip when I don't say anything but keep staring at her. I am fighting the strong urge to grab her and lock her in a tower but then I notice her fidgeting with her damp hair and fingers, a tell that she's on edge or scared of my reaction. The thought makes me close my eyes as violent shudders wreck me.

"You've given this a lot of thought." My voice is low and gruff. I pitched it low because I was afraid it would come out thin and whiny, like the voice screaming in my head. I take Candice's wrist and although she tenses, she doesn't snatch it away.

"I want to keep you here with me, even if it means holding you at gunpoint, kidnapping you, and keeping you in a mansion in the woods." I feel her pulse jump against my fingers. "Yet, to see that fear on your face right now cuts me so deep, I can't breathe properly. I've seen how wary you've grown around me, always waiting for me to snap or take out my frustrations on you. You've taken it all silently and I'm afraid that if I push this time, I will break you beyond repair. I don't think I can live with that on my conscious." I laugh but the sound is a short, sharp crack of ice.

"I have killed people without mercy and slept soundly afterwards, I have done so many horrible things without blinking. I have hurt you again and again and you quietly took it but each time, a little of the fire in your eyes dimmed. I wasn't fully aware of it until I saw the fire in your eyes that first night in your apartment in Turffontein. I have watched it slowly take root again since. I don't want to take that away from you again. If Mozambique and me staying away from you is what it will take to keep that fire burning, then I will let you go. Even if it causes me a thousand deaths."

I watch painfully as Candice sags in relief and pulls in greedy gulps of air, as if she was holding her breath the entire time. I keep drawing circles around her wrist to ground myself.

"I have conditions." Her pulse jumps again but she holds my stare without wavering. Then she gives me a tiny nod to continue. "I will continue taking care of you and the kids financially, and that means I have to approve of the home that you choose. My kids will not stay in a drivel ever again. If you need any help getting them into any school, I will help you. I'm also getting you household staff. The children get to be with me two weekends each month."

Her breathing has eased but I put up my hand because I'm not done.

"This condition is nonegotiable: There will be no divorce. You take however long you need apart, but you will still be my wife."

A battle of wills ensues as we stare at each other. I am channelling Minister Sisulu, who is used to getting Bills that benefit him gazetted, the lawyer in him making his negotiation skills sharp.

"I do not file for divorce for a year, provided that you actually work on your demons. Go to therapy, or I walk right out of here without your name and a penny from you," Candice counters, her gaze steady, even as her pulse jumps like crazy.

"Therapy isn't for me, No—"

"Take it or leave it. You gave me your conditions, I accept all of them; this is my only condition, and it is final."

I can see the stubborn will in her eyes. Nompumelelo always said Oyama took her strong will from me but I knew she took it from her mother, even her razor-sharp wit. My Adam's apple bobs as I swallow before letting go of her wrist and proffering my hand to seal our agreement. Her hand is soft and warm against my clammy palm.

"One more thing," Candice tries to tear her hand away but I keep it in place, "I will be with you when we deliver the news to the kids."

Chapter 44

Candice

I let out a sob of relief because I am so scared of approaching the kids with this. The sob escalates as all the pent up emotions break out of me like a burst dam and Daniel holds me in his arms. I think he's crying too, I don't know. A large part of me doesn't want to leave him, it wants to believe that he can change while I'm here, in his arms.

That part of me is the scared part, Daniel has been my safety net for so long, I'm undergoing a complicated pregnancy and I need him now more than ever. But the small stubborn part tells me that if I don't fly now, I never will. If I don't see my dreams through, they will always remain locked inside of me. I'm scared, sad, relieved, hopeful, and heartbroken.

"We will be alright, you want to know how I know that?" He's now holding my chin and making me look into his teary eyes. His face is tear-streaked and he is not making any effort to hide his tears or his pain from me.

"I know it because you are not just a morning star to me, Masase." The name sounds foreign coming from his lips, I love the way he says it.

"Wami, to me, you are iKhwezi, Venus—a planet outshining even the brightest of the stars in the night sky." My cheeks heat up, a hint of a smile draws the corners of his mouth as he continues. "When I need to come home, you are the morning star beckoning me from the darkness—iKhwezi lokusa. When I have my moment in the sun, you are there, silently cheering me on, even when most don't see you—iKhwezi lesibini. When it is time for me to put in the work, you are the star that guides me to milk everything from my work—uCelizapholo. When my loins ache, you are all I see and need to get me to fulfillment—uMadingeni. So, night and day, whatever the distance between us, uliKhwezi lami, and you will always guide me home."

He holds me until we have to bathe and go fetch the kids. I don't take them to Turffontein, Denise would flip and I need them relaxed as I uproot life as they know it. At first, they are excited to be finally back 'home' with their father. I see Denise's wide smile as Daniel hugs me and places a soft lingering kiss on the side of my head. It widens as he takes my hand and faces them.

"Your father and I have something important to discuss with you," my voice falters, and Daniel squeezes my hand, giving me the strength to take a deep breath and tell my children that I've always had a dream to open a beauty bar along the coast and that an opening came up in Mozambique and I am taking it. That we have to move there as soon as possible. The sale of my mother's house went through last month and I have enough money to get space by the seafront, since Daniel is now getting us a home.

I watch the smiles slide away from their faces—the confusion and agitation on Oyinqaba's face and the anger and twisted hatred on Denise's face cuts me up. I reach for her but she pulls away from me, angry tears sliding down her face.

"I hate you! You can't even get Daddy to stay with us, like Monwabisi's mum or Aleja's mum; even Oyama managed to get a daddy who is always there for Amandla, and now, you want to completely take us away from the daddy that we barely spend time with? I hate you! I hate you! I wish that I wasn't born from you!"

I sob and clutch my stomach, feeling the pain deep in my gut. Daniel makes me sit down, I tell him that I'm fine, I am more afraid of history repeating itself. He understands and takes off after Denise, who bangs the door so loudly, Oyinqaba flinches and buries his face on my lap. I pray through my silent tears that Denise doesn't have any suicidal thoughts, that my unborn baby stays strong for me, that Oyinqaba isn't set back by all of this, and that the pain goes away. It only intensifies and I feel like I'm wearing an electric belt that keeps tasing my lower back.

* * *

"You will find me at the hospital, Candice." When the line goes dead, I take a deep, calming breath, just like my doctor told me to and try not to alarm my sweet baby boy.

I take a couple more breaths until I feel the belt of pain lessening and Oyinqaba, bless his precious soul, is copying my breathing technique. I want to send him upstairs to go and call his father but when he is upset, his stutter becomes worse and his words come out a jumbled mess.

The pain has subsided and when I stand up, the sofa is dry—that's a good sign. I send another quick prayer before mounting the stairs with Oyinqaba at my heel. I let out another long breath when we finally get to the top and I rub my aching back.

"Please God, take care of my babies," has become a short mantra that I keep saying under my breath.

When I reach Denise's room, the door is slightly ajar and I can see her slumped on the floor, her head on her father's lap. He keeps stroking her hair, the gesture warms my heart as does the tail-end of the conversation that floats to me, "... on me. I should do better, not your mother. We can't blame Mummy, she's always taking care of all of us and now it's time that we take care of her. Okay? I promise you that it won't be forever, but I need you to look after Mummy while I am not with you. Can you do that for me?"

There is a lot of sniffling before a tremulous and muffled, "Yes, Daddy. I promise." comes out.

Oyinqaba gets into the room before Daniel can say anything else and he looks up from hugging them both, his frown deepening as he looks at me. I try smiling at him in reassurance but it comes out as a grimace.

"We need to get to the hospital, now." I'm proud of myself for not doubling over in pain.

I turn and start my slow descent while Daniel helps Denise and Oyinqaba to wash up their faces; Oyinqaba always copies what his sister does. By the time they are done, they find me in the car. Denise's eyes are a bit puffy but she looks presentable, and Oyinqaba looks cute in his denim overalls that match Denise's.

"Are you okay?" My face probably resembles a beetroot right now but I blow air from my puckered lips and nod.

I can tell that he wants to press harder but I put the navigation on and close my eyes from the million questions in Daniel's eyes. The drive passes in a blur of pain and me half-listening to Denise teaching Oyinqaba how to recite the alphabet. My back is sleek with sweat.

Chapter 45

Candice

I feel drained by the time we pull up outside Life Brenthurst Hospital. I silently let out another small prayer of thanks when there is no bleeding on the leather seats and the pain has subsided considerably. I don't want to entertain the thought of this baby not making it.

I view the text I just received of the room number and I walk in while Daniel brings the children at the rear. I would tell them why we are here but I don't trust myself to talk right now. I'm anxious and in pain; I'm using all my energy in trying to regulate my breathing. Daniel keeps looking at me during the elevator ride up but I ignore his inquiring eyes.

Breathe, Candice. Breathe.

We finally get to our floor and I lead the way. When we get to the private ward, we find the Levines and the ecstatic new parents. I feel the tension in my gut lessen when I look at my baby, hair damp with sweat and plastered on her face as she looks down at her suckling baby boy.

Thank you, God.

"Thank you for calling me," I tell Mpumi as she hugs me and kisses me on the cheek.

"We are both her mothers and she wanted you here." She nods towards

Oyama, who hasn't stopped beaming, even though she looks tired.

I kiss her sweaty forehead and peek at my grandson; he's a strapping baby and looks content as he feeds. I feel an arm around my waist and tear up when I see Denise pressed against me as she looks at her nephew. Her arm tightens around me as he opens his eyes, blinking at the light and frowning his annoyance at being gawked at.

"He doesn't look too happy to see me, Mummy," she grumbles, and we all laugh. Trust Oyama's baby to scowl a mere hour into his life.

My heart is full as I watch my family's excitement over the new addition. My own pain and discomfort is the furthest thing from my mind right now. I wasn't there when Amandla was born and I consider it a blessing to be a part of this birth, a sure sign of how far we've come with Oyama and the healing that has taken place between us.

"Sibonakaliso, that is his name. The proof of our love and our token of the gods' presence in our lives." I can see Oyama becoming emotional as Sipho says this.

I watch as he takes her in his arms and whispers something to her. They are perfect for each other and I pray that they have the strength to stand together always.

After sterilising my hands, I accept my grandson from Mpumi and whatever pain I was in dissolves instantly. He's studying me as I study him and it has an odd yet calming effect on me. I take his little hands and kiss every finger as I bless him in my heart and ask for Makhulu to look out for him and guide him as she was supposed to guide me.

When I pass Sibo to his grandfather, I tell him that I need to use the bathroom. Daniel is too preoccupied with the baby to see that instead of using the one in the private ward, I slip out.

There is the doctor who was just in the ward just, checking Sibo's vitals and that Oyama wasn't in any pain. I go to her and her warm smile makes it easier for me to tell her that I'm in the first trimester of what is potentially a risky pregnancy, and that I was in great pain earlier but I managed to get it down by doing some of the exercises that my doctor suggested, and I would still like to check that everything is fine with my baby. She's very understanding and tells me to follow her, even though it is against hospital protocol.

When my baby's heartbeat sounds loud and steady over the machine, I let out the tears that I was holding in. My little fighter kept it together for me and I'm grateful.

"Everything seems to be okay, except for your blood pressure, which is a bit high. I would advise you to go to your doctor tomorrow and have it checked. Take it easy, Mummy." I thank her, and she places a reassuring squeeze on my shoulder.

She leaves because she has to do her rounds and I wipe the cold gel from my tummy. It feels wrong to be going through this without Daniel but my gut is telling me not to tell him. I will be alone in Mozambique, I might as well start practising for that now. I got through today, and the baby is still fine.

When I get back to Oyama's room, everyone is still cooing over the baby and they didn't notice my absence. Visiting hours come to an end and we are kicked out. I'm happy, now I can leave without the fear of missing out on Sibo's birth.

Chapter 46

"Everything is in place on my side," I assure Shefu in the secure video conference call that Joshua set up. "I'm ready for the next phase, meeting the money people. They hold the real power and pull the strings of the goose we got last weekend."

Secure or not, our communication still has to be cryptic, in case this somehow comes out in the future. I have a lot riding on this collaboration now, Candice's words from the lodge are imprinted in my mind. While I couldn't do anything about my mother's death, and I found a replacement in the plan for Nompumelelo, I'm willing to burn it all down for Candice.

My great-uncle saw it in my eyes, that's why he allowed the lobola and registration of our union, and death better think twice before trying to come between Wami and I.

After I get the money people on board, then I can start implementing my exit strategy; thanks to the scarecrow's networks, I'll be able to move in the shadows. She must be turning in her grave, the thought makes me smile as I listen to Joshua outline every angle, possible outcome, and mitigation system for each possible outcome. The man is anal about micro-managing and that has led to me grudgingly respecting and trusting him in such a short period of time.

"Gentlemen, until the next meeting is set up, remember, no communication. For all intents and purposes, we do not know each other past surface level," Joshua concludes the meeting, and then I'm alone in my study.

Without Mandisa hovering around or Monwabisi's peals of laughter sounding throughout the place, the whole place feels too big, too empty. I've already packed a few essentials, I'll be moving in with Candice and the kids until they leave for Mozambique. After some introspection, I realised that it's better this way, to get them as far away as possible before this deal is concluded, in case things go sideways. Joshua has already told me that he knows security, ex-militia type, in Mozambique; at least I'll know that they are safe. He also promised to hook me up with some surveillance system, he muttered something about having to do the same for a Vimbai and Nosihle. Before I could ask him what he meant about that, Shefu joined the video conference call and then we got into business mode.

I'm packing away my laptop when my study door is rudely opened without so much as a knock. I exhale, as Mbuso's protruding gut makes his presence known, a second after, his overpowering scent enters the space. I sit back, and interlock my fingers, and school my features to benign boredom. My cousin thrives on getting a rise out of people and my passiveness irks him, if his flared nostrils are anything to go by. I casually reaching for the gun stuck under my desk. Seconds drag by and I simply stare at him, refusing to bend for him even a little.

"You think you can just fuck over Mandisa's family like that? Do you know the repercussions that that will have on the Sisulu name?" His hiss is meant to be intimidating, his eyes narrowed into tiny slits. It's like facing off to an alcoholic puffed-up version of me, my father. Our fathers were brothers and Mbuso looks more like my father than his, and he hates that everyone's always pointed it out. My cousin sets an imposing figure, he's almost my height and where I am lean and lithe, he is fat and muscle rolled into one mean combo.

"Mandisa's family fucked me over first, they gave me a whore to be my wife." My tone is casual but my words land exactly where I wanted them to, causing Mbuso to lunge at me. He's slow and predictable, so I am able to shove the desk right into his gut, causing a loud wheezing sound to leave his mouth, his eyes bulging in pain and heat up in rage.

I know that Mandisa ran to him the moment I made it known that I knew their secret. It wasn't hard to put it all together; when a wife who cringed when you tried touching her is suddenly throwing herself at you and seven months later, you have a healthy baby boy, then there must be something worth looking into. I was indifferent to Mandisa's lies and she mistook that for stupidity.

"You know, one thing I do want to know is when did you start fucking her? After or before she was presented to me in a tight, neat little bow? Or were you fucking all the candidates?"

"Mandisa was meant to be mine. All of this...," he gestures around my office, "was meant to be mine. Your father and all his rats were ex-communicated from the family, and my father's offspring were raised as heirs but you managed to crawl out of the sewer and mess it all up for me."

The laugh that erupts out of me isn't feigned. I laugh until I wheeze, tears squeezing out of the corners of my eyes. When I finally manage to contain my mirth, I come face to face with Mbuso's enraged scowl.

"Oh, you were serious? Mbuso, you couldn't even hold on to the NCOP seat in parliament that your surname guaranteed you, let alone get to my position."

Mbuso lets out an angry roar and pushes my table away but stops short when he sees the gun I'm holding almost loosely in my hand pointed directly at his crotch. He still moves one brazen step towards me and I tighten my grip on the gun.

"You'd never hurt me; if you do, you'll be cast out from the family," he sneers, but also doesn't move even an inch.

"Your family cast me out before I was even born, yet, here I am today—alive, and in a position that you envy so much, you have to fuck my wife to feel vindicated. What was the plan? Fuck Mandisa and turn her into your spy, then use the information to take me down? She nagged enough about wanting to know my every move, you failed to train your spy well." The last part has his nose flaring, and I let loose my most manic smile, the one I keep hidden behind diplomacy and tact.

"Leave, before I give into the urge to kill you and use your body as manure for my flowers out front."

Mbuso stares at me, not quite meeting my eyes and then he says the dumbest thing, signing his death certificate, "You can't keep that whore under lock and key forever, she's eager to run away from your suffocating presence. When she does, I'll be there, and I'll make you watch as I tear her apart and maybe I'll let my men also have a taste of that slut that has your balls twisted."

Outwardly, only my manic smile widens to a deranged grin but inside, I'm seething. I knew that Mbuso sent whoever attacked Candice's rundown flat but to hear him speak so callously about hurting my woman makes me see red. I want to shoot his crotch until the magazine of this gun is empty but I rein in the bloodlust strumming through my veins, not yet. Plus, I can never be tied to his death.

"You need your hooligans to do it for you because you cannot see your speckled manhood under that gut. Or maybe you've popped so many of those blue pills, that you've become soft even after using them," I goad him and when he steps menacingly towards me, I take off the safety latch on the gun. I silently dare him to make the mistake of coming for me while my demons are baying for his blood.

"Maybe I'll film it when I fuck your whore seven ways to Sunday," he sneers, and like the coward that he is, he makes as hasty a retreat as his beer gut allows him.

I take out my burner phone and dial the number under the letter 'J'. It rings twice before it's answered without a word uttered.

"Change of plans. Please send security detail to my precious cargo now instead of when I send it away to the tropical side. Eyes and manpower on it, immediately. Please," I let my desperation bleed into the last word. If anyone hurts Wami because of me, I wouldn't be able to live with myself.

"Consider it done."

I end the call and then I call Ntsikelelo, he answers after one ring, "S'khulu."

"I need the kill team, I have to get rid of a cockroach discreetly."

Once all my plans are in motion, I get out of the house, driving in agitation, and the fear that I might be too late making me fly past two red lights. I make sure the guard at the gates know not to let anyone in, not even deliveries, and even though they assure me nothing is amiss, my breathing only evens out when I find my entire world cuddled up with our cubs in the lounge, watching 'The Princess and the Frog'. Nowami's warm smile dims a little when she sees my face. The kids are just excited to see me and while they want to cling to me, right now, all that I need is their mother. Sensing this, Nowami distracts them with a task and she drags me upstairs to our bedroom.

"What's wro—?" I seal her lips with mine before she finishes her question, and she moans, yielding without question.

With the kids downstairs, I have to be quick. I don't bother with taking off our clothes; my hand bunches Nowami's panties before tearing them from her while she expertly opens my belt, freeing my aching balls—all the while, neither of us breaks our kiss. I hoist her up and she crosses her legs behind my back, bringing her moist heat up against my raging hard-on, I thrust into her in one fluid movement and swallow her mewls and my groan. I pound into her with desperate urgency, needing the reassurance that she's here, that she's mine, and she's safe.

She lets me pour all my frustrations and pent-up rage into her and I feel her getting wetter with each savage thrust as she also scratches my neck. I welcome the sting of her nails, as it drives away the images of Mbuso hurting her. This heaven, that is her walls tightening around my penis, is mine alone and I will die before anyone can hurt her like that again.

I don't let up even as her back arcs and I swallow her screams of ecstasy, and I feel her walls tightening again. It's intense, it's reassurance, and love all rolled into one. When Candice comes up for air after her third orgasm, I bite down on her soft, pale neck as my vision darkens around the edges, goosebumps pepper my skin and I shake as a release that transcends me to heaven wrecks through me, leaving me spent and vulnerable.

"I love you, and I need you to give me all your days while you're still here, please." I don't hide the cracks in my voice, the fear coursing through me.

Nowami craddles my face, her hands warm as her thumbs wipe away the stray tears on my face. "I'm here, Daniel, and I don't think I could stop loving you or deny you anything. God knows I've tried."

Her words calm down my demons, my heart stops racing, and I want to kiss her again when we hear two pairs of footfalls pounding up the stairs. By the time the door is flung open and Oyinqaba comes hurtling in like a giggly hurricane, our clothes are righted but I refuse to let go of Candice, even when our children run in circles around us. Seeing her laughing and safe, settles me. This—her, my children—is my home; only, Oyama isn't here to complete us but I know she's safe with her own little family.

Chapter 47

I can't believe that I'm even thinking this, but Daniel's control issues have served me well this past month. He has found the perfect house for us, the kids now have vacancies in one of the most elite schools that side, whatever we are taking with us has been packed and shipped, and I didn't lift a finger in all this.

The only thing where I put my foot down was my beauty bar; he only got me a meeting with his estate agent and she came to see me about what I wanted. Within three days, I had found two vacant stores by the beach. She showed me the space via video call and I loved it. As of today, I am the owner of both and the adjacent wall between the two is being demolished, while the 3D plan that I chose for the place is being perfected. I should be able to hold the grand opening in the next two or three months. That gives me enough time to settle in with the kids.

At first, I was scared and anxious but now that everything is in motion, excitement is brewing, and even Denise has latched onto my excitement.

"What's a beauty bar, Ma?" she asks, as I paint her nails for their farewell slumber party with the famous four or whatever Oyama calls the Levine twins, Amogelang, and Amandla.

"More or less a mixture of a beauty parlour and a spa. It will cater for hair, nails, facials, and the general pampering of women. Stop fidgeting, or I'll get nail polish all over the couch." She pouts and tries to stay still but she's giddy with excitement.

"Will I be getting my hair and facials done for free?"

"No, you will have to pay like everyone else. Now, put your hands in the nail dryer." I laugh when she attempts to pull the puppy eyes at me.

I have to do Oyinqaba's nails too and he wants the same colour as Denise. Daniel will flip and the thought makes me grin widely as I apply the cherry blossom colour. Daniel has been staying with us for the past month and it has been pure bliss. At first, I thought it was some ploy to get us to stay, but he's kept his word. He only goes out when he needs to go to physical meetings, but other than that, he does virtual meetings and work in the mornings from 5 a.m. until 11 a.m. while the kids are having their online lessons, and then we have his undivided attention.

I answer all of Denise's questions, I think she's preparing to brag to all the other kids, and Oyinqaba only wants to know if there are dolphins in the Mozambican waters. I find Oyama waiting for her siblings in another one of Sipho's hoodies and shorts, she lives in those hoodies when she's not in scrubs or going out. My granddaughter is with her and I'm told that my grandson is with Mpumi, Nomusa, and the rest of the gang.

I can't resist the temptation of seeing those adorable chubby cheeks. If I weren't already pregnant, Sibonakaliso would make me broody. He's the light-skinned version of his father, he's also a little solemn baby, quietly sucking on his fist as he looks at me like he can see all of my deepest and darkest secrets.

"Are you sure you don't want to stay and join the slumber party?" Oyama asks, as she stays longer in my hug than she normally does. It's refreshing to see her being even a little clingy.

"I have to go visit your grandmother, maybe someday, when you're not breastfeeding anymore, we can go together," I offer tentatively.

"I'd love that." My baby smiles briefly at me and I almost get teary but I hold it in until I am alone in the car.

After leaving Oyama's estate, I turn my car to the other side of town. Aside from intense morning sickness shortly after waking up and in the evenings, I haven't had any other complications with Tshimangadzo; a little nickname for my surprise blessing that I am sure will not make it to his or her birth certificate. I'm starting to feel a bit like my old self again, I put on my "Alone Time" playlist, which is songs that Denise wouldn't be caught dead in the car with them playing. She once scrunched her nose when I was playing Mandoza's 'Nkalakatha' and said, "Mummy, that's so ghetto!"

I scroll until I reach Lebo Mathosa's tracks, 'Free' comes on and I sing along softly, absorbing her need and mine to break away from the chains holding us back. Of all musicians, I relate most to Lebo. I was wild once, too, with a dress sense as daring as hers and then I sort of morphed into a more sophisticated version of me. She died so young and that makes me sad, but I'll carry her with me. 'Brand New Day' comes on and I drum my fingers on the steering wheel as I wait to off-ramp onto Ergo Road.

On the long drive to KwaThema Phase 1 Cemetery, I listen to Lebo Mathosa and Brenda Fassie because my mother loved her so much and I need to feel closer to her. I breathe in deeply as I look for a place with at least some shade to park under, before I start my search for my mother's final resting place. I've only been here twice since her burial and it has been years since I last came to visit her grave.

It takes me over 30 minutes to finally locate the headstone that I had them put up after my first cruise ship job. It's simple and elegant, just like her.

In loving memory of
Gladys Lupfuno Ndou
Mother, Daughter, and Sister
1965-1996
"A mother holds her children's hands for a while, but their hearts forever."

When I first chose that inscription, it was just so that her headstone wouldn't just be left bare. I was still harbouring some resentment against her for her ill-treatment of me and leaving me with alone with a new-born in this cold and cruel world. As a long-serving mother myself now, the words make perfect sense. I clear my throat, trying to rid myself of the tears clogging it.

"Hi, Gladys. I'm sure you are happy to know that my children have given back some of the grief that I put you through and then some. I think my first daughter likes me now, even though she still calls me 'Candice'. I don't know why you never allowed me to call you 'Ma', I longed for it so badly. Guess I'll never know why you were so angry at me. In your own weird way, you were always pushing me to be a better version of myself. I'm sorry for disappointing you, I did go back to school and I got that certificate you preached about. I also made a lot of questionable life choices—like, a lot—but somehow, I am still here. I have the most gorgeous children..." I choke on my words when the image of Gladys beaming as she held Kungentando in her arms pops into my mind.

"Denise has your fire and I wish you could have held her in your arms, Oyinqaba is the sweetest little boy; I honestly don't know where he gets it from. I'm having another baby coming and I was shocked and disappointed at first but then, this baby has given me the wings I've needed to fly. To be the best version of me. This isn't goodbye, because you and Makhulu live in my heart but I just needed to talk to you; to tell you how sorry I am, and how scared I am to uproot my life and that of my children."

I stop rambling and push the sunglasses to my hair as I dab my eyes. I stay for a while, wishing I had brought some flowers. The smooth granite feels cold against my lips and my hands linger on the inscription before I put my sunglasses back on and I turn and leave the cemetery without a backwards glance.

I have a good cry in the car when Brenda Fassie's 'Mama' comes on. From this point on, I will try to be the best version of myself for my Mama; she's not here to bitch to me about calling her that.

* * *

I'm passing Brakpan when a call comes in and I answer it over my Bluetooth.

"Hello, Sisi. I got your number from the agent that sold us the house." I suck in a short breath because I had made it clear that I didn't want to know who bought my mother's house. I politely lie and say it's okay, and ask how I can I help her.

"My son, he's five, he was playing in my bedroom and one of the wooden tiles came off." This is exactly the reason why I wanted them to only deal with the agent and I'm about to tell her that but she continues her narration. "I hadn't noticed it was loose and I was about to put it back when I noticed that there was a small parcel inside it and a letter addressed to 'Candy'."

A chill whooshes up and down my spine at the timing of it all. I had never noticed a loose tile, neither did the tenant who lived there for years before he relocated last year, and I had to decide whether to get another tenant or just sell the house.

"Thank you for calling me. I'm actually in the vicinity of KwaThema. Is it okay if I come by and collect it?"

She's amenable to the suggestion and I do a U-turn at the next possible turn and I head back to my mother's house. When I park outside, I can see the open curiosity of the residents. It's too bad that Sis' Thuli's sister relocated back to KZN some years back, so I don't have any ties with the neighbours that remained. All the memories of my spiral after Gladys' death rush up to the forefront of my mind, threatening to take me under.

"You are not the girl who was broken anymore. You are not your past. You are not the girl who was broken anymore," I repeat the mantra, and try to do the breathing and counting coping mechanisms that my therapist taught me.

"I am smart. I am loved. I am at peace. I am happy."

When my breathing has steadied, I finally unlock the door, not ready to face my past but doing it anyway, to fully close this chapter of my life.

Chapter 48

Candice

The new owner of the house is short and plump, and smiles and laughs easily; she even hugs me, as if we have known each other forever. She hands me the small box and the letter. I try to hide how shaky my hands are and I give her son a R100 bill for coming across this letter. I decline the offer of tea by lying and saying that I still have to collect my child from crèche.

I ignore the neighbour who makes a snarky comment about how all the people I ran around with have succumbed to AIDS but I'm still here, probably leeching on some poor rich woman's husband. I'm grateful that I am not showing yet, because that would give them even more fodder for their gossip.

Driving back to my complex passes in a blur of nerves, I keep on throwing a glance at the letter. When Daniel comes back in the evening, he finds me thumbing at the still-sealed letter and I jump when he kisses me on the temple.

"Hey, it's okay. It's only me." I let out a sigh of relief. He flew to Mozambique this morning to check that everything was in order.

"The house is all set, and the renovations on your beauty bar started as scheduled," he responds to my query but he's eyeing the letter that I am holding. "Who is that from?"

"My mother. Apparently, she hid it under a loose tile in the house, and the new owner's son stumbled upon it."

"Are you going to read it?" he asks, and I tell him that I don't know and how scared I am of a piece of paper.

"You don't have to do it alone," he assures me, and I manage to give him a watery smile in return. "Wait here."

I want to ask him where else I would even go, but he's gone, bounding up the stairs as if he's Oyinqaba. I wait for about five minutes before Daniel comes and sweeps me off my feet. I protest that I've gained weight, but he doesn't even break a sweat as he carries me up the stairs, my mother's letter clutched to my chest.

Daniel undresses me as if he's undressing Denise carefully taking the letter from my cold clutches, and I'm grateful for that because right now, I feel like that little girl who longed for her mother's love. Hopeful for a glimpse of that love in the letter but afraid that it will tear me apart even further. He guides me to the bathtub and I smell the lavender oil as I sink into the hot water.

"Tell me about your mother," Daniel says quietly, as he pours some shampoo on his hand and then massages it into my scalp. His hands knead with skill, and I feel some of the tension that his request brought up ease away.

"She wouldn't let me call her 'Ma'," I admit to him quietly, and his hands still for a second before he goes back to massaging my scalp but he doesn't say anything. "Gladys was strict. She was more of a mother to the children that she nannied than she ever was to me; they adored her, they got all her softness while I got all her hard edges. The only time she was tender with me was when she did my hair once a month."

I hate the pathetic tremble in my voice but Daniel doesn't stop rinsing out the soap from my hair. I shut my eyes tightly and I see an image of my mother huffing as she threw a case of mangoes and avocados on the table one day when she was coming from work. She didn't say where she got them but they tasted like home, Maebani, and I had told her the previous week that my pregnancy cravings were mangoes and avocados from my grandmother's trees.

"She did have a sweet layer to her but you had to dig very deep to find it; or at least, I did. She loved Brenda Fassie and when she thought I wasn't looking, I'd catch her dancing. Whenever she was off work, she would deep-clean our house, cook enough food to last me a month, wash and iron my clothes and uniforms. She had no friends. Looking back now, she always had this nervous energy and she had to be doing something at all times. It drove me crazy."

I'm still talking about all the things I remember about Gladys when Daniel makes me stand and dries me with the big fluffy towel, and then bundles me up in my robe while he's wearing his own. The blankets are already turned down and he still tucks me in as if I'm a baby. He hands me the letter and I stare at it as if it's a live snake. Daniel settles in next to me and offers me his hand. Once I tear open the letter, I put my left hand in his and he squeezes it gently in support. I take a deep breath and let my eyes go down the letter.

My Darling Candice

Seeing the endearment in her bold neat handwriting chokes me up, Gladys never called me 'darling' and I didn't know how much I needed to until reading that line. I sob and Daniel holds me after carefully taking the letter from my clammy clutches again. I cry until I have hiccups and he rubs my back, telling me that he's got me, that I'm not alone. The deep rumble of his voice anchors me and finally, the tears recede and I stop crying.

"Please read it for me." My voice is croaky and I need Daniel's calm voice to get me through this letter. He takes it from next to me and smooths it before pulling me to his chest. Then he starts reading.

"My Darling Candice

I don't know if I will ever get the strength to tell you this or even give you this letter, but all I know is that it has taken all of my strength to pen it down. Today we exchanged harsh words and that is normal for us but today it made me sad because I see how angry you are my child. I wish there was something I could do to take some of that anger away but I cannot change the past.

You want to know who your father is and why I abandoned you all those years until your grandmother died. The answer to both is Bertus Botha. Your father. I grew up in the village that you love so much and one day we went to the dance that the chief had thrown for his guest, an Afrikaner missionary who was going to build a new school in the village. What started off as an exciting day for me slowly turned into my worst nightmare.

The chief had arranged for his missionary friend to pick up any maiden as his "reward" or a bribe, I don't know my child, I just know that I was the unfortunate maiden. I fought. I fought so hard but in the end you were conceived in the most painful manner. He gave me his watch as "payment" it's what I put in the box with this letter.

My mother knew and didn't do anything about it and she refused to give me the herbs to get rid of you, get rid of my pain and shame. I hated her for that but she made the best decision because now I cannot imagine a world without you.

When my pregnancy became public knowledge, I was ridiculed and shamed even by my own siblings and that caused a further rift between us because my mother in her fear, didn't correct them when they called me loose. I gave birth to you, then I turned my back on everything that reminded me of that awful period in my life. My roots, my family and I took you with me to Gauteng.

As you grew, so did my resentment and when the need to hurt you grew too big, I made the decision to take you to my mother. I knew that she would give you the love that I couldn't find in my heart to give to you.

I realise now that you weren't the cause of my pain and instead of looking at you and seeing your pale skin and curly hair, I should have seen how just like me you are, you are more a part of me than that dreadful beast. From today onwards I vow to do better by you and I hope that someday you won't be angry at me and the world anymore. I'm sorry, my child.

Love

Your mother

Gladys ."

Chapter 49

Daniel

I'm woken by the sound of water. I rub my blurry eyes and check the time; it's a little after two at night. Candice isn't snuggled next to me on the bed. After reading her mother's letter, she was so distraught that I ended up slipping her some of the meds she was prescribed when she suffered from PTSD after Denise's birth into her juice. They put her to sleep just after seven and now, she's up. I walk gingerly towards the sound of water, barefoot, and I find Candice with yellow glove-clad hands, scrubbing the toilet bowl as if it were contaminated.

"Candice," I call her softly so as not to startle her but she continues to scrub the poor bowl with vengeance.

"Candy?" That doesn't get me any reaction either and I step up until I'm towering over her.

"Nowami, it's 2 a.m. Please come back to bed." My voice is still gentle but firm, and she looks up at me, offering me a big, sunny smile meant to reassure me but her eyes are off, vacant.

"I'm coming. I just need to clean this toilet, it's dirty." Her voice is high with nervous energy and I have to forcefully take the brush and gloves off her.

"Nothing is dirty, you're not dirty. Come on, Baby, you need to rest before our journey tomorrow." She resists and then the next minute, she's sobbing—painful, heart-wrenching sobs that make my heart ache.

"She had every right to hate me, I reminded her of the monster who hurt her, not only with my presence but also because I kept asking for that monster." Her words are hoarse from crying but I hear them clearly and they land square in my heart.

"She had no right to hate you, you're nothing like that monster. And screw her for treating you like you were anything other than the precious gift that you are."

My words renew the floodgates of tears and I let her cry as I carry her back to bed and cradle her against me. I hate how she's taken on the burden of her father's choices and is excusing her mother's abuse. I hold her until the sobs die down and I think she's sleeping but then she says something that breaks me.

"You were right to keep me in the shadows, I do nothing but steal people's light, you wouldn't have gotten so far if people knew me as your wife." I temper the violent urge to shake her until even the thought goes out of her mind. Instead, I do something that I've never done before, I allow Candice to see me.

"I was fourteen when I lost my virginity." My voice is a scratchy whisper and Candice turns to look at me, her eyes wide and softened by the bedside lamp. "That's a lie, my virginity wasn't lost, it was taken from me violently by a woman who was old enough to be my grandmother. I didn't know it then, but Phindiwe had approached the woman to get her husband to sponsor me for my political career and she agreed, only if I became her little plaything; her gigolo. I can still smell the whiskey that she loved to drink, I can feel her claws as she forced me to drink it. It must have been laced with something because I became hard instantly and… and…" The memories threaten to drag me under but Candice's soft sobs and her hands stroking my face keep me tethered to her.

"Shhh, you don't have to tell me, I understand," she pleads with me, but the gates have been opened and the little boy in me is clawing to be let out after being trapped inside my mind for so long.

"I didn't understand what was happening to my body. Sure, I had begun having morning wood but my father wasn't around to tell me what the changes in my body meant; he was too lost in his own misery. Even though I had the worst erection, I didn't want her touching me, I didn't want the things she did to me. She whipped me when I was crying; my voice was still high-pitched, I was just a boy. At some point, I blacked out, I was there physically but my psyche detached itself, and when I came to, she was still there on top of me, doing things that disgusted me but the worst part was that I still ejaculated. That night, I couldn't close my eyes without seeing her on top of me, without hearing the lewd sounds that she made, and so I got out, I waited for my father at his drinking spot and I killed him. It felt like I was taking back some of the control that had been stripped away from me."

When the words stop, I feel Candice's tight hug. Even as she's shaking and crying, she's holding me as if she can shield me from the memories, and I welcome her cries because it feels a lot like she's mourning the childhood that I never had from that day. I hold and comfort her, I don't tell her that that wasn't the worst thing that the scarecrow did to me. I don't tell her about the times she would invite her friends and the times they would make me lick them while I was chained like a dog. I'm afraid that if I let her see those depraved parts of me, she will never again look at me with stars in her eyes.

I hold her as she cries herself to sleep, I stay awake, wrestling with my demons until morning comes. Candice's alarm wakes her up and she is instantly worried when she finds me awake.

"You stayed up the whole night?" She scrunches her nose in that cute way that Denise does when she's worried.

"I woke up about five minutes ago and I've been watching your pretty face since," I lie, and I don't regret it because her shoulders ease and she blushes prettily.

"Stay," I beg in a moment of weakness, even though I know that it's best that she and the kids are far, far away, where Mbuso and all my other enemies cannot get to them. It's the boy she held and comforted yesterday who doesn't want to let go of the person who has seen him and didn't go running for the hills.

"I want to..." she whispers, as if it's a dirty confession, and then I remember how I found her cleaning that toilet bowl insistently. Staying will break her further, I will break her further, and I would rather kill myself than ever dim her light again. So I swallow all the pleading and manipulation that rises inside me and I take her lips in a short sweet kiss. I can taste her salty tears as well as the sweetness of her, my Candy. Wami...

I let my lips communicate to her what my voice can never say out loud. That I'm grateful that she's held me down for so long. That she's seen all of my demons, all of my brokenness, and she still stayed, and that I don't want that for her anymore. That I love her and I need her to be the shining star that I met in that bus all those years ago.

When it feels like my lips can't pour everything I have to say into her, I let my body do the talking. Each stroke is slow, measured, and lingering. If I had only one day on this Earth, I'd want to spend it lost inside her like this. Candice accepts me and she also wines her waist, every moan and every cry tells me that she feels the same, that I'm not alone in these feelings ebbing between us.

She doesn't tell me how much she loves me, but I can tell from the way she clings to me as her walls pulse around me and she screams her release, and when she squirts, I know that I've touched the deepest parts of her and I allow myself to fall because I know she'll still catch me, no matter where, in the world, she is.

Chapter 50

Candice

"How have you been?"

I suck in some air and let it swell around my mind, round and round it goes. I hold it in until my lungs feel like they might explode, as if I'm submerged in the ocean, and only then do I let it go. I try to focus my blurry eyesight and at first, Celeste appears in fragments behind the screen. When my vision is clear, I can see the patience and kindness in her eyes. I will my mind to take me back to her office with its sparse furnishings and a couch that is the most comfortable in the world.

"Take your time," she encourages me, and I finally let the question sink in.

"At times, it felt like I was drowning, gulping copious amounts of salty water, and so I threw myself into making sure that the kids are okay, that they are settling in well. They are doing fabulous now; they love their new schools and have made new friends. So, I am forced to now focus on me, and I've been putting off this session as much as I could but I need to speak to someone before I snap again."

"That's why I'm here, so that you can talk and not drown. We will circle back to why you used the word 'drowning', but let's start with the letter. You sent me an email telling me that you received a letter from your mother that shed light on a lot of things that we've been grappling with."

Trust Celeste to jump right into the fray. I take the letter from the drawer beneath where I positioned the MacBook. I try to smooth the edges out, I've read it maybe a hundred times over the past month and each time, with a different emotion. I read it out loud for Celeste and she listens without interruption. When I'm done, she doesn't say anything, she just watches me as I struggle to control my emotions, and then she softly tells me to drink the water that is in front of me.

"You know, there were times when I begged her to go and leave me with my father, and for years after she died, I thought I was suffering because she denied me a relationship with my family. Now… the very thought of him makes my skin crawl and I want to poke his eyes out for what he did to my mother. What he probably did to a slew of other girls out there." I'm breathing heavily after my venting rant, my hands scrunched into fists but with my nails digging painfully into the soft flesh of the inner part of my hands.

"Have you looked for him?" she asks, but she's eyeing my clenched hands with that look instead of looking into my eyes. I slowly relax them, and I wince when I notice that I have drawn some blood.

"I didn't, but Daniel did and he sent me an email with just his file attached. He's so old, he was probably in his late 40s when he raped my mother. He has thyroid cancer and any day now, he could die; that gives me a little satisfaction, that he's dying. No known kids or spouse. He's in some elderly home, being taken care of by the church. May the cancer eat him up until even breathing is painful and then he can go to hell for all I care!" Celeste cocks her eyebrows but doesn't say anything, just steers me away from my volatile emotions.

"Are you and Daniel talking?"

"No." I let out a painful breath. "That was the only email that he sent, and he didn't add any text to it. He calls Denise every day, they video call, and his secretary arranges their meetings every second week. The kids are with him today."

"Isn't that what you asked of him?" I feel the juvenile need to roll my eyes, but then I remind myself that Celeste didn't make up these terms, I did.

"I did, and for once, he's respecting my wishes to the T but it hurts because I miss him. I kind of…" My voice trails off when I realise that I am about to give up how much of a stalker I am.

"Go on. You kind of what?" Trust Celeste to pick up on every nitty-gritty.

"I kind of hoped that when Mandisa announced their divorce, the day before yesterday… that he would call or text or even email. I caught myself a lot of times before I dialled his number. The media interest in who could be his next wife isn't helping matters. Has he come for a session with you yet?" I ask, and Celeste purses her mouth before shaking her head 'No'.

"He keeps cancelling or postponing his sessions, but he's supposed to come in today," she tells me, and I'm not surprised. Daniel hates being vulnerable to anyone.

"When he comes, he's going to offer to pay you off in exchange for you to tell me that he's attending therapy. When he does that, please call me." Celeste gives me another noncommittal grunt and then asks me another question.

"Is it the media interest giving you anxiety or is it manifesting your insecurities?"

I scowl at Celeste but she only smiles almost serenely at me. I hate how she always seems to hear the words that I leave unsaid.

"I am anxious that he might take another wife to fill in Mandisa's spot." Saying the words makes me sick, it feels like déjà vu.

I was pregnant with Denise when Mpumi divorced Daniel, and when he told me that he was marrying Mandisa so soon after marrying me, I became depressed and that, combined with PTSD, led me to Celeste's office. She saved my life, and I've been with her since.

"What would you do if he did take another wife? You don't want to be in the limelight and he has a certain image to uphold." I suck my teeth because the thought has plagued me since I saw Mandisa's press statement via a media site.

"I cannot stand the thought of him with another woman. I guess I would have to make peace with the fact that I am not enough for him, that I have never been enough for him." Celeste gives me a curt nod, neither cementing nor dissenting from my admission.

"Now, let's go back to why you uprooted yours and your children's lives in the first place."

"To find myself. Who I am outside of my marriage. To reconnect with my dreams and everything that I let go of when I became Daniel's baby-maker."

"Are you doing that? Besides the new anger that you harbour against your father, fussing over your children and stalking Daniel and his other wife on media sites, I don't see you putting much effort into finding yourself. Everything else is ancillary, the core of your struggles is your identity. You are hiding behind everything and everyone else, instead of finding yourself; the you that is drowning. What are you so afraid of, Candice?" Celeste's words are said evenly but I still tear up.

"My beauty bar is opening in two weeks," I hedge stubbornly after dabbing my eyes.

"That's a huge step that should either excite or scare you, but you haven't mentioned it, not once, until your hackles were raised. I'm not fighting with you but I feel like something is holding you back. I thought finding out who your father is would help you let go, but you are still shying away from yourself. Make me understand why that is Candice." There is a gentleness in the way she's talking to me that makes me break down and sob.

Celeste watches me, not saying anything, until all my tears are exhausted and I fumble around the desk until I find some tissues. If this was a physical session, she would have handed me her box of tissues by now. When my face is presentable, I take a deep, steadying breath and I look within myself, staring my deepest fears in the face.

"Every time something seems to be going right in my life, it is cruelly... tugged from under my feet. When I was on top of my class and I was supposed to get awards for that term, Makhulu died suddenly and my mother whisked me off soon after her funeral on the day when I was supposed to receive the awards. When I thought I would start a new life with my baby and Daniel, that, too, was ripped from my hands—not once, but twice. When my life was finally settling after my Matric, I was so excited to be going to Polokwane—that, too, was snuffed out, as I had to flee from

Vhutuhawe." My throat is clogged again and it is taking everything within me to force the words out, "It's almost like I don't deserve any greatness or anything good in my life, so I make do with the scraps that life offers me. I'm tired, Celeste. Tired of dreaming, and when I can almost taste that dream becoming a reality, life comes hurtling in and casts me aside. At first, I used to think it was because I didn't have a father to shield and protect me but now I realise that it's because I am a product of vileness. I am a curse." Through my hazy view, I see Celeste dabbing her eyes. A silence stretches between us while we both try to compose ourselves.

"I wish you could see yourself from my eyes, Candice. Not everyone would still be standing after everything that life has thrown at you. Yet, here you are, still standing, still dreaming, and with so much love within you for those you hold dear." We are both emotional and Celeste takes a deep breath, trying to be professional again.

"I need you to look after the little Masase within you; show her the same love that you have shown your children, that you have shown Daniel, and everyone you have ever loved and cared for. Every day, I want you to do a little something for Masase; remember, she's a little bruised, a whole lot broken, so I want you to love and shield her just as fiercely as you do the rest of your children. Every day, I want you to write down what you did for Masase on that day. Okay?"

As I nod, the tears that were hanging capriciously on my eyelids come rolling down my cheeks. I wipe them with my hands before I offer Celeste a watery smile. I rub my growing belly. This baby has withstood so much of my pain.

"Ms Khumalo, Mr Sisulu is here for his appointment," the voice of Celeste's assistant sounds from the background.

I remind Celeste to call me when he offers her money and she brushes me off. We end our session and I take a much-needed walk on the beach. I'm trying to reach out to the little girl inside me who used to race barefoot on the red soil of Maebani, the wind pushing against her hair and face.

Chapter 51

Daniel

I read through Mandisa's press release, just to make sure that she didn't deviate from the script that I pre-approved. She fought against the divorce, probably because her boyfriend told her he has a plan, but Mbuso was found dead from an overdose in a famous whore house in Hillbrow and Mandisa quickly changed her tune. I like it when things come together. I just have to get the scarecrow's husband's crew firmly on my side, then I can start initiating my resignation.

The past month has been a whirlwind of whispered conversations and furtive glances, a delicate dance of ambition and risk. I been to countless polo matches just trying to persuade them that we are perched on the edge of opportunity, the air thick with potential—one that could shift the balance of power in the whole Southern African region. Most of the old geysers are prickly about change, but I've spent countless hours crafting my pitch, honing my arguments to assuage their fears—none of them stand a chance.

In those initial meetings, I laid out the groundwork with a mix of calculated charm and unyielding confidence. The potential for profit is staggering, when I told them that, I could almost see the numbers flashing before their eyes: Stability breeds investment, and a regime change could usher in a new era of untapped resources and lucrative contracts. I had to convince them that their bottom line won't just remain intact; it will flourish.

I think back to the hesitations I sensed in their expressions, the flicker of doubt that crossed their faces when I first broached the subject. They worry about the fallout, the unpredictability of such a move. But stability is a mirage in our region—one that can only be achieved through decisive action. I just need to press them a bit more, show them the roadmap to prosperity; perhaps I can turn that doubt into enthusiasm. Those I can't persuade, I can threaten with all the videos I have of their wives and, at times, them.

The stakes are higher than mere financial gain. This is about influence, about shaping the future, and positioning themselves on the right side of history. I'm almost sure I have their support in the bag, but the thing about politics is you can never be sure about something until you actually have it in the bag.

"Daddy, when are we leaving for Amandla's house?" Denise's question brings my head from behind the screen of my MacBook and I check the time—shit, it's almost 12. I got so caught up with work that I almost forgot that I promised to take my kids to Oyama, and then finally go to that blasted therapy session that I've been putting off.

"I'm ready now, Baby. Get your brother, and let's go." I move from my temporary office for the past month. I've moved in permanently into Candice's townhouse. I needed to be closer to her, to smell her scent, even though it has faded with time. Also, it's best for the kids to come back to a place they are used to, not the cold monstrosity I used to live in. I'm on the fence about whether I will sell that house with all its ghosts or rent it out.

"I can't find him upstairs!" Denise screams from upstairs and I go to my man cave, a room that Candice set up for me, because I know that Oyinqaba loves hiding there, because of the top-of-the-range gaming screens. I find my son perched on my Vegas Xtreme highchair, his little tongue sticking out of the corner of his mouth in concentration.

"Nqaba, it's time to go, Nyana," I say gently so that I don't startle him. He turns to me with that big goofy smile and climbs into my arms like the little monkey that he is.

"Ta-ta. What's that, and why does it show Mummy's new home?" my son asks innocently, pointing at the 'Live' emoticon on the screen that is camouflaging the live stream of the CCTV footage from the hidden cameras and drone footage of Candice's new house in Mozambique.

"It's Tata's new secret game and we don't have to tell the girls about it. Okay, Son?" I hand him my little finger for a pinkie promise and he solemnly takes it. He's growing so quickly and he speaks better each time I see him.

Every other weekend isn't cutting it for me anymore. It helps that I watch their daily CCTV footage every night before I finally fall into an exhaustion coma.

I listen to my children as they tell me about their new schools as I strap them into both of their car seats, even though Denise grumbles that she's now too grown for a car seat. I'm closing their door when I turn and I see Phindiwe parked just up the driveway. She looks at me longingly, as if she wants to say something, but her pride won't allow her to grovel, not when she's convinced herself and all of our siblings that I'm ungrateful and that's why I cut her off. She puts on her glasses and drives away, and I get into my SUV and drive away.

Oyama is waiting for us when I drive up her driveway and she has my grandson strapped to her front. She looks just like her mother after she had just had Denise, and that makes my heart ache. Where Candice's face would light up when she sees me, Oyama has the blank look that I've wielded like a weapon my entire life, it makes me both uncomfortable and proud. Her face does soften when Denise dashes into her outstretched arm, giving her a side-hug, while Oyinqaba is hugging her legs.

I take out the small car that I got for the little man, that's almost identical to the one I got his sister but his is in blue and black. Oyama's eyes narrow at my gift, unimpressed. She still thanks me but I think it was for Denise's benefit because once she tells them to go on inside, she turns to me with the same narrowed eyes.

"You're doing it again," she states without preamble, and I'm genuinely confused.

"Doing what?"

"Trying to bribe your way into my children's lives, yet you've never even had a conversation with Amandla or held Sibonakaliso outside of that hospital visit after he was born. Or, maybe I should count myself lucky that with Sibo, you blessed us with your presence, while it took you years to even look at Amandla or say her name without your face twisting into something nasty. If you refuse to have a relationship with my daughter, I will not allow you to have one with my son. I will not have my daughter feel shitty because you have something against the way I chose to defy you and have her, while you're fawning over her brother." With that, she turns and leaves me with my mouth hanging.

I think about Oyama's words all the way to the therapist's office. It wasn't what she said and how she said it that got to me, but it was the pain in her eyes, as if she wasn't talking just about her children. I don't hate my granddaughter… she's just a manifestation of my failure as a parent. I couldn't protect Oyama. I swore that no child of mine would ever go through what I went through and yet, she did, right under my nose.

When I heard that Oyama was pregnant, it was easier to believe that she was sleeping around at such a young age, that she was a teen being naughty, and the truth broke me. I brought Mhlanguli into her life. I was the one supposed to be taking care of her when she slipped out to go to that nightclub with Lola. I'm to blame for that night, and Amandla is a constant reminder of that failure, and then I feel guilty because she's such a precious little thing, and I bought her that car because it was the one thing that I bonded with Yaya over.

I'm on edge when I get to Dr Khumalo's practice and the receptionist goes to announce my presence. I don't intend to stay long as I shake the doctor's hand. She has a firm grip, and she points me towards the couch. I sit up, refusing to relax into the obscenely-comfortable couch.

"Mr Sisulu," she states, and then eyes me as if she can see past the mask I have on.

"Dr Khumalo," I respond in kind, and because I have a tonne of things to do, I get down to why I'm here. "My wife, Candice, has been your client for close to a decade now and she believes you can help me, I don't. But I love my wife and I want to stay married to her. So, how much would it cost for you to report back that we've had these sessions to her, and we both do something else that's worthwhile with our time?"

I don't expect the sudden laugh that breaks out of the doctor. She laughs until she grabs a tissue from the box next to her and then she's dabbing her eyes after having removed her glasses.

"I assure you, Dr Khumalo, I don't joke when it comes to my time. How much? A million? Two million?" She lets out a whistle at the figures that I mention, and I lean back, smug—everyone has a price.

"I see, please excuse me for a moment," she says, while putting back her glasses and reaching for her iPad. I watch bemused as she dials someone and I listen to the dial tone. The phone is answered after a while and I hear the distant sound of waves crashing and wind, before a door closes and then the therapist is talking.

"He offered me two million," Dr Khumalo says, and then she turns the iPad around and suddenly, I'm face to face with Nowami. It's one thing seeing her from the CCTV footage but it's another to see her glowing in real time, her eyes lit up in amusement. She's let her hair be curly and wild; her skin is tanned and has the bronze glimmer of sunscreen, and I want to reach out into the screen and kiss her.

"Daniel, you have to stop offering people money from my estate without discussing it with me first." Her words are laced with laughter and if I wasn't so hungry for any scraps of her that I can get, I would be angry.

"I was going to pay her from my own separate account." I sound petulant, even to my own ears, and Nowami doesn't hide her laugh this time, and it warms me all over. Or, maybe it's the way her full breasts jiggle as she laughs, I want to bury my face in them and never come up for breath.

"Even that is my money. You promised me you'd honour my only ultimatum, Ta' kaOyama." Her voice is gentle, but there's no mistaking the steel underneath it and I feel chastised.

"I don't think I can do it, Nowami. I'm not like you, who's able to confront her feelings." I might as well confess because I've been caught red-handed.

"You are the strongest man I know. I also try to run away from my feelings, and in our session, which was just before yours, Celeste called me out on it. I need you; I need you whole and healthy, Daniel. I'd rather love you from a distance than be with that version of you that was careless with my feelings, careless with my love. Please find it in you to try, not for me, not even for our children, but for the little boy inside you who was hurt and alone. You don't have to hide him and his scars anymore. Allow him to heal, Myen' wami; ngiyakuncenga." I can't see her because somehow, the screen has become blurry. I only realise that I'm crying when the therapist hands me the box of tissues and I nod to Candice; not trusting myself to not sob the moment I open my mouth.

The doctor takes the iPad from me while I get my emotions in check, and she looks at me with kindness but there's no pity there and that eases my raised hackles somewhat.

"Now, would you like us to begin the session, Daniel? Can I call you 'Daniel'?" I nod to both, and then clear my throat.

"I don't know where to begin," I admit, almost sheepishly.

"Wherever the hurt began," Dr Khumalo says, and suddenly, I feel too hot, and she watches me when I take off my tie and jacket and loosen my cufflinks.

"I was four years old when I realised that my family was the laughing stock of the shanty town where we stayed..."

Chapter 52

Candice

Dear Candy,

I hope this letter finds you in a moment of peace, a rare stillness amidst the chaos of our past. As I sit down to write to you, I can almost feel the warmth of your tiny hands and the innocence that radiated from your bright, curious eyes. Celeste suggested I connect with you, my inner child, through regression therapy, and at first, I was sceptical. It felt strange to delve into memories I had buried deep, but she assured me that these moments, however painful, play an integral role in shaping who I am today.

When I finally allowed myself to drift into that sea of memories, it was as if I was swimming through a kaleidoscope of my life, each moment frozen like a snapshot of time. I had anticipated encountering Masase, that comforting figure from my childhood, but instead, I was drawn to you. There you were, so small and fragile, with skin like cream and a rosebud mouth that I longed to cover in kisses. The urge to gather you in my arms and shield you from all the hurt was overwhelming.

The first memory that surfaced was of you taking those tentative first steps toward Mama. I can still see you wobbling, your little feet barely able to carry your excitement. Yet, instead of the joyful encouragement you so deserved, you were met with harsh words and a frown that crushed your spirit. I watched as tears brimmed in your eyes, and when you stumbled and fell, she simply turned away, leaving you alone in your pain. My heart broke for you then, and even now, the weight of that moment lingers heavily on my soul. I wished so desperately to scoop you up, to tell you that everything would be all right, but the hurt was too profound.

The memories continued to unfold, each one more heart-wrenching than the last. I saw you during potty training, the confusion and shame washing over you when accidents happened. It wasn't fair; you were so little, trying to figure everything out in a world that seemed so big and scary. When she hit you, the impact of her anger reverberated through my very being. Every lash against your tender skin felt like a dagger aimed at my heart. I remember the way you crawled toward her, seeking comfort, only to be pushed away and hurt again. The moment you hit your head on the corner of the bench, I felt a surge of protectiveness like never before. I scooped you up then, holding you tightly as if I could absorb all the pain you had endured, but even in that embrace, I felt utterly powerless.

As the memories swirled around me like a tempest, I felt your anguish manifest in my own sobs. It was a painful reminder of the wounds we both carry. I longed for it all to stop, for the cycle of hurt to end, but the memories kept coming. I saw you clinging to her skirts as she prepared to leave you in Maebani, your heart filled with desperate pleas for her affection, for her love. It was gut-wrenching to witness how you yearned for her approval, even in the face of rejection. She simply brushed your hands aside, leaving you in a sea of sorrow, without even a backward glance.

But then, just when I thought I couldn't bear it any longer, someone else came into the picture. They picked you up, cradling you in their roughened hands, and I whispered softly, "You are safe now, she will love you." In that moment, I realised that while the past cannot be changed, there is still hope for love and healing.

Emerging from that session, I was a sobbing mess, but I also felt a strange sense of clarity. Days later, Celeste encouraged me to write you this letter, and I am grateful for the opportunity. I want you to know, with every fibre of my being, that it was never you. You were never unlovable or undeserving of love. The hurt inflicted upon you was a reflection of your mother's own pain, a cycle of anguish that should never have touched your innocent heart.

You deserved love then, and you still do now. I wish beyond measure that I could hug you a million times over, to shower you with kisses and remind you how precious you truly are. You are worthy, Candy, of kindness, affection, and all the beautiful things this world has to offer.

As I write this, I promise to carry you with me, to honour our shared journey, and to nurture the love that should have always been yours. Together, we will heal, and I will strive to be the protector you have always needed.

With all my love,

Your older self

Chapter 53

Daniel

I keep having this dream. Each night, it's the same haunting vision. I find myself in a dimly-lit room, and there she is, my mother, sitting curled up on the floor. Her arms are wrapped tightly around her legs, as if trying to shield herself from the world. There's a weight in the air, a palpable sadness that clings to me.

Each time, I feel an overwhelming urge to reach out to her, but I'm rooted to the spot, helpless. Then the mood shifts—her silence breaks, and she begins to wail, a heart-wrenching sound that pierces through me. I can see her hands clutching the top of her head, fingers tangled in her hair, as though she's trying to grasp the pain that consumes her.

I wake up in a sweat, heart racing, the echo of her cries still ringing in my ears. The dream lingers, shadows of her sorrow following me into the waking world, and I can't shake off the feeling that I'm meant to save her from whatever it is that haunts her.

I stretch myself, trying to ease the creaks on my neck, a result of falling asleep in front of the monitors again. I've taken to sleeping here since Candice's scent completely faded from the sheets. Watching her soothe the kids into their nightly routine before she hands them the iPad to call me is my favourite time of the day. I long to see her naked, I made sure to ask that no cameras were installed in her bedroom and bathroom because I don't know who controls these feeds and I don't want them to see my woman naked.

I'm about to go grab a shower and carry out my assignment from Dr Khumalo when I catch a glimpse of Candice on the screen. She's wearing yoga pants and a sports bra, with a yoga mat under her armpit. What stops me dead in my tracks is the bump beneath her breasts. It feels like someone poured icy water down my spine. How did I miss this? She's been wearing a one-piece swimsuit with her yoga pants and I didn't think much of her weight gain, the glow, the full breasts. The first instinct that rises to the forefront of my being is to leave everything behind and be with her—to hell with the plan or her stupid boundaries. Candice's pregnancies have gotten progressively bad—she even had to be on bed rest with Oyinqaba—so when she said she's taking the shot, I was fully on board because I had been there, watching her suffer and doing everything I could, but it didn't feel enough. Who is rubbing her back and her feet or holding her hair while she throws up?

Then the burning need to be there for her morphs into disbelief and denial. Candice can't be pregnant. She would have told me, just as she excitedly handed me both Denise and Oyinqaba's positive tests after they were conceived. Then doubt creeps in, what if she didn't tell me because it's not my child? Is that the reason she was insisting that she wants to be as far away from me as possible? I rubbish the thoughts before they take root but the sting of betrayal still lingers: She knowingly kept the news of this pregnancy from me. It explains her sickness around Sibonakaliso's birth. I rub my chest, trying to alleviate the physical ache in my heart. Were we so far gone that she would keep this from me?

All the questions swirl around my head as I watch her stretch while facing the ocean from her garden. The rays of the rising sun bounce off her skin, setting it to a golden-orange glow. I can't take my eyes off her stomach, where she's growing a life, where my seed is being incubated. I close my eyes and try to feel the pain of this moment without shoving it into one of the compartments in my brain. Dr Khumalo has been encouraging me to allow myself to feel every emotion fully. I still think therapy is hogwash, but she's not half bad because somehow, it's easier to talk to her, to tell her moments that I have kept to myself for fear of being weak. She, in turn, calls me out whenever I try to manipulate the narrative to make myself look better and she gives me bloody assignments, like the one I have to do today. I take one last look at Wami and then drag myself to shower upstairs.

I drive while on the phone with my PA, going through my schedule for the week halfheartedly; my heart and mind is with Nowami and our growing family right now and the assignment that I have to carry out. I assure my PA that I'll look at the proposals that she emailed me and then I put on Hugh Masekela. Dr Khumalo has been teaching me to give my father grace, to try and see him as a human who was broken by his family and the system that kept black men inebriated to further break them. Most days, I hate him, but some days, like today, I wish he had been present enough to know me and guide me.

The security at Oyama's complex allow me in after calling them to confirm my visit. I'm about to drive off when the security asks for a selfie with me. I give him my best election smile and then drive off. My son-in-law opens the door for me, with his son strapped to his front and my granddaughter glued to his side. My hands itch to take the baby from him but remembering Oyama's words, I force my attention to Amandla instead.

"Hi, Amandla. How are you?" I feel shitty when the little girl's eyes widen and she looks at Sipho furtively before turning to me and taking my offered hand.

"I'm good, Mkhulu. What did you bring for me? Is it in your car?"

"Amandla!" her dad reprimands her, while I laugh heartily; she's her mother's daughter, alright.

"I didn't bring anything today, but if you parents agree, I'd like to take you on a date soon and we can go anywhere you want." My words make her face light up so much, it makes my heart ache again for all the time I've missed because I was a giant prick.

"Really?" She scrunches her nose in suspicion, then says almost flippantly, "I want to go to San Diego Animal Sanctuary and Farm. It's one of the top petting zoos in the world."

"Amandla, that's not what Mkhulu meant, he—"

I cut Sipho off, and I take Amandla's hand and link our fingers in a pinkie promise. "Deal. We can go together next month, when it's school holidays. That is if your parents agree." The excited squeal that she lets out tells me that I have many petting zoos in my future.

"Go and get your mother," Sipho orders Amandla, and then he leads me to the lounge. It is tastefully decorated; simple, but also feels lived in from the toys and the books in one corner. I stretch my arms, and luckily, Sipho gets the memo and hands me a sleeping Sibonakaliso. He's the cutest little boy I've ever seen, after Oyinqaba.

"I need to ask you something pertaining a dream that I keep having," I tell Sipho, the weight of the vision still heavy on my chest. "I dream of my mother, sitting with her arms wrapped around her legs, looking so lost. Then she starts wailing, her hands clutching her head. At times, she's walking around, looking lost, and I try to reach for her to guide her but all I can reach are her piercing cries. It's haunting."

Sipho leans back in his chair, his brow furrowing as he processes my words. "You know," he begins thoughtfully, "I think there's more to this than just a dream. It sounds like your mother is trying to communicate something important."

"What do you mean?" I ask, curiosity piqued, cradling the baby carefully to my chest, ensuring that his neck isn't turned in an awkward angle.

He takes a deep breath, meeting my gaze with a seriousness that makes my heart race. "She might be trapped, unable to find peace. She struggled to feel accepted, especially in this place. Maybe she needs you to help her move on, to free her spirit."

I blink, his words settling over me like a heavy cloak. I never shared my mother's background with him and I doubt that Nowami would have either. "Free her spirit? But how? What can I do?"

"You need to acknowledge her pain, honour her memory, and perhaps perform a ritual or something that signifies letting go. She can't rest if she feels bound to a place that never accepted her," Sipho explains, his voice steady and reassuring.

I ponder his words, feeling a mixture of fear and hope. "You really think that would help?"

"I do," he replies, a gentle smile breaking through his seriousness. "Sometimes, we have to confront the past to set the future free."

I'm still trying to digest his words when Oyama comes into the lounge in a hoodie that looks almost like a dress on her because it's so big. Her pajama shorts peek beneath the hoodie and some tattoos trail down her legs. She looks like she was just woken up.

"Did anything happen to Candice or Denise or Oyinqaba or Monwabisi?" she asks, without greeting.

"Your mother and brother and sister are okay. Monwabisi is with his mother," I reply, a touch gruff because I'm rethinking my assignment. My armpits have begun to itch.

"Then, what the fuck are you doing here?" she asks, her brows raised in confusion.

"Nokwindla!" Sipho admonishes her the same way he admonished Amandla. My ego is telling me, To hell with Dr Khumalo, I don't need to sit here and be treated with such disdain. I close my eyes and count back until the urge passes, then I look at my daughter.

"I'm here to apologise to you." My words are met with deathly silence, only broken by Sipho getting up and taking the baby from me. Then, before he goes out, he says something to Oyama that I don't quite catch but it makes her shoulders drop, and she comes and sits where he was sitting, curling her feet beneath the hoodie. Then she stares at me, waiting for me to continue.

"There's so much that I did wrong with you," I push past the sudden lump in my throat, "Taking you from your birth mother, not telling you about Candice until you heard Mpumi and I arguing, and it only got worse from there. I failed you when Mhlanguli… When he hurt you like that. It was my fault, I should have looked after you better, Mpumi wouldn't have slipped up like that, and I hated myself for that failure. Every time I looked at Amandla, it was a constant reminder that I failed you, and that wasn't fair on her or on you. I swore I'd be a better father to my children than my father was to us but I'm worse, because I can't hide behind alcohol. I'm sorry that I made you feel like you didn't matter to me as much as your siblings. I'm sorry that I didn't try harder to reach out to you, you deserved better, and if you'll have me, I'd like to start over. I want to be the kind of father that you deserve, one you can be proud of."

Oyama's stare is unwavering and it feels like she's looking into my soul. "Why now?"

"I've been attending therapy, and Dr Khumalo told me a few hard truths. I can't fix the past but a good starting point is admitting my mistakes, taking accountability for how my actions hurt those that I love, and some talk about boundaries, which I think is a lot of shit, but I'm trying." I laugh nervously at my lame attempt at levity.

"I appreciate your apology. I'm trying to process it, but I'm not sure I trust the sentiment behind it and whether it's genuine or a bid to get back with Candice." I suck in a breath, but before I can assure her that I meant every word, she continues, "I need time to process it and your actions to back up your words. I had to build walls around my heart after you tore it to pieces again and again. A simple apology won't erase that, neither will it lower my walls; but if you're trying, I can also try."

Her words are harsh but I see the lone tear that falls from her eye and I know that inside, she's still that fifteen-year-old girl who needed me to love her harder; instead, I let her down. So, I release a breath and lower my hackles. Maybe one day, I'll tell her that we're a lot alike than she knows, but right now, I need to heal my little girl, not burden her further with my own trauma.

"Can I give you a hug?" I ask tentatively, and Oyama hesitates for a moment before she crawls onto my lap and I cradle her just as I cradled my grandson. I sit there, blinking back my tears, and my heart expands when her hand rests on my chest. Maybe there's redemption for the bond we once had.

Chapter 54

Candice

Dear Naledzi ya Masase,

Oh, what a dazzling little star you are; illuminating the world around you with your boundless energy and infectious joy! I have taken great pleasure in sharing stories about you with Denise and Oyinqaba, recounting your delightful escapades in Maebani that seem to dance across my mind like vibrant images.

They listen intently as I tell them about that unforgettable day when you, filled with unrestrained enthusiasm, attempted to climb the towering pawpaw tree. Your small hands grasped the rough bark, determination glinting in your eyes. What a sight you were! If only that mischievous boy hadn't come along to shake the tree, sending you tumbling back to the ground, where your laughter rang out like the sweetest melody.

I share with them the tales of your insatiable curiosity, that wonderful spark that drove you to run everywhere, as if the world were a grand adventure waiting to be explored. You had such a strong dislike for shoes, relishing the feeling of warm earth beneath your feet, and there was a special thrill in escaping into the shade. Makhulu worried endlessly about the harsh Limpopo sun on your fair skin, her face etched with concern, but you would fidget and squirm until, with a resigned sigh, she would finally relent and allow you the freedom to dash off once again, your spirit uncontainable.

I reminisce about your incredible throwing skills in magava, where you effortlessly returned all the stones to the circle with a precision that seemed almost magical. Denise, eager to learn the game, begged to play, and we began indoors. But when we nearly shattered my glass coffee table, we had no choice but to venture outside to the beach. Denise is surprisingly good at throwing, but she simply cannot hold a candle to you—my extraordinary star. The way her eyes light up when she hears your name, how she thinks you are so cool because of the games I've taught her, fills my heart with warmth and pride.

Recently, I have taken to exploring the stunning landscapes of Mozambique, a place I know you yearned to see. You did, after your adventures in Maebani and Gauteng; spending nearly a decade working on a cruise ship, and I can only imagine how enchanted you would be by the palm-fringed white sandy beaches and the alluring remote islands. Just last week, we had the incredible fortune of spotting an actual sable in Gorongosa National Park, a sight so breathtaking that it made my heart flutter with joy.

While the children were spending time with their father, I escaped for a blissful weekend at the Bazaruto Archipelago, immersing myself in the crystal-clear waters while snorkelling and discovering the vibrant underwater world. It was during this delightful excursion that a cheeky samango monkey snatched my half-eaten sandwich right from my hand. I couldn't help but burst into laughter, a sound so reminiscent of yours that it felt as if you were right there beside me, sharing in the joy of the moment. Once this baby arrives, I promise to take you on an exhilarating ocean safari in Tofo, a charming little village along the coast, where the waves sing and the sun dips below the horizon in a breathtaking display.

Something truly magical happened recently. I decided to tell Denise about the time you were unable to receive your awards because Makhulu had passed away, and you had to move to Gauteng. Her eyes sparkled with interest, eager to absorb every detail about you. I believe she thinks I'm rather cool now, all thanks to your wonderful legacy. Just yesterday, at her award ceremony, Denise boldly requested the microphone. With a beaming smile, she explained to everyone that she has a special award for a bright little girl from Maebani who dreamt of becoming a doctor and ultimately became a skin doctor, instead.

You should have seen the crowd, their faces lighting up with admiration as they clapped for you, my beautiful little star. I made my way to the stage to accept the award on your behalf, and I know you might roll your eyes at me for how emotional I was, but I simply couldn't help it. The award bore your name, along with the name of Luvhivhini Primary School, complete with the school badge, and as I held it in my hands, I felt an overwhelming sense of pride and love. You would have been so proud, my darling.

Denise recently suggested that I should write a book about you and she even had a title: Masase's wild adventures in Maebani. It's catchy, isn't it? Denise reminds me so much of you, your fearlessness and your smarts, and I told her that we should write the book together. Her smile was blinding, and I truly have you to thank, Masase.

From the depths of my heart, I want to thank you for being one of the brightest lights in my life, a radiant beacon that continuously reminds me of my own strength and intelligence, of all that I can achieve when I set my mind to it. I find myself laughing more with my children, relishing the stories I share about you, and I hope they will carry these tales forward, telling their children and generations to come about Naledzi ya Masase—the morning star who shone brightly, chasing away the darkness with her laughter and light.

With all my love,

Candice

Chapter 55

Daniel

I stand before the Speaker's desk, the weight of the moment pressing down on me like the humid air of a summer afternoon in Pretoria. The chamber is quiet, the usual bustling energy replaced by an uneasy stillness, as if the very walls are holding their breath. I can feel her gaze, sharp and probing, as she studies my face.

"Minister Sisulu," she begins, her voice steady yet laced with concern, "this is unexpected. You were on the brink of greatness. A rising star, they said. What has prompted this decision?"

I swallow hard, struggling to find the words that have been swirling in my mind for weeks. "It's not a decision I've made lightly," I reply, my voice barely above a whisper. "I've enjoyed serving the people, pushing for progress, but… it's time for me to step away."

She raises an eyebrow in a way that resembles Phindiwe so much, it makes my heart ache, the hint of disbelief flickering in her eyes. "Daniel, you're not embroiled in any scandal. There's no public outcry. Why now?"

A bittersweet smile tugs at my lips, memories flooding back. We've shared laughter, debates, and the occasional late-night strategy session that blurred the lines between politics and friendship. She's one of the good ones.

"You know me well enough to understand that sometimes, it's not about the noise outside," I say, my heart heavy with the weight of unspoken truths. "It's about what's happening inside. I've lost my passion. The fire that once drove me now feels like embers. I can't lead when I'm no longer inspired."

I don't mention how the goal posts have shifted, the dice has been cast and I'm going to continue leading, albeit in the shadows. She studies me with a mixture of empathy and frustration, her brow furrowing. "You were destined for greatness. You could have been president one day."

I chuckle softly, the irony cutting deep. "Destiny is a fickle thing, isn't it? I've come to realise that greatness isn't always about position or power. Sometimes, it's about knowing when to step back, to let others take the mantle."

Her silence hangs between us, thick and heavy. I can sense her disappointment—both in me and perhaps in the political landscape itself. "And? What will you do now?" she finally asks, the question tinged with genuine concern.

"I don't know," I admit, the honesty lacing my words like a fragile thread. I've done my part and orchestrated support for Shefu and now, I wait in the shadows. "Perhaps I'll find a way to serve outside these walls. Or, maybe I'll simply take a moment to breathe. I owe myself that much."

There's a poignancy in her expression as she nods slowly, understanding dawning in her eyes. "You've always been more than just a politician to me," she says softly. "You've been a friend, a voice of wisdom. If this is truly what you must do, then I support you."

I feel a swell of gratitude, mixed with the ache of finality. "Thank you," I reply, my voice thick with emotion. "That means more than you know. I hope one day, you'll understand why I had to do this."

As I turn to leave, the echoes of the chamber follow me, a bittersweet reminder of the path I've walked. I glance back at the Speaker, her silhouette framed by the light pouring in through the windows. There's a moment of connection, a silent understanding that transcends words. I may be stepping away, but the memories, the friendships, and the dream that has shaped my every waking moment up until this moment remain heavily yoked with my spirit.

Yes, I might have been on this journey to get power and exact revenge but I was damn good at my job and I'm going to miss the rush, the chaos of the House, the thrill of my motions being moved to Bills. The heat of debates and then the drinking sprees that occurred afterwards to 'cool down'. Handing in my resignation letter to the head of the Party went by with a bit of reluctance, back and forth, Jimmy enjoying the pretense of not knowing the true reason behind my resignation a little too much. He's always been one for theatrics—a show pony, if you will.

My phone lights up with an email reminder from my PA. She's taken my resignation the hardest, and if she wasn't such a sharp political mind, I might have kept her on my payroll but she has a long successful career ahead of her in politics, not in the shadows with me. I got her a gig with a female MP who's decent. I've grown fond of my PA ever since she extorted money from Mandisa by claiming to be pregnant with my child.

As I close the email thread, my eyes linger on my wallpaper. It's a picture of me with Amandla hanging on my neck like a monkey at the San Diego Animal Sanctuary that was taken on our one-on-one date there. Oyama wasn't keen on the date but she ended up relenting. I'm still working on getting Oyama to go on a date with me; baby steps.

Traffic is hell on the N14 and I almost speak myself out of continuing to my destination, but that's just my cowardice speaking. My latest session with Dr Khumalo comes to mind.

Dr Khumalo leant forward slightly, her expression compassionate yet firm. 'It's crucial to understand that while your actions were deeply harmful, they are not the entirety of who you are. You've faced significant trauma yourself, and that can sometimes manifest in ways that are destructive.'

'But I should have known better. I should have been in control,' I said, frustration creeping into my voice. 'I can't keep blaming my past.'

'You're right; taking responsibility is vital,' she replied gently. 'But, it's equally important to recognise the patterns that led to that moment. Blackouts can be a response to overwhelming emotions, often rooted in unresolved trauma. Your experience at 14—being violated—created a fracture within you. It's understandable that in moments of stress, you might lose control.'

As hard as it was, I had to look back at the husband I was to Nompumelelo, and I outlined all of the horrible things I did to her, and Dr Khumalo didn't even flinch. 'You are still capable of growth and change. Understanding your trauma doesn't excuse your actions, but it provides context. It's about finding a path to healing and making amends, not just for your ex-wife but for yourself as well.'

I took a deep breath, the weight of her words settling in. 'But, how do I apologise? What if she can't forgive me?'

'That's a possibility, and it's important to prepare for that,' she said. 'An apology should be sincere, acknowledging the pain you caused without expecting anything in return. It's about taking accountability and showing her that you understand the depth of your actions. Change begins with awareness and the willingness to confront uncomfortable truths. Together, we can work through this.'

* * *

Well, here goes nothing, I think as I pull into Nompumelelo's house. This house is a beautiful blend of both Nompumelelo and her husband, Jarred. It carries a warmth that only radiates from two people who are truly in love. Another time, that thought would have stung, but I realise that, for so long, I was more in love with the idea of being with Nompumelelo than actually being with her; I put her on a pedestal, yet totally ignored her autonomy and feelings as a person. As Candice told me, I was callous to other people's feelings as long as my vision was served.

I called ahead, so I find Mpumi and Jarred waiting for me at the door and after a few awkward greetings, they lead me to the lounge. The last time I was here was after I was informed of Oyama's pregnancy, and there's more pictures now on the wall, beaming faces of their family and a well-lived life that brings a pang to my heart.

"Daniel, I was surprised when I received your call," Mpumi opens up the conversation once she's offered me juice, and I twirl the glass nervously.

"It's long overdue. I know I apologised before, but I don't think I realised then the weight of all the wrongs I did to you. This apology also extends to you, Jarred, I'm deeply sorry for stealing your child's life. There's no excuse for the pain that I caused you, and Mpumi, the last time... the last time I touched you, I knew it was wrong the moment I saw what I'd done and saw you coiled away from me. It's no excuse but I wanted you to know that... I was sexually abused from the age of 14. Phindiwe pimped me out to some wealthy man's wife in exchange for their support with my political career." I almost stop when I hear Mpumi's sharp intake of breath but I soldier on. the words coming out in a rush.

"It was... It was horrible, and I started blacking out after one particularly rough session where they chained me down like a dog and had their way with me. It was a shame I carried secretly with me for years. At times, when triggered, I do black out and when I come to, the damage is done. I have hated myself for that moment, but my ego wouldn't allow me to tell you all that before. It won't take away your pain or fix the past, but from the bottom of my heart, I'm sorry."

I'm so focused on Mpumi's wet face as she silently cries while looking at me that I miss Jarred standing up and aiming at me. His right hook lands nearly on my left cheek. "This is for *my child!*" My head snaps to the side and I temper down the instinct to strike back or hide my face. The hook on my left face is worse than the first, bursting my lip. "And this is for hurting my woman, you fucken *dick!*"

Jarred pulls back his arm and lands another hit, on my lower stomach, this time. I grunt as I fold. "And this is for Amandla and Yaya."

I feel the air leaving my body for a moment and when I come to, Mpumi is shouting at Jarred, who seems unbothered, and I retch, before turning over and spitting out blood. Mpumi looks alarmed, and Jarred is starting to look concerned, until I bare my blood-streaked teeth at him in a manic grin and say, "You punch like a bitch."

Chapter 56

Candice

15-year-old Candice,

Hi, Candice!

I can almost picture you rolling your eyes at that exclamation mark because I know it feels like there's very little to be happy about right now. You might feel like you've become exactly what your mother has always derided you for, and now, you find yourself pregnant at just fifteen. It's as if the weight of the world is pressing down on your shoulders, and I can only imagine how you dread the moment when everyone starts asking why you keep wearing that oversized jersey. You can only tie your breasts and stomach for so long before the dragon lady, as you like to call her, notices something is amiss.

Your worst fears materialise before you: You have to drop out of school, and Gladys drags you to Daniel in a way that feels unbearably humiliating. When he doesn't deny the baby, as you had feared, it's almost worse than you imagined. Brace yourself, Candice; he's going to marry someone else just a week before you give birth. And to add to the heartache, he plans to take your child a day before Gladys's funeral, raising her with his new wife. It's a lot to bear, I know.

But, before you let that anger consume you, I want you to understand something vital: This turns out to be the best decision for all of you in the long run. Your child will grow up surrounded by love, while you return to school and ultimately earn two qualifications in beauty therapy. You end up owning your own beauty bar, a place where you pour your heart and soul into helping others feel beautiful. That child you are carrying, Candice, becomes a little medical prodigy, diving into fascinating scientific research. She recently celebrated the birth of her second child and is happily married, living a life full of possibilities.

So, why am I sharing all of this with you? It's simple: You have been angry for so long, and I want to remind you that this anger didn't break you. I know that sometimes, it twisted you up inside, making you feel as though it would claw its way out of you to live a life of its own, a life of destruction. Yes, you spiralled out of control, faced unspeakable violations, and were beaten to an inch of your life.

But, by some miracle, you made it, Candice.

You made it through life without the love of a father, who, I'm afraid to say, turned out to be a total disappointment. He died yesterday, alone and miserable, and I chose not to visit him. He didn't deserve anything from me—not my presence, not my anger, nor my forgiveness. I'm sorry for making this about me; I know you don't need to hear that right now, so, no rolling your eyes!

The anger didn't win, nor did the bitterness swallow you whole. You found peace with Gladys, and now, I think of her as 'Mama', even after all these years. It's been over twenty years since she passed, and I've come to realise that, at one point, she was just as angry and isolated as you felt. You have three beautiful children now, and there's a fourth on the way. I know you swore you wouldn't have another child after the first, but each new life has chipped away at your anger, bringing you a little more peace each time.

When I look in the mirror today, I don't see or feel that anger anymore. You held onto it for so long that it nearly crushed you, but only in letting go of it completely did I come into my full power. I deeply regret that I allowed you to wallow in self-doubt and loathing for such an extended period.

I'm truly sorry that you sought love in the arms of a man who was just as broken as you were. I'm sorry that, for so long, you couldn't see beyond your mistakes, hurt, and anger. I'm sorry that life seemed to conspire against you, and even when things did go your way, you would often sabotage yourself.

But I also want to express my immense gratitude for you, Candice. At just fifteen, you withstood pain that could have knocked down an elephant. You kept fighting to stay afloat, even when it felt like you were drowning in despair. I am grateful that you didn't listen to Mapura and try to have a backdoor abortion; you always were the smart one.

Now, I'm going to wrap my arms around you and hug you until you squirm and bat my hands away. I'm going to kiss you because you need all the affection I can possibly give you. Beyond the anger, the hostility, and the bitterness, I see you, Candice.

I truly see you.

Love,

43-year-old Candice

P.S. I love you.

P.S.S. I'm relieved that the trend of removing all your eyebrows just to draw them back on stayed in the 90s. You were right not to jump on that train!

Chapter 57

Daniel

"What happened to your face?" Are the first words Candice says for our combined therapy session, but I'm too busy cataloguing how her face has plumped up in the past three months to respond. I take in her healthy, luminous complexion and how bright her eyes are, even though they are currently narrowed at me.

"Daniel!" she snaps me out of my perusal and I've forgotten what she asked, so I say the one thing that's on my mind.

"You're glowing..." Her sharp breath-intake is damning, as is the way her eyes dart to Dr Khumalo before she bats those long lashes, thinking of a way to change the topic. It hurts that she's keeping our child a secret, but I'm trying my best to not take more than she's willing to give me at the moment.

"You look like you face-planted a wall," Candice says, and I just shrug, still stung by the fact that she won't tell me that she's pregnant.

Dr Khumalo clears her throat to get both our attention and start the session. It's the first joint session that we're having and I'm nervous. The room feels tense as I sit across from the screen that shows Candice, the therapist's voice cutting through the silence.

"Do either of you know what trauma bonding is?" she asks, her gaze shifting between us. I glance at Candice, whose eyes dart away, a sign that she's retreating into herself.

I clear my throat, feeling the weight of my past pressing down on me. "It's when two people bond over shared trauma, isn't it? Like, a connection formed through pain?"

"That's right, Daniel," Dr Khumalo replies, nodding. "And both of you have experienced a significant similar pattern of trauma in your youth. Sexual abuse, parental neglect... These experiences shape who you are. Candice, you've often shrunk yourself, haven't you? Avoiding conflict, wanting to stay in the shadows, putting everyone's feelings before yours, and keeping your voice down. When I first met you, you'd say 'sorry' about twenty times each session."

I steal a glance at Candice. I can see the tension in her shoulders, the way she hunches slightly, as if trying to become smaller, less noticeable. It stings to see her like this, and I feel a surge of protectiveness mixed with guilt because in a way, I let her stay in the shadows because it benefited my ruthless plans.

"And Daniel," Dr Khumalo continues, turning her attention to me. "You've inflated your presence, perhaps as a way to cope. That need for validation, that desire to be seen at any and all cost. The need to hide behind power and riches—there are traces of narcissism in your behaviour."

Her words hit me like a slap. I shift uncomfortably in my chair, a mix of shame and defensiveness rising within me. "I didn't choose to be this way," I say, a bit too forcefully. "It's how I survived. I had to be bigger than everything that happened to me. How else was I going to fit into politics? There was no space for the nerdy little boy who grew up in a shanty town, the poorest of the poor. I had to work twice as hard as everyone in the room so that I could stand out and be picked."

Candice's voice is barely a whisper when she speaks, "And I had to disappear. My skin bothered my mother, she hated when people would bring it up, and now, I know it was because of the white part of my DNA. I just learnt that if I shrunk into the shadows, no one bothered me. It was easier that way." There's a sadness in her tone that cuts through the room like a brand new, sharp knife. I want to reach out and touch her, to bridge the gap that has grown between us, but she's in another country because she needed to get away from me before she lost herself fully.

The therapist watches us intently, her expression compassionate yet firm. "You both carry scars from your past, scars that have influenced your relationship. But it's important to ask yourselves: Beyond your trauma bond, is your love worth salvaging?"

"Yes!" The word comes out confident and pushy. Then I look at Candice, her eyes glistening with unshed tears. I want to tell her that I love her, that I'm willing to fight for us, but the words suddenly stick in my throat. Instead, I say, "I don't know. I… I just… I don't want to hurt you anymore."

Candice nods slowly, her gaze unwavering. "I don't want to hurt either of us. But I'm scared, Daniel. Scared of falling back into old patterns where I'm living in the shadows, waiting for scraps of your light to live on. I know I made you and myself believe that I want that. That I was content, but the few months I've been here have shown me that I wasn't living then, Ta' kaOyama, I was surviving, and I can never go back to that. I'm scared that you'll take another wife and the thought of it is crippling me…"

I want to tell Candice that there hasn't been any other woman since she left and that there never will be. I'm done with that version of me, but I know my words won't mean much, so I intend to show her instead.

The therapist interjects gently when Candice hasn't continued speaking, even after she finishes dabbing her now blotchy face with tissues. "Fear is a natural response, but it doesn't have to define you. Acknowledging your trauma is the first step towards healing. Can you both commit to working on this together?"

"I want to try," I say, my voice steadier now. "I don't want to dim your light anymore, and I won't be taking any other wife. I need to know which of my actions make you feel small and figure out how to stop hurting you."

Candice meets my gaze, her expression softening. "I want that, too. I want to know who we can be, without the weight of our past."

Dr Khumalo smiles, sensing the shift in the room. "That's a good start. A willingness to confront your trauma and support one another is crucial. Remember, healing is a journey, not a destination."

The session is only an hour long but it is intense, and it leaves me vulnerable and feeling raw. I drive straight home, ignoring all the pending work that I need to sign off on before my notice is served and my resignation is announced. I'm agitated and drained, I forgo my nightly sojourn of watching the CCTV footage and climb into bed.

I toss and turn, Candice brought up how my sleeping around made feel small and unsafe, then I had to admit that I was a gigolo for not only the scarecrow, but that she'd passed me around to her friends and to cover that shame, I had to make it look like I was a philanderer rather than a gigolo. Dr Khumalo reminded me how my fixation with appearance stems from my need to be in control but I only had a semblance of control until I faced all of my issues head on.

I don't know when I fall asleep but I see my mother almost instantly. This time, she's facing me and it's almost eerie the way that she's silently looking at me but I can feel the heaviness of her despair through the tightening around my chest. Then she lets out one sharp cry, that's when I see that she is crying but her tears are blood.

I wake up with a start and freak out when I check my pillow and there's blood all over the Egyptian cotton pillowcase and sheets. I jump away from the bed and switch on the light and that's when I see the blood that's dripping from my nose. I haven't had a nosebleed since my mother's burial. I clean myself as much as I can then I hightail out of the house, still in my PJs.

I bang at her door, uncaring that it's a little after 3 a.m., I bang until Phindiwe opens, looking regal in her Japanese kimono nightgown. She takes one look at me, and opens her arms. I start sobbing the moment I feel the warmth of her embrace, and she shuts the door behind me, probably with her foot.

* * *

Phindiwe, our siblings, and I brought our mother's spirit to Devende, the village that she came from, close to the Kosi Bay border post. We rented a villa in Ponta da Ouro and we made a holiday out of it. It was the first family holiday we've ever had and Phindiwe decided that next year, we will come back and bring our children. If she thinks I'm buying them a property down here, she should keep dreaming. I've paid my dues and her children can buy her whatever else she wants.

She's still Phindiwe, bossy, militant, and when she tried to pry into my issues with Mandisa, and subsequently, Candice, I told her firmly to butt out, and she did. For now, we are taking tentative steps at reconciliation. It felt good to be around my family, even though I left them at the break of dawn to drive to Sommerschield to watch Candice and our children like a creep. I know it's an important weekend for them, Candice is having a maternity shoot with the kids in the morning and then, in the late afternoon, it's the opening ceremony for her beauty bar.

I drive past Grandeur International School, where Denise and Oyinqaba go to school, and after a short ten-minute drive, I see my R30 million investment almost immediately. Set apart from the other beachfront properties—hidden beneath blooming acacias, frangipani, and bougainvillea, lies a dusky pink monstrosity because my wife refused to have it in the white colour that it came in—is my family's home. Pride settles warm and welcome as I watch the camera crew set up from the security house that Candice isn't aware of just a couple of yards from our property. I sleep easier knowing that someone is looking out for them twenty-four-seven.

I wait until they are engrossed in the shoot before I walk down to be closer. It's utter chaos. Candice is incandescent and ethereal in a flowing red chiffon crop-top and matching skirt that has a long tail. I cannot take my eyes off her, head thrown back as she laughs at something that Oyinqaba said. Then the screams turn chaotic when Oyama makes her entrance with her two children and I stand, unseen, but my heart brimming with gratitude for the beautiful family that I wouldn't have had if I hadn't offered to carry the girl with the wild curls in a crowded bus back in the 90s.

Chapter 58

Candice

I feel a deep contentment as I trail my fingers at the life-size portrait from my recent underwater maternity shoot. The photographer and his team mounted it for me on the wall just next to the meandering staircase. It's perfect. Holding the shoot in the ocean instead of a pool was a gamble but it paid off; the pictures are gorgeous! The portrait is my favourite—the red chiffon floating around me and the aquatic life makes the portrait seem ethereal. I look and felt like a goddess.

I grin as I look at the smaller portraits of Oyinqaba with his snorkelling goggles and Denise holding baby-blue boots. There's another big portrait that holds Oyama, Amandla, Denise, and Oyinqaba all cradling my belly while I held a sleeping Sibonakaliso in my arms. That moment is one that I could relive forever, and the photographer managed to capture the content serenity on my face. The shoot was fun and the highlight of my pregnancy. Now, I just feel heavy and I want this baby out. The doctor is surprised that the baby has hung on this long.

My little fighter.

I feel restless, so I take all the letters tied in a ribbon that I've written to myself at different stages in my life, a large clear jar that Denise bought for me, and leave the house. I take the short scenic walk to the beach. I can hear the birds chirping on the treetops. There is no sound of cars or motorcycles on this side of town, as most people prefer to walk. It's peaceful and perfect.

My heart soars as I see my bar gleaming in the peak of sunset. 'Eileithyia', claim your beauty, is written in elegant, bold letters on the glass walls. A lot of times, women lose themselves in childbirth and rearing, I opened the bar to offer them an escape and a means for them to tap into their beauty beyond being a mother.

With a small playing pen for children, it is fast becoming popular among tourists and locals alike. A place where the kids can play while the mother gets some much-needed pampering was a stroke of genius on my part. I based it on my experiences and needs as a mother of four.

I have been depressed shortly after giving birth before, and I know a day out and full-on pampering would have helped me some. We launched the bar on the same day as the maternity shoot, which happened to be a day before Mother's Day and the launch was a success. Oyama managed to attend it as well as Nomaswazi and they seem to be bonding well, I was just sad that they couldn't stay for more than the weekend.

I don't head towards it because, at this point, my manager is likely to chase me away with a broom. I take my shoes off and sigh contentedly as I feel the cool sand tickling the soles of my feet. I love these long solo walks on the beach at sunset and sunrise; Denise disapproves, though. She says I'm likely to give birth at the beach.

The ocean breeze ruffles my hair and I run my hands through my short curls, trying to tame it. I cut my hair and decided not to put any more chemicals in it. I love my curls; they are wild and untamable, reminding me a bit of me in my teenage years. I shield my eyes with one hand as I look at the burning orange-amber of the sinking sun. The other hand is clutching my letters and jar.

Moving here was the best decision, I talk to my neighbours now—or at least the people who stay around the beach, because our house is a bit isolated on top of a flat hill. We don't have to hide here, and Denise is thriving and popular, Oyinqaba can speak clearly with very little impediment now, and both of them have picked up some Portuguese phrases. All I can do is greet, thank, and apologise in Portuguese; very soon, they will be holding conversations in the colonial language.

"Olá!" I wave at a mother that I met at Oyinqaba's school, and she smiles brightly at me.

"Boa tarde." She waves back, and thankfully switches to English to ask me how my baby is doing. We chat for a few minutes before I continue down my path.

I'm wearing a flowing chiffon dress. Ever since the shoot, I've fallen in love with the lightweight material; I can't stand anything restrictive, and that includes bras and panties. I've been focused on me and I have to say I love it, even though parts of my self-discovery were excruciating. I soldiered through them and now, I feel like a weight has been lifted off my shoulders and deposited into my gut. This is my heaviest pregnancy yet.

I get to the tiny cove that's a bit hidden from the beach and I kneel on the wet sand. If I sat down, getting up will be a mission, and I cannot bend over. I open the jar and kiss each letter as I put it inside the jar. The letters fill the jar, I must have written over 70 letters; when I was feeling too low to even get out of bed and as I found myself again, the letters kept coming. I hold the jar and I say a silent 'Thank you' before I walk a little ways into the water and place the jar.

At first, it doesn't sink, the jar floats, being pulled gently by the current, and I watch until some waves take it under. Out of my sight. Denise told me this theory that she got from Frozen 2 that water holds memories and so, I don't want my memories to die—the painful ones as well as the happy ones. They all make up me—Candice Masase Nowami Sisulu. I shiver as the temperature drops and I turn back to the beach.

* * *

I'm leaving the cove when I stop dead in my tracks. There is Daniel, fidgeting nervously with the simple wedding band that I slipped on his finger at home affairs. I haven't seen or stalked him in over four months. He looks older, is the first thing that jumps out at me. The silver-grey hairs have accumulated around his temple and longer beard, as well as the worry lines around his mouth. He carries ageing elegantly. He is also drinking in my face as openly and unabashedly.

His eyes widen when they reach my swollen belly; it has dropped considerably this last week. My surprise blessing is almost ready to come out. My doctor is just surprised that I managed to carry full-term.

Daniel clears his throat and I watch his Adam's apple bobbing rapidly as he draws closer to me. He stands a foot away. The linen shirt that he's wearing flaps in the light breeze. This is the moment of truth. I kept pushing back telling him until I even stopped thinking about it. He offers me his hand and I look at it curiously.

"Hi. My name is Daniel Sisulu—a father of four, about to be five. I recently got divorced, my other wife left me, and I stepped down from Parliament, and I just moved here from South Africa." I give him a bemused look, my mind still stuck on the bit about him stepping down from Parliament.

"You resigned?" He fidgets with his ring again and tries offer me a brave smile as he offers me his hand once more.

"Officially, I finished serving my notice two months ago. Packing up my life took a bit longer than I anticipated and there was also the issue of bringing back my mother's spirit… I'm sorry, I am blowing this thing, I want us to start on a clean slate." I continue looking at him as if he's grown an extra head.

There is so much I want to say and ask. Before he drops his hand again, I take it and give him a short handshake.

"Hi, Daniel. I'm Candice. I own a beauty bar, I have three children, another one is about to join them any time now, and I am estranged from my husband. I moved here a couple of months ago myself, and it's been the hardest but also the best decision of my life. I found myself again." I'm proud of the confident lilt in my voice.

"You own Eileithyia? Wow, it's a great place. I saw it as I was coming down the beach. Do you mind if we go and sit somewhere? You look like you could use the rest." I am preening like a peacock, and I don't take his offered hand but fall into step with him.

"What made you quit politics?" I run my fingers through my short curls as I wait for him to contemplate and answer my question.

"I am not sure if I would have gone into politics if it wasn't for the need to redeem myself in the eyes of my father's family. I was so hell-bent on getting their validation that I hurt and lost everyone who genuinely cared about me. It took my wife uprooting her and my children's lives while pregnant to make me realise what I was missing out on. I realised that I was going to grow old alone, because the very people I was trying to get validation from are living their lives; none paying any attention to me. I also made new friends who have been teaching me that real power lies in the shadows, not in the spotlight."

"That's a mouthful to a stranger that you just met," I say cheekily, and he barks a short, sweet laugh. He doesn't have his usual guard up.

"A stranger that I intend to wife, if she'll have me. I have to put it out there, though, that I am in between jobs, and I don't really have a place to stay." I crinkle my nose, and he grins down at me, the lines around his eyes resembling crowfeet.

"I don't date unemployed hobos." We laugh, and when he takes my hand in his, I let him, and we walk slowly on the beach.

He's carrying his sandals with the other hand and his off-white pants are rolled up to show his lean legs.

"You said something about your mother's spirit. How did that come about?" He looks at the darkening water before he settles his watery gaze on me.

"I kept having this dream, every night, where I would see her sitting with her arms folded around her legs or the one where she was wailing, her hands would be on top of her head. I told my son-in-law about the dream and he told me that I needed to free my mother's spirit, she couldn't rest in a place that never accepted her. I resisted at first but when her tears turned to blood in my dreams, I had to do something. So I did. She was dancing along the shoreline in my last dream of her."

A breeze ruffles my hair again and I give up trying to tame it. My house is now looming in the distance, and I stop walking.

"My stop is there. I can't invite you in, though, because I don't want to confuse my kids. The only man I will introduce them to is the one I eventually marry." I can't see his face clearly in the fast-fading light but I can feel the intensity of his stare.

"Can I take you to dinner one of these days?" He's fidgeting with his ring again.

"If you woo me properly, I might consider it." His teeth flash in a smile.

"May I?" His hands are hovering around my stomach. I nod, and feel his gentle hands as they massage it.

The little traitor starts a stomping marathon on my bladder. Daniel is saying things that I don't quite catch, except for "…sorry…". He doesn't stop whispering until the baby settles down. I catch him wiping his eyes with the back of his hand and I feel like a heel.

"I'm so—"

He doesn't let me finish, he kisses me softly on the corner of my mouth and then, without another word, turns, and goes past the house to the road. I watch him for a while before I slowly turn to the house, a secret smile playing softly around my lips.

Chapter 59

EPILOGUE

Daniel

The air is heavy with anticipation as I stand behind Candice, my heart racing in sync with her breaths. The gentle sound of waves lapping against the shore fills the space around us, a soothing rhythm that echoes the strength and determination I see in her eyes. She's in the water, the infinity pool that Denise demanded I have installed, that's shimmering like a sheet of glass, reflecting the first rays of the sun that peek over the horizon.

"Breathe, Wami. Just like we practised," I whisper, my fingers gently tracing her damp hair away from her face. She nods, her brow furrowed in concentration. The doula and Oyama are nearby, my daughter's presence means the world to my wife while the doula offers her calm, and is reassuring Candice, offering her encouragement and guidance.

"Keep your focus, Candice. You're doing brilliantly," the doula says, her voice steady, cutting through the tension. I can hear the soft splashes of water as Candice shifts, her body responding to the waves of contractions.

"Ugh, it's so intense," she breathes out, her voice a mix of frustration and determination. I can feel the tremors in her body as another contraction rolls through her.

"Just a few more, my love. You've got this," I reply, forcing a smile to keep her spirits high. Her grip tightens around my hand, the warmth of her palm grounding me as much as I hope to ground her.

She leans back, drawing in a deep breath, and I can hear the soft, rhythmic sound of her breathing—inhale, exhale, and then a low moan escapes her lips; a sound that reverberates in the air, raw and powerful.

"This is the last time, Daniel. I'm driving you to get snipped tomorrow," she grunts menacingly, but sounds more breathless between contractions.

I chuckle softly. "That's the spirit, Love. Just keep riding the wave."

My efforts provoke a hiss from Candice and I hear Oyama mutter something that sounds like "Idiot!" but she coughs to cover it when I look in her direction. The ocean stretches out before us, the water golden from approaching daylight, but my focus is solely on Candice. She is a vision of strength, her beauty enhanced by the vulnerability of this moment. I wasn't sure she would want me to be a part of this moment, since our tentative dating started last week; it's taken all my strength to be able to leave at the end of each night and go to the security house, instead of being in bed with my wife.

The past week has consisted of me carrying a bunch of flowers and waiting for Candice to emerge, protruding belly first, out of our home and then we walk slowly towards the beach and we talk. I have learnt all of her cravings, given her countless foot rubs and back massages. Oyama came a day after me and she's been taking care of her siblings; Amandla is on holiday and her whole family came to wait for the baby, even Sipho came.

Only last night did Candice allow to sneak me in after the children had gone to bed and we went past the slow, tentative kisses that we've shared this past week. It felt like heaven finally sliding into her heat after months of fisting my cock with my hand almost every night, and I was close to coming when I thought Candice was squirting, but it turned out to be her water breaking.

Fun times.

I had to get Oyama to call the doula and my daughter gave me sass about being old enough to learn to keep it in my pants. Like I said, fun times.

"Almost there, Ma. Just a bit more," Oyama encourages, moving closer to Candice, her hands poised to assist.

Candice's face contorts for a moment, and she gasps, "I can't do this!"

"Yes, you can!" I say firmly, squeezing her hand. "You're the strongest person I know. Just breathe."

With one final, powerful contraction, she lets out a primal scream, a mix of effort and release, and suddenly, the water stirs around us. I can see Oyama spring into action, ready to catch our little one.

And then, amidst the soft cries of the new-born and the gentle splash of water, the first rays of the sun break across the horizon, painting the sky with hues of pink and gold.

"It's a boy!" Oyama announces, her voice filled with joy as she lifts the tiny being from the water. Candice looks up at me, her eyes wide with disbelief and joy.

"Did we really just do that?" she breathes, her expression a blend of exhaustion and exhilaration.

I nod, tears brimming in my eyes as I gaze at the little one, his tiny body glistening in the sunlight. He has a strong pair of lungs. "Yes, we did. He's perfect, just like you."

While Oyama and the doula fuss over our new son, I take a moment to admire my wife, her strength radiating in every inch. She is breath-taking, and in this moment, I know I will do everything in my power to protect this beautiful life that we've made together.

"What's his name?" Oyama asks, and before I can answer, the shrill ringtone of my phone elicits a screaming match from my son and I wade out of the heated pool to go and retrieve my phone. It's Joshua.

"Turn on the news." Is the only thing he says before ending the call. I scroll to my DSTv app and turn on the live news stream. I watch, a slow smile spreading when I see Shefu, in his decorated uniform, talking while facing the camera, his mean mug passive and relaxed, just as Joshua coached him to be.

"To both our people and the world beyond our borders, we wish to make it abundantly clear that this is not a military takeover of government. What the Zimbabwe Defence Forces is actually doing is to pacify a degenerating political, social, and economic situation in our country, which, if not addressed, may result in a violent conflict…"

I tune out the rest, having gone through the speech at least ten times last week. I look back at Candice, bathed in the beautiful glow of dawn as our son suckles from her heavy breasts, still in the pool, and the stress of the last year falls away completely. We're going to thrive in this dawn of a new era.

The End.

About the Author

Busisekile Khumalo is a celebrated South African author whose compelling narratives resonate with readers both locally and internationally. With a string of ten bestselling titles, including The Harvard Wife and Nomaswazi, she is dedicated to amplifying African voices, particularly those of women, through her literature.

Busisekile's mission is to empower African women by reshaping how they perceive themselves and their roles within society.

You can connect with me on:

- http://www.busisekilekhumalo.com
- https://x.com/khumalo_busie
- https://www.facebook.com/busisekile.khumalo.7
- https://www.tiktok.com/@busisekilekhumalo

Also by Busisekile Khumalo

NOMASWAZI
BUSISEKILE KHUMALO

Busisekile Khumalo
Fallen
CANDLE

BUSISEKILE KHUMALO
HER SILENT
Screams

BUSISEKILE KHUMALO
HER SILENT
Screams
MAGNIFIED

BUSISEKILE KHUMALO
THE END OF
HER SILENT
Screams

BUSISEKILE KHUMALO
SUNSHINE
&
SHADOWS

BUSISEKILE KHUMALO
RUBIES
&
RAIN

www.ingramcontent.com/pod-product-compliance
Lightning Source LLC
Chambersburg PA
CBHW031344070726
47496CB00017B/1655

* 9 7 8 1 9 9 7 4 5 9 6 7 5 *